IN THE BLOOD

DEDICATION

In memory of Barry Unsworth 1930-2012

IN THE BLOOD

Jenny Newman

This edition published in Great Britain in 2024 by Best Books and Films
(an imprint of Psychology News Press)

www.bestbooksandfilms.com

This book is also available as Kindle and Ebook

ISBN 978-0-907-63390-7

Typeset by Keyboard Services, Luton
Printed by Balto Print in Lithuania

The Opening Meet

Chapter One

1945

IN the summer after the war, strangers appeared in our valley, weird-looking people who couldn't speak our language. The men had bandaged heads or stumps for arms or legs. Blank-eyed, washed-out women pushed their wheelchairs or helped them hobble along on wooden crutches. Pretending to be long-lost mams and dads, they found their way to isolated farms or knocked on doors of cottages stuck up lonely tracks. They were looking for vackies whose parents had failed to collect them.

Some said the kids would be sold into the army, then sent to clear up rubble from the bombs. Others said they were sent off to Australia or some other place too far to get back home.

My mam had died in the blitz. As for my dad, he'd done a bunk long before the war. But I wasn't at risk. The *Saeson* picked on homesick boys and girls – the lonely ones who hadn't fitted in. Not kids like me, who knew each hound, its talents and capacities, and every stream and covert in our valley. The god had led me to Capel y Bont, Iolo always said. My place was here with him. This was where I'd stay.

I was washing tripe for the hounds on a chilly afternoon when clouds like dirty sacking hung above the yard. October, when the trees turn to the colour of foxes. A motor car chugged up our lane. I stayed beside the netting, liking the slosh of water in the bucket. The engine noise grew louder. Rooks flapped in rowdy circles, watchful birds with an eye to local welfare, mobbing the big brown motor car that stopped outside our gate.

If I'd had any sense I'd have listened to their warning. Instead, I watched the foxhounds trotting from their lodges, me, a heedless twelve-year-old, protected from the world. Or so I thought. The car door slammed. Hounds surged towards the netting. My pack. My family. The only one I wanted. Each hound was woolly and white, low hocked, with perfect shoulders, each one Welsh and touched by Gwyn ap Nudd. Gwyn the god who oversaw the rituals of the hunt: that the animal's death was honoured, its precious soul appeased; and that no animal was killed before its time.

Footsteps clicked on the tarmac. A stranger appeared at our gate. Not your usual *Saesnes*, worn and pasty-faced. This one tittuped in pink high heels that matched her coat and handbag.

'Sut alla i'ch helpu chi?' I called as she fiddled with the latch. Can I help you?

She gave a gormless shrug. Why should I bother translating? We never spoke English here, and not very often at school, although I remembered snippets from the time before the war, songs my mam had taught me back in Liverpool. *And when he was down he was down. Oh Maggie, Maggie May, they have taken her away. Simple Simon met a pie man.*

The woman smiled, as if not sure I'd smile back. Her pert little hat had wings like a tiny bird's and a swirl of flimsy gauze above her eyebrows. Her scent pretended it came from violets and roses. It really smelt of factories and shops and stuck a sugary finger up your nose. The hounds had caught it, too. Their hackles rose.

The woman stepped into the yard. 'Are you sure they can't get out?'

I didn't reply. Knew I was being rude. And, what's more, I liked it, swirling the tripe round the bucket until it drowned her scent with its juicy, cow-muck pong.

She shut the gate behind her. *'Be ydech chi isio?'* I asked, then struggled for the English. 'What is it that you want?'

Head up and elbows bent, she picked her way towards me. For

4

a grown-up she was small, I saw as she drew near, with anxious eyes, pencilled brows and fluffy, pale blonde hair. Already the pack had massed behind its leaders. Alert and sharp-eyed, they moved towards the netting. Aneurin, wise as any Master; Eleri, his brilliant, ugly niece; and my favourite hound, the erudite Caradog, more than a match for a flimsy afternoon vixen. A vixen, what's more, that had strayed from her terrain. Two dog hounds and one bitch: *she means no good,* they said.

The woman looked me up and down, taking in my plimsolls, scabby knees and shrunken sweater.

'Tell me your name,' she said.

As if I'd fall for that.

'It's you, Jacqueline, isn't it?' she said.

The air around me stilled. Somebody had told her. A sneak of a teacher or maybe the woman from the *Swyddfa Bost,* coughing up children's addresses for the *Saeson.*

'Come here to me, dear,' the woman said, stretching out her arms. I backed towards the netting.

'Come here to me, dear,' she said again. 'I've come to take you home.'

Before I could move, the farmhouse door swung back. Iolo, shirt sleeves rolled, was standing on the step. My heart jumped. He was joined to us all by an invisible thread: spoke to us every morning from his bedroom window. At night he'd appear, a hurricane lamp in his hand, the minute a bitch began to whelp or one of us shivered with colic. Now his canny huntsman's eyes took in the prying woman, the big brown toad of a motor car crouched outside the gate, then me, still clutching my bucket in the corner by the kennels.

The woman swung towards him. 'I'm right! It's her,' she said.

'Fe ddylech chi wedi fy rhybuddio eich bod chi'n dod.'

The woman's shoulders sagged. 'Does no one here speak English?'

Light on his feet for all his solid build, Iolo loped across the yard towards her. They faced each other, one small and pale, the other broad and dark. Iolo would send her packing, like he'd sent the school inspector and the nosy nurse who'd come to treat my scabs.

But no, here he was, not meeting her eye exactly, but switching into English as he asked her for her name.

The woman stuck out her chin. 'You know perfectly well,' she said.

Liar, cawed a rook high in the elms overhead.

'Where's your proof?' Iolo asked.

The woman snapped her fingers. 'Bernard!' she called. 'Come here!'

A man had entered the yard without me seeing, not bothering to shut the gate behind him. Burly and thick-waisted with a broad red slab of a face, he too looked like a townie in his rowdy, blue-checked suit.

'We'd best go inside,' said Iolo.

The steam from a pot of tripe simmering on the stove mingled with the smell of cooked potatoes. The grown-ups settled themselves around the table while I hovered by the outside door.

'Why didn't you answer my letters?' the woman asked Iolo.

Iolo shifted in his chair. 'We never got any letters.'

'Your postmistress said she delivered every single one.'

That goggle-eyed old tattle with her yellow teeth. No one would side with her against Iolo.

'Besides,' he said, 'your way of life's not right.'

'What do you know about that?'

'Children talk,' he said. 'We had plenty here from Bootle.'

'Kids will say what they think you want to hear.'

'They said enough to make me think that you're not fit to rear her.'

'You can talk! Your postmistress says your wife left years ago, and she wondered why I hadn't been informed. And some of her customers said you made Jacqueline sleep in the kennels.'

Iolo shook his head like a hound who has swum through a river. 'Only because she needed to. Jackie has to hunt.'

6

'Hunt? With dogs? Can't you see it's cruel?'

'Hunting's part of nature,' said Iolo.

The woman drummed her fingers. Their words dashed to and fro, two engines starting and stopping, Iolo's voice gone pebble-hard, the woman's high and strained, and me in the doorway, trying to follow the English.

The man tugged out two pieces of paper and thrust them at Iolo.

'*Damia,*' Iolo muttered as he read. '*Damia.* Yes. I see.'

The light grew murky on the kitchen wall. Out in the yard, the hounds had fallen silent as if each one was seeing what he saw.

The man held out his hand. Iolo returned the papers, then forced his big strong fists into his trouser pockets. 'How do I know they're genuine?' he asked.

The man rolled up the papers and slapped them on his palm. 'Give us the girl at once or I'm getting the police. Chief Inspector Tudor is waiting for my call.'

Iolo turned towards me. 'She's your mam.'

Iolo, touched by Gwyn. How could she have taken him in? 'My mam is dead,' I said. 'You told me so yourself.'

The woman's cheeks flamed red beneath her white-blonde hair. 'You told her that? You wicked, evil man.'

'He's right,' I said. 'My mam had dark brown hair.'

Iolo spread his hands. 'She's dyed it, *cariad.* But that don't mean to say she's not your mam.'

'Even so,' I said, 'my real mam was tall!'

I caught a knowing look between the *Saeson*, the sort that teachers pass above your head.

'You've grown, that's all,' the woman said. 'You've been away five years.'

Not knowing what else to do, I leant on the doorpost and scratched, clawing, nails outspread, at an itch behind my lug.

The woman's small pink mouth curled in disbelief. 'She's covered in ringworm,' she said, 'probably caught from them dogs.' She turned towards me. 'Jacqueline, go and get your things.'

'But I'm going to stay here.'

'Do what she tells you,' said the man, 'or we'll go without them.'

Behind the wire, Caradog stood, ears flat. No cawing from the rooks, no yelping from the hounds, just a high-pitched whistle deep inside my head. Caradog at my heels, I dived inside the lodge. What the woman called my 'things' lay scattered where I slept, pressed spine to spine against him. A fox's brush; a piebald stone I'd found at Rhyl; a badger's claw, half-worn down from digging. I bundled them into my pillowcase and ran back to the kitchen. The woman pulled a packet from her handbag. 'Look, Jacqueline, pet, I've brought you sweeties!'

I saw garish pinks and yellows. Here was yet more proof! I hated Liquorice Allsorts. Always had. I shook my head and turned back to Iolo. 'If my mam had been alive she'd have fetched me weeks ago.'

Iolo stood and stroked my neck as if I was a pup. '*Cariad*,' he said, 'she's had a difficult war. She told me just now – and petrol in short supply.'

I could tell from his voice that he hadn't believed a word.

'He's right,' the woman said with a quiver in her voice. She reached to slide her arm around my waist. 'Oh, pet,' she said, 'don't stiffen yourself against me. I came as soon as I could, honest I did. I've been finding us both a decent place to live – a lovely house in the country, up in Westmorland, the home of a gentleman called Major Wetheral.' She tightened her grip on my waist. 'You like the country, don't you, Jacqueline, pet?'

'What about my dad?' I asked. 'Will he be coming too?' A last resort. I wasn't sure he'd ever lived with us, just knew that he was tall and thin and drove a motor car, and once I'd seen him hug my mam and swing her off her feet.

The woman dropped her voice. 'Never came home,' she said.

I should have run. Taken them all by surprise. Dashed through the yard and into the hills above the kennels. Lived like the hound I'd learnt to be, stealing farmyard chickens, sleeping under hedges and scavenging in dustbins till the motor car chugged down the lane.

Instead, I threw my arms around Iolo, pressed my face into his sweater, caught his smell of wool and old digestives.

'*Cariad*,' he said, '*mae'n ddrwg gen i.*'

The first time he'd ever said sorry. 'Sorry for what?' I croaked. Even then, I thought that he would save me. But no. He ducked his head. 'She's got the proof.' His hands were slick with sweat.

'But she'll stop me hunting.'

The man grabbed my elbows from behind. His grip closed like a trap.

'Be gentle with her,' said the woman. 'She's done nothing wrong.'

My legs lashed out of their own accord and kicked the man on the shins. He hit my ear so hard the air around me fizzed and spun.

Iolo lowered his head, as if herding a cow through a gate. 'There's no need for that,' he said.

The man yanked my collar, his face so close I smelt his dinner-time pasty. 'You'll do as you're told,' he said as he dragged me into the yard.

Iolo's big brown hands were dangling by his sides. '*Calon bach*,' he called, 'I'll come and see you soon.'

'No you won't,' the woman said, her voice gone high and clear. 'You show your face round there and I'll summon the police.' Her eyes ranged round the sagging roofs, the broken loosebox door and the searching eyes behind the netting. 'You Welsh are bloody savages,' she said.

Stumbling a bit on the cobbles, she beckoned to the man who still had a grip on my elbows. Iolo spoke as I was dragged towards the gate. Not spoke. He almost sang, dancing the words in a stream, in a ribbon of light. Iolo touched by Gwyn ap Nudd, the huntsman in the stars. 'I'll never forget you,' he said, 'and nor will the rest of the pack. We'll send you a message, *cariad*. Believe me, we'll find a way. Remember this: Gwyn's powers know no bounds.'

9

As he spoke, the pack began to howl, the kind of yelp they give when one of them has died, hanging stifled on a fence or savaged by a badger. Eleri, high as a capel boy, gave the note to the rest, then came Rhodri's hefty baritone, supported by the older members of the dog pack, followed by the bitch pack, alto and soprano. Their high-pitched, mournful note was throbbing with my pulse, flowing through my body and drilling through my brain. I collapsed onto my haunches, pointed my nose at the sky and, before I knew it, I was howling, too, great gouts of sound pouring from my throat.

The woman gave the man a small, despairing shrug. The man cleared his throat as if about to spit. 'You've fooled yourself,' he said. 'Dump her while you can. Take her with you and she'll scotch your plans.'

The woman wiped her eyes with the tip of her handkerchief, edging round her sticky-looking lashes. 'How can I - ' she said, then swallowed and tried again. 'She's mine. I know she is. How can I leave her here?'

The rooks bounced up from their branches with clattering wings. One hand on my collar, the man made a gun of the other, swung round towards the trees and aimed it at the birds. 'Bang!' he said. 'Bang! Bang! You're dead, the lot of you.'

He bundled me into the back of the car. The woman slid in beside me. Iolo watched, head sunk between his shoulders. The man pitched his hat into the back. It stank of smoke and Brylcreem. I buried my face in the seat. The engine started up and drowned the hounds' unbroken yelps.

Iolo had said Gwyn's power knew no bounds. So why had the god let the *Saeson* march into our yard? And why had he let me be kidnapped just like all the other kids?

Chapter Two

One Month Later

THE gates clanged shut behind us. The woman gripped my wrist. I flinched. Felt worry in her fingers.

'I really need this job,' she said, 'so please don't try escaping. We've had enough of that. You're going to like it here.'

I scuffed the gravel with my toe.

'Do you hear me, Jackie, pet?'

'Yes.'

'Call me Mam, for heaven's sake.'

How could I call her Mam? My real mam was dead.

The woman gave my wrist a shake. 'Yes, *Mam.*'

'Yes, Mam.' The word sat like a stone in my mouth. Yes, *Lizzie,* I said beneath my breath. A name I knew she hated. She was always *Elizabeth, if you please,* and sometimes *Liz* to one of her favourite uncles.

Gloomy in the dusk, a drive stretched ahead. Leaves dodged in and out of the ditches on each side. Army tanks squatted in the fields beyond. Next to the tanks, two lines of trenches gaped. The war. Not over here, like it was in Wales.

She gave my wrist another shake. 'Hurry up. We're late.'

Close to, I caught her sickly flower scent, now mingling with the fug of the afternoon train. Twin rows of elms locked branches overhead. She'd lied again, had said we'd go to a beautiful place in the country. Instead, at the end of the tunnel of trees, a big stone barracks loomed.

My suitcase bumped my legs. *'Dydw i ddim yn hoffi fan'ma,'* I said. I don't like it here.

11

'Jackie, pet, try and speak in English.'

'Dwi wedi anghofio. I've forgotten it all.' Not exactly true. During the month I'd spent with her in Liverpool the words in *Saesneg* came crawling back like rats into a feed bin.

She dumped her suitcase on a ring of gravel. Ahead of us, a flight of steps led to doors so wide and high they might have been made for a giant. Huge windows loomed on either side, all staring at me and her. *You're trespassing, the pair of you. Get out of here at once!*

The woman squeezed my hand.

I scuffed the ground again. A smell bounced up to meet me: of petrol, rubber boots and chilly, rained-on soil. I jerked her hand so hard she let me go.

'Jacqueline!' she cried.

I dropped my case and tore across the gravel.

'Jacqueline,' she cried again. 'Come here to me at once.'

Her voice wheeled overhead. I dodged away. She'd never catch me in her silly shoes. The smell of rubber led me to a path around the side. Out of sight, I dropped onto all fours, bashing through the weeds that poked between the flagstones. An oily pong of weasel swamped the smell of boots and drew me round the farthest corner of the house.

A broad stone terrace ran along the back. Dark and empty-looking, the house reared on my left. Somewhere deep inside, a doorbell rang. A blackout curtain blocked the nearest window. The next was smeared with tar. Through the third I glimpsed a pile of gas masks in a corner, and a stack of metal boxes, each marked with a red cross.

She's going to sell you to the army, said a voice inside my head. Straightening up, I saw a lawn beyond the flagstones, falling away through the twilight, scared of the house. I'd ford the stream I could hear at its foot, cut through the stand of oaks and into the darkening fields. There I'd get the god back on my side by living like the hound I really was.

I swung towards a flight of steps that led down to the lawn. A hand gripped my collar.

'Where d'you think you're going?'

Lizzie, calm as you please, spinning me round to face her. And I hadn't even heard her clacking heels.

'Ow!' I yelped. 'That hurts.'

'Trying to escape again? You stupid, stupid girl!' She turned her small white face on mine. Was I thick or what? That Welshman was depraved, he should never have been allowed, a decent set of neighbours would have summoned the police.

On and on she went, her voice all sad and choky. I cut her out, distracted by a worry on my hackles. Somebody had got us in his sights. A soldier, rifle cocked, his finger on the trigger? At Lizzie? Me? Or both? I scanned the lawn for cover, noting blobs of shade and ragged bushes.

Lizzie handed me my case. 'You're not even paying attention!'

'Somebody's watching!' I whispered.

She glanced up at the rows of sightless rooms. 'There's nobody there or they'd have answered the door.'

A yellow square landed on the flagstones at our feet. We looked up at a lighted attic window. A small, stick-like figure stood behind a row of bars. As we watched, it rapped its knuckles on the glass.

'Is that Major Wetheral?' I whispered.

'Of course not. He's six foot tall.'

The figure pointed at the way we'd come. Ignoring it, Lizzie clacked to the opposite end of the house. I followed, still sensing the eyes on my back. She paused to dab more scent behind each ear, her favourite way of wrecking my precious sense of smell. A hound who cannot smell cannot think, let alone escape and find its way back home.

'Have you been here before?' I asked her.

'Just the once.'

We'd stopped beside a flight of steep stone steps with a basement window at its foot. 'I'm going to say I worked in a pub,' she said, 'so for heaven's sake don't talk about the uncles.'

As if I'd want to talk about the creepy Uncle Dennis. Or lanky Uncle Eric with his quiff and grabby eyes. Or fleshy Uncle Bernard who'd helped take me from Iolo, with his gifts of nylons and marbled belly pork.

'And for Pete's sake act as if you're normal and don't go acting like a dog or sniffing round the room. Our noses aren't for smelling with, you know, just for breathing through, or blowing if you have to, and that means with a hanky.'

Dazed by the effort of acting like a girl, I followed her down towards a lighted window. Inside the room, a tattered blackout shade hung above a big, bald man behind an ironing board. Lizzie knocked on the door beside the window. The man looked up. She smiled. The man slammed down his iron. A few seconds later, the door creaked back enough for me to see that he'd plonked a bowler on his ears.

'Are you one of them divels?' he asked.

'Pardon me?' said Lizzie.

'I asked: are you one of them divel reporters?'

'I'm here about the job.'

The man's eyes travelled upwards from her peep-toes, taking in the buttons on her flared pink coat and stopping at her flimsy little hat. 'Where have you come from?'

'Liverpool. On the 4.35.'

'And where are you staying?'

I caught a whiff of panic beneath Lizzie's Odor-O-No. 'Major Wetheral said we could stay here.'

The man opened the door a little wider.

It met me as we stepped inside the room. A smell of blood and musk mixed with bedraggled fur. I closed my eyes to sift it. An elbow jabbed my ribs.

'Stop that!' Lizzie hissed. The door slammed shut behind us. 'Would you be Mrs Arbiter?' she asked.

Not a man. A woman. Thickset as a mastiff. Beefy hands designed to wring a chicken's neck. Bring a mallet down between a rabbit's ears. Lisle stockings rolled around her ankles. A cardigan and skirt of dingy black.

14

Lizzie dumped her suitcase by the door. 'I'm here about the job, as I'm sure the major told you.'

'He never said owt to me.' The mastiff's jaws clamped shut.

'Well, I'm sure he will. When's he getting in?'

'In? He's gone to Lunnon. Went of a sudden this morning. Fed up with them reporters, like as not.'

Lizzie's small pink mouth drooped at the corners. 'How long will he be gone?'

'Nobody knows. Mebbe a week or more.'

'Can I wait till he returns?' Lizzie asked, her manner gone from sure-of-itself to nervy.

Mrs Arbiter tightened the strings of her pinny. 'I can't agree to that with him not here.'

I left my suitcase next to Lizzie's and, forcing myself to stay upright, dodged past her into the room. Eyes half-shut and nose in the air, I tracked the musky scent beyond the pool of light around the ironing board. A battered kettle simmered on a cranky-looking range, thickening the smells of blood and death. Steam wafted to a rack beneath the ceiling, the kind with six long bars hauled up by ropes. High in its shadows a coat was hanging lengthways, lining downwards, like a drowning man. I caught a glimpse of scarlet, a row of shiny buttons and a silky shimmer through the bars. Though I'd never seen a coat like that, I knew it from its reek of man's and horse's sweat, of mud and blood that mingled with the musky pong of fox. A coat you wore to witness life and death, a magic coat that changed you when you put it on. I saw the hounds, the horses and the pelting fox.

'Come here to me!' called Lizzie. 'Come here to me at once!' Small and worried-looking in her fancy clothes, she stood with Mrs Arbiter beside a scrubbed pine table.

'What's up wid her?' asked Mrs Arbiter.

The smell of Lizzie's anxiety grew stronger. 'Jacqueline was a vackie,' she said, 'and only home a month. But soon she'll be her lovely self again.'

Mrs Arbiter fixed me with a greenish, goosy stare. 'There's plenty of kiddies were vackies and it ain't done them no harm.'

'Not sent to a man whose wife had run away, a man who'd never heard of soap and water. He made Jacqueline sleep in a kennel with his dogs.'

Wrong. Iolo didn't *make* me. It's the way to catch the dreams the jump from head to head.

'The major is an MFH,' said Mrs Arbiter.

I caught my breath. Praise be to Gwyn. The major owned the coat.

'MFH?' echoed Lizzie.

'Master of Foxhounds,' I told her.

The skin on Lizzie's pencilled brows grew tight. 'I didn't know the major liked to hunt.'

'Like it? He fair lives for it,' Mrs Arbiter said.

'I don't want Jacqueline anywhere near his dogs, or chasing helpless animals, come to that.'

'Has nobody told you? Servants' kids don't hunt.' Mrs Arbiter's upper lip grew stiff. 'Even if you're taken on – as may not be the case - you can be sure the lassie won't get near the major's hounds. If she sets foot in the kennels his staff will send her packing.'

'Quite right,' said Lizzie with a little nod.

I shut my trap. The major's mind would change. And soon. The god would see to that.

Mrs Arbiter pulled an iron off the range. 'When were you last in service?'

'Till 1933, when I got married.'

'And where's your husband now?'

Lizzie gave a sad little smile. 'Dead behind enemy lines.'

Another lie. She'd told the girls that he was still alive, and what to do if he turned up one day.

Mrs Arbiter spat on the iron. 'What's your name, did you say?'

'Elizabeth Elton.'

'And where exactly was this place you worked?'

Silence, apart from bobbles of spit hissing on the iron. 'Lord Blencathra's castle,' Lizzie said at last. 'And what a job that was. His butler was a stickler, and his housekeeper, too. There was nothing us maids didn't learn about running a stately home.'

'And did Lord … the butler give you a character?'

'Of course he did.' Lizzie tilted her chin. 'There was nobody like me, he said. When it came to washing and scrubbing. I was the best.'

Mrs Arbiter held out her hand. 'I'll pass that to the major.'

Lizzie shook her head. 'Sadly, it got lost the night the docks were bombed. And now the butler's dead, as I'm sure you know, and His Lordship died at Amiens.'

Mrs Arbiter folded her arms across her bib, as if she saw straight through all Lizzie's lies. I scratched my legs, still itching from the fuzzy seats of the train.

'So where did you go next?' asked Mrs Arbiter.

'Back home to Liverpool. When my Eddie was called up I trained to be a VAD – that is, after Jacqueline went to North Wales.'

While Lizzie talked about the injured men she'd nursed, I leant against the table and looked around the room. No hoof picks on a row of hooks or wellies by the Aga, no woolly socks steaming on its rail, no copies of *The Foxhound Kennel Stud Book* or jars of ointment on a nearby shelf. So where was the major now and why had he left his hounds? What sort of a Master didn't sit in his kitchen?

Mrs Arbiter slammed the iron onto a pair of long johns. They jumped as if the man was still inside them. 'You'd mebbe do better getting a job in a hospital.'

'Not with a kiddie. They wouldn't take me on.'

Mrs Arbiter drove the iron over a darn. 'Are there no other jobs in Liverpool?'

'I had a job in a local pub and a cosy little home.'

Cosy? A house of sooty brick with gaps on either side like knocked-out teeth?

'So why did you leave?' asked Mrs Arbiter.

'Jacqueline's not cut out for city life and I want to do the best for her, you see.'

The kettle lifted its lid with an unbelieving clink. Mrs Arbiter dumped the iron on the board and shovelled tea into a pot warming by the hot plate. 'I still don't understand why you've come to Westmorland.'

Lizzie bit her lip. I smelt the long johns singeing. But I wasn't meant to use my nose. Careful not to sniff, I breathed in through my mouth. Back turned, across the room, Mrs Arbiter lifted the kettle. Surely even Lizzie had smelt the bitter pong. I buried my nose in my sleeve. Smoke drifted from the board.

'Mae rhywbeth yn llosgi!' I shouted.

Lizzie frowned. 'Speak to me in English.'

'The gentleman's … knickers are burning.'

Mrs Arbiter clanked down the kettle. At last she'd smelt it, too. She flapped away the smoke and snatched the iron off the board. 'Oh Lordy! What have I done?'

A v-shaped burn was pointing at the buttons, just like the one I'd left on Iolo's winter vest. Aware of the god on my side, I grabbed the long johns. 'I can get rid of that mark,' I said in English.

Mrs Arbiter stared, as if surprised to hear me speak.

'Have you got any borax?' I asked.

Without a word, she pulled a blue and white box from a cupboard, found a bowl and pointed at the sink. I took the box, tipped powder into the bowl and made a nice thick paste with water from the tap. Mrs Arbiter settled her hat on her forehead and watched me slather the goo onto the wool.

'She's a handy lass.'

'I've trained her well,' said Lizzie.

'So she wants a job and all.'

'Good heavens, no. She's only twelve.'

Mrs Arbiter raised the twin brown lines she'd drawn above her eyes. 'Only twelve? Lord bless us. What a beanpole.'

'When I went to pick her up, she didn't know who I was. She said her mam was tall and had brown hair - couldn't see that in five years she'd grown a foot or so. What's more' - Lizzie paused to touch her fluffy hair – 'she'd no idea that I'd become ash blonde. That Welshman had destroyed my letters, cards and Christmas presents.'

Mrs Arbiter poured two cups of tea. 'You'd best sit down,' she said.

Lizzie unpinned her hat and settled herself at the table. 'Worst of all, he'd told her I was dead – had died on the night of the Liverpool blitz.' Lizzie's voice ran on. How I'd been covered in ringworm – my clothes were stiff with dirt – how she'd had to drag me to the motor car. When we got home she'd had to bathe and disinfect me. Then she'd caught me shinning down a drainpipe and had to bolt my bedroom window before I went to sleep. And not a stitch to wear, apart from the rags I stood up in. Lucky she had a pretty dress for me to wear.

True. I wore it now, a horrid thing with scratchy lace around the neck. It had belonged, Lizzie had told me, to a girl called Christa. She'd also found a pair of Christa's shiny shoes, and lacy socks and frilly vests and knickers. The dress's armpits smelt of tired sweat. Had Christa run away and left her stupid clothes behind?

Mrs Arbiter pulled out a chair and settled herself at the table. 'You can stay if you like,' she said with a sigh, 'at least till the major gets home. I won't tell a lie. It's hard getting staff to live in, especially since the army knocked the place to bits – not that it wasn't falling apart already, and Polly grown so useless I don't know where to turn.'

I yawned. We'd left at nine o'clock that morning. Our first train had been crammed with men in demob suits. The next train chugged for hours past farms in rumpled fields.

'You can help get the rooms into shape,' Mrs Arbiter said to Lizzie. 'That will mean cleaning the windows, polishing the floors, beating the carpets, vacuuming the sofas, not to mention the high and low dusting – and a lot more besides.'

As if caught in a spell, Lizzie was nodding her head off. At what she'd called her cosy little home she'd lain in bed till ten o'clock each morning and left all the cooking and cleaning to the girls.

High on the kitchen wall a box had started to rattle, its square wooden frame surrounding rows of dolls' house windows, each with curly writing underneath its sill. A stick whizzed in the window above the words *Di. Ro.* Mrs Arbiter's head jerked in its gumboil hat.

'That'll be Master Oliver,' she said.

If Lizzie had been a hound, she'd have pricked her ears. 'It said in the papers that he was killed in the war.'

Mrs Arbiter jabbed a fork into an opened tin, skewered a pear and plopped it into a dish. 'That was Master Jack, a different lad altogether, brave as they come and a divel after hounds.' She opened the cupboard underneath the dolls' house, slapped the pears on a tray and grabbed a rope that dangled to one side.

'I think we might have seen Master Oliver at a window.'

Mrs Arbiter hauled the tray up the shaft. 'Very like. Half-French, you know. A sissy, gowling sort.'

'I read that his mother's scarpered back to Paris.'

'Aye, and he took it hard. Now he's landed home from school. Glandular fever, they say.'

Lizzie clinked her cup down on her saucer. 'How could a mother abandon her child like that?'

Something in the cupboard creaked and groaned. Mrs Arbiter opened the door as the tray rocked down again. A dish of roast potatoes, barely touched. A heap of brussels on a dirty plate. Hunger made a cold, hard fist inside me.

Mrs Arbiter held out her hand. 'Ration Books, if you please.'

Meek as you like, Lizzie dug in her handbag. 'Here's mine. The Welshman said that Jacqueline's was lost.'

Mrs Arbiter leafed through every page then sliced a loaf and scraped each piece with Stork. We got two each and two cuts each of Spam. I'd never liked the sour cauli taste of Piccalilli but when I'd wolfed my meat I took a second helping, scraping my spoon round the jar.

Though the bossy black hands of the mantelpiece clock said only half past eight, Mrs Arbiter lit a Tilley lamp. 'Pick up your cases,' she said.

We followed her through a door beside the range, down a dark passage and up some twisty stairs. The legs that carried her big square body looked bony and strong as a horse's. I stamped on every step, liking the bang on the wood.

'Hush that noise,' Mrs Arbiter said. 'The walls between them and us is paper thin.'

She paused and patted her chest as we reached the landing, a space like a little round room with knobs that gleamed on the woodwork.

'Them's the family's rooms,' she said.

I saw that the knobs were on doors cut in the panels. We set off again as soon as she'd caught her breath, up to the second landing and two more pannelled doors, one on each side of the entrance to a third and steeper flight.

'Major Wetheral's bedroom,' she said, 'and Lady Wetheral's rooms. At least, they used to be.'

At the top of the stairs we stepped into an attic corridor. On the left it stretched towards a distant corner, on the right towards a row of low and narrow doors.

Mrs Arbiter shone her lamp along the lefthand passage. 'Whatever else you do, don't go wandering down there. I don't want Master Oliver kicking up a fuss.'

So that was where they kept him. How would he make a fuss? We followed Mrs Arbiter through the last door on the right. The room was crammed with two beds, a chest, a coffin wardrobe and a mean little fireplace clamped round an empty grate.

'Polly's next door, having an early night.' Mrs Arbiter set the lamp on the chest beside a pitcher and basin. 'Crying herself to sleep, like as not. Since the war, girls have got a bit more free and easy.'

'You mean she's in trouble?' asked Lizzie.

'Little pitchers have long ears,' Mrs Arbiter said.

'A twelve-year old should know the facts of life.'

'A kiddie's a kiddie. You don't want 'em learning too early.'

'Better than too late.' Lizzie nodded at the wall.

'It wasn't her fault, poor lass. He said he was going to marry her. But she's not the first he's jilted and nor will she be the last.'

'You can't trust a man till you've got him to the altar – and some of 'em not even then.'

Mrs Arbiter pulled a pile of sheets from the wardrobe and flopped them onto the chest of drawers. 'The servants' lavs is down below so you'll have to make do with the po and mind you put out the lamp before you turn in.'

Chapter Three

LIZZIE leant back against the door and puffed her cheeks. 'So the major's buggered off. Bloody typical.'

'Didn't he know we were coming?'

'Of course he did.'

'Why was he fed up with the reporters?'

Lizzie kicked off her shoes and rubbed the blisters on her toes. 'That stuff about his wife has been in all the papers. Embarrassing, if you ask me. He'd been a bit of a hero.'

'I did well with the borax, didn't I?'

Lizzie didn't reply.

'Didn't I, *Mam?*'

'Well enough,' she said, opening the window, 'but why did you go scoffing all the Piccalilli? You can't get hold of that stuff for love nor money.' She shook out a sheet speckled with iron mould, floated it onto a mattress and made a hospital corner.

A howl flew in from outside and circled the room, born on a gust of muddy country air.

'What the hell was that?' she asked, staring at the window.

It came again, the panicky cry of a hound cut off from its pack. 'A foxhound bitch,' I said.

'Has nobody told you not to use that word?'

'It's what they call a lady hound.

'Lady hound! It's just a bloody dog.'

Wrong. Hounds are never known as dogs. 'Some stupid *Sais* huntsman must have gone and lost her.'

'I thought you liked them hunting folk.'

'Only when they're Welsh.'

The bitch howled again on a high-pitched, silvery note. The god would be expecting me to find her. Maybe that was why he'd brought me here.

'Why can't it belt up?' asked Lizzie. 'It's giving me the willies.'

I peered through the window in between the bedheads. By the light of a strong half-moon, I made out our way from the station: past the pub, the row of shops, the cottages, the school with netball posts and the soldier on his pillar, and then the double gates, the drive, the fields on either side. 'Can I go and look for her?' I asked.

'So you can try and scarper again?'

She needn't have worried. I knew I'd lost my bearings. A girl without a pack has only half a brain. I'd lost track of where we were or which way back to Wales. A movement caught my eye above the grass beyond the drive. Not the hound. Blodeuwedd in her owl shape cruising over trenches, piles of earth, a burnt-out jeep and tangled rolls of wire.

'Are we in some sort of camp?'

Lizzie handed me a jar of ointment for my ringworm. 'The army used it during the war. Now they're clearing off.'

'How did you get to know the major? Did he used to be an uncle?'

'I told you before. You've not got to talk about them.'

'But did he?'

She busied herself hanging her frocks in the wardrobe, a shiny pink tea dress, a polka dot shirtwaister and the green and white skirt she called her whirlaway. 'Mind you own business,' she said.

'Where did you meet?'

'If you have to know, he came into The Fleet.'

I'd seen the pub by the docks. The Spanish Fleet. Did the major stand at the bar in a topper and red coat? 'What had he done with his hounds?'

'Search me,' said Lizzie, shutting the wardrobe door. 'He was on leave from the Border Regiment.'

I scratched a scaly spot on my legs. *'Dwi isio mwythau.'*

'What's that supposed to mean?'

I knew the words in English. They meant: I want a hug. But *cael mwythau* meant more than that. Home. *Bara brith.* Caradog's sweaty paws. Iolo's jacket with its smells of wool and old digestives. Lizzie filled a china basin from the jug. Its splashing sound made me want to pee. The cold rim of the po bit my bum and my pee rattled noisily onto the metal. I stood and dragged off my dress with its scratchy collar, then wriggled out of my stupid lacy vest. That morning, Lizzie had bundled my pillowslip into my suitcase, the one my real mam had packed when war broke out. I felt inside it for my lucky badger's foreclaw and held it as I pulled on Christa's nightie.

Lizzie set a bottle on her locker. *Pinkhams,* said the label. She tipped a few glugs of the mixture into her toothmug, letting loose its bitter, woody smell.

'If you were really my mam,' I said, climbing into bed, 'you'd of come to see me during the war.' The sentence popped out like a nosy cub from its earth.

She sat on the side of my bed and pulled a Kensitas from its pack. 'Do you know nothing? We none of us had any petrol.'

I looked into her wrapping-paper eyes, the kind you could stare at forever and never learn the truth. 'Maisie Haydon's mother came five times.'

'Black market petrol, knowing her.' Lizzie struck a match. 'And what with you gone queer and me not liking the country the doctors said I'd better stay away.'

'Why did you bring us here if you don't like the country?'

Her worry-lines softened as she stroked my hand. 'I've changed since then,' she said, 'but don't think I didn't miss you, or that I ever once forgot your birthday.' The skin beneath her eyes grew moist. 'I spent every penny I made on lovely dollies, a golliwog and a manicure set in a beautiful plastic case.'

More proof she wasn't my mam. I'd always hated dolls and

wouldn't know what to do with a manicure set. Two smoke rings hung in goblin circles round her head, yet another way to wreck my sense of smell. I buried my nose in my sleeve.

Lizzie crossed her legs with a rasp of nylon stockings. 'Oh, pet,' she said, 'why are you doing that?'

Pet! How I hated that word. No animal is a pet. I raised my face. 'I want to go home,' I said.

She stood and crossed to the window. 'That wicked, wicked man.'

Iolo wasn't wicked. He came to kiss me every night. As Lizzie stood at the window, staring into darkness, my thoughts flew back to the night my real mam died. I'd been woken by the usual click of a latch. But for once Iolo stayed beside the door.

'*Cariad,*' he whispered, 'you'd best pull on your clothes.'

'Why? What's the matter?'

'Hurry up.'

The hounds were howling in their lodges as we left the yard and a bright, full moon was sailing through the sky. A bombers' moon, as people called it then. At the end of the lane, Aled, my cob, whickered behind the gate. A little group was waiting on the verge. Soddy Murphy had buck teeth and a limp from when he had polio. Shifting his weight from foot to foot, he was standing with his cousins, three girls with teeth like Soddy's and hair tied with blue ribbons. All four of them came from the street next to mine, and their mothers, identical twins, visited twice a year and brought me presents.

Led by the butcher's sister and the lady from the hen farm, we left the lane for a field full of cattle. They hoisted themselves to their knees as we drew near. Ewes began to bleat as we reached the mountainside and lambs in their woolly cardigans dashed anxiously to their flanks. More people huddled on the ridge high above the kennels, a row of still, black shapes against an orange sky. All stood, backs turned, not moving, hardly speaking as we panted up the slope towards them.

I recognised each one: the minister, two teachers, three farmers and their wives, the butcher and the man who owned the garage.

'What's happening?' Soddy was asking. 'Why's the sky gone red?'

'Jerry is bombing the Liverpool docks,' said the butcher.

A hole opened inside me. The docks was where we'd lived. 'Me mam. Me mam,' I heard myself shout.

Iolo laid his hand on my neck. 'Don't worry, *cariad*. They were given lots of warning. Your mam will be safe in the shelter.'

For once he was wrong. Mam never went near the shelter. Too scared of the dark. She always dived beneath the kitchen table.

Soddy started crying. A cousin stroked his head, smoothing the thin white hair that lay in all directions.

'Those children shouldn't be seeing this,' the older teacher said.

Planes like minnows floated black against the orange. At least, I think they did. Next weekend, I saw the pictures in the paper. But could anyone have seen them from that mountain-top, let alone the bombs that showered from each plane? And yet I saw them then, tumbling like nails.

Next night, Iolo walked into the lodge as I lay by my favourite hound. '*O cariad,*' he said, and sat beside me on the bench, 'your mam is dead and so is Soddy's mam.'

I stared into the flame of his hurricane lamp.

'Cry if you want to,' he said.

I buried my face in Caradog's neck, smelt his smell of scurf and warm bone. How could I cry for a mam who'd never come to see me?

'They'd all of them managed to get to the shelter,' I heard Iolo say, 'but it got bombed as well. There was none of them left alive.'

The curtain blew into the room and the lamp went out with a pop. Lizzie stayed by the window, smoking and swigging her potion. Out in the darkness, the hound howled on. Still clutching the badger's claw, I clamped the blankets over my ears. *Hiraeth.* Homesick. Longing. Feeling out of place. Another word that Lizzie wouldn't understand. O mighty Gwyn, I prayed as I drifted off to sleep, make the major's lazy huntsman go and find his hound.

Chapter Four

NEXT morning, I woke to yelps more desperate than before. I jumped out of bed and tugged on my vest and knickers. Lizzie had placed a little clock beside her bed. Half-past six. She herself had vanished – maybe scarpered back to Liverpool. Last night's scummy water slopped cold against my face. I dried it, slipped on my dress and opened the door to the passage. How had we got upstairs?

Round the right-hand corner, pictures lined the walls. Scents of honey and lavender polish thickened the air. I stopped. Not what I remembered. Before I could turn, a door swung back at the opposite end. Skinny against the light, a figure stood on the threshold. Master What's-his-name escaping from his room.

'Hey! What are you doing?' he called in a hoity-toity voice.

I froze. He slopped towards me on thin white feet in backless leather slippers. As he drew near I saw he wore a camel dressing-gown and a grown-up frown beneath his floppy fringe.

'*Galw draw i ddweud helô,*' I said.

He jerked his chin as though about to peck me, cross and glittery-eyed from life behind bars. 'Are you the girl I saw yesterday?' he asked.

'I might have been.'

His thin white fingers fiddled with the cord around his waist, his nails clean and pointy like a girl's. 'And who was the woman?'

'Me mam. She's come for a job.'

'Then she's made a mistake. Tell her there's no work.'

So nobody had let him know she'd been allowed to stay.

'Go on,' he said. 'Chop chop.'

I spun away.

28

'On second thoughts,' he called before I reached the corner, 'you could come and wait with me. My breakfast will arrive – there's always far too much - and afterwards I'll show you all the birds' eggs I've collected.'

Is that why Lizzie had brought me? To make friends with the major's son? I bolted round the corner to a door I hadn't noticed. It opened onto stairs that plunged down into darkness. Ears out for the slip-slopping boy, I felt my way down to the landing. Fingers stiff against the walls, I passed the knobs on the panels, then followed the smell of frying down to the kitchen.

A girl in an old black dress stood pressed against the Aga, her white cotton cap skew-whiff, pom-poms missing from her slippers and her waistband fastened with a safety pin. Polly: I knew from size of her tummy.

'What are you doing here?' she asked, swinging round to face me.

'Nothing. I want to get outside.'

'Outside? Have you asked your mam?'

'I can't. I don't know where she is.'

'Where d'you think? She's in the servants' hall.'

Polly's face, broad and shiny beneath her grubby cap, looked honest enough to make me think she might be telling the truth.

'Where's the outside door?'

She pointed at a chair. Her flesh bulged round the straps beneath her dress and its cuffs were fraying round her beefy wrists. 'So your ma used to work as a maid.'

'No,' I replied, not sure I was doing right. 'She worked in a pub. A pub called The Spanish Fleet.'

Polly bossed the sausages round the pan. 'I was wondering where she got that fancy skirt.'

Stupid of me not to check our wardrobe. She'd never have left without her pretty clothes. 'She's got better things than that,' I said. 'A coat and matching hat and shoes and handbag.'

A banger burst and Polly speared it with a fork. 'A matching hat and handbag and she wants a job up here?'

'She wants it because…' I should have kept my trap shut. 'She wants it because I think she needed work.'

'What about the pub?'

My head felt hot from the jumble of lies inside it. Or lies mixed up with truth. No telling which was which. 'She might have got a bit tired.'

'From pulling pints?' The girl's blue eyes were opening my brain. 'If she gets tired that easy she won't last long round here.'

'She doesn't get tired. Not normally,' I said.

'You wouldn't catch me landing here if I had a job in a city. She'll be off again soon enough, you can bet your life she will.' The girl jammed the sausage meat into her mouth. 'And she's a widow, you said?'

'Yes, I think she is. Yes, my dad is dead.'

'If he's dead,' said Polly, 'why aren't you wearing black?'

Before I could think up an answer, Lizzie walked into the room, her lipstick smudged and brows too dark against her small white face.

'I was coming to wake you,' she said.

She wore a cap like Polly's, except cleaner, and the same sort of dingy black dress, except that hers looked baggy, with sleeves that reached her knuckles. Polly loaded the tray inside the corner cupboard. Toast, bangers, bacon, eggs: the brekkie I might have shared. Did the major's son have a special ration book? Studs and hobs were clattering down the passage beyond the kitchen, wafting in a tang of brushy air. Lizzie's eyes grew narrow as I moved towards it.

'Get back here,' she said. 'It's time for breakfast.'

Turning from the outer door, I tracked her down the passage and into a long low room with a table down the middle. Men in worn tweed jackets were shoving their caps in their pockets, their faces berry brown below the mark made by the bands and white as a baby's above. They clumped to the table in pockets of chilly air and swung their gaitered legs above the benches. I wriggled into a space across from Lizzie and in between a plump young man in cords and a man with a face as creased as a worn leather glove.

Mrs Arbiter stood by a chair at the top of the table shovelling porridge into chipped white bowls. Polly filled cups with tea that slopped as I passed them along. The men cut their porridge into squares and stabbed them with their knives. Straight-backed, her hair fluffed around her cap, Lizzie said no to porridge and puffed on a Kensitas, her lips and nails bright among the browns and duns. Now and again, a man would glance at her sideways. Mostly they ignored her, talking in words I'd never heard before. Fozzy and tup. Tethera and neep.

But I understood them when they got onto the hunt – how the deputy master couldn't hunt a thimble and people out of pocket because of that damn fox, strolling round the farms as if he owned them, dragging off the biggest gander in the yard then coming back for more a second night.

Not a fox. No dog fox would risk a second night. The killer was a vixen with a late or sickly litter or with cubs she'd taken over from a missing dam.

'And now we've lost a hound,' said the leathery man, 'and wouldn't you know it's that daft bloody dog hound from Bala.'

'Llywelyn!' I burst out. And I'd thought he was a bitch.

Lizzie leant across and spoke to the man directly. 'Please forgive her,' she said. 'She forgot all her manners in Wales.'

Ignoring her, the man swung round to face me. 'Who told ye his name?' he asked.

Llywelyn was a dog hound whose cry had never darkened, bred by Dai Meredith, Iolo's second cousin, and famous for his silvery, bell-like notes. 'Nobody,' I said to the man. 'I knew it for myself.'

His sharp, unsmiling eyes staring at my stupid tartan dress. 'There's not many lassies could tell a hound from its cry. And not many kennel men, either, come to that.'

'I used to hunt three valleys away from Dai Meredith.'

'So you'll be used to wild, white gormless hounds. And the major thinks our line should be outcrossed!'

Men were guffawing up and down the table. What was so funny? I waited till they'd stopped. 'No Welsh Master ever lost a hound,' I told the man, 'not even in the war when they was fed on broken biscuits.'

'Here it was us that got the biscuits,' said the man. 'The major would see us starve before he'd underfeed his pack.'

Mrs Arbiter stood to the right of an empty, high-backed chair, doling out black pudding and fried bread. 'That's enough of that,' she said. 'The major does his best.'

The man stabbed a lump of porridge with his knife.

'Can I go and look for him?' I asked.

'Leave him be,' said the man. 'I'll find him soon enough. Teach him a lesson an' all.'

I cut a square of porridge and tried to force it down. Llywelyn was a fearless stallion hound, descended from mighty Glog Nimrod and cousin to Aneurin. Dai Meredith had lent the major of his best. 'Are you a whipper-in?' I asked the man.

'Nay, lass. I'm the huntsman.'

Like all huntsmen touched by Gwyn the god, but this one only lightly. Not a wizard like Iolo who could read a foxhound's mind. More your normal grown-up, slow to cast and late to find. A man who, if he knew his pack, would only know the centre and never the minds of the hounds who worked the edge.

Mrs Arbiter settled herself to the right of the empty chair. As she was stirring her tea, Polly burst in from the kitchen. 'Master Oliver wants to see you straightaway.'

Mrs Arbiter tugged off her pinny. As she puffed towards the door, a wormy feeling slithered through my chest. 'I think I saw him in his dressing-gown,' I said.

Lizzie's cup clattered in its saucer. 'Jacqueline! Are you sure?'

'Yes. I turned the wrong way.'

'Oh, pet, you'll get me sacked.'

At last the huntsman caught her eye across the table. 'Don't worry, lass. You won't get sacked, not from here you won't. The last maid walked with three months wages owed.'

Lizzie stubbed out her cigarette, her red mouth slipping sideways. No man was meant to tell her what was what. Not seeming to notice, the huntsman clanked down his knife. 'Looks like I'd better get searching.'

I jumped up from the bench. My chance had come at last. But no. Mrs Arbiter marched back into the room. 'You've been going where I told you not to.'

So the boy had snitched. 'I want to look for Llywelyn,' I said.

'Bob will deal with him.'

'But I can call him in Welsh.'

'Welsh or not, we have to make sure you know where you cannot go.'

The hand of Gwyn was on me as I dodged towards the passage. The housekeeper grabbed my collar as I passed. 'What a little tyke,' she said and swung me round to face her.

Up in a flash, Lizzie came between us. 'You've got to excuse her. That's what she learnt as a vackie.'

'She's going to learn different here,' Mrs Arbiter said. 'When I'm done with her this morning I'm going to telephone the school.'

Still gripping my collar, she tugged me into the passage. Long as a village street, it stretched ahead, its cabbage-coloured walls sucking light from the bulbs on the ceiling. Lizzie on one side, Mrs Arbiter on the other, we marched past a row of doors, all of them shut, until I'd lost all hope of hearing Llywelyn. Next came a passage with even more doors than the first, walls even darker and lights even further apart, its ceiling so low I could have jumped up and touched it.

Mrs Arbiter chose a key from the bunch at her waist. 'This used to be Mr Arbiter's pantry,' she said, turning the key in a nearby door.

Mr Arbiter was Dead. I knew from her solemn voice. 'And here's where he sat when he squared the major's accounts.'

A chill bounced off the marble counter. Mrs Arbiter laid her hand on a chair, high-backed with long curved arms like the empty one at breakfast. 'Died at El Alamein,' she said. 'He was the major's batman.'

His ghost breath froze my neck. She shooed us back to the passage and into another room a few doors down, windowless like the pantry, with shelves round all four sides. Lizzie rattled the matches in her pocket: a sure sign she needed a smoke. Mrs Arbiter said it was good to have supplies to hand and that every year they bottled damsons from the orchard, droning on and on about the different sorts of fruit.

I looked at rows of bottles the colour of old blood and jars of fruit blanketed by mould.

Mrs Arbiter poked my arm. 'Are you listening? If I send you here for raspberry jam I won't want strawberry or damson.' She led us out and turned the key in the lock. As if anyone would nick her mouldy fruit! The next room ponged of bleach and sweat. She took up her post beside a window that leaked cobwebby light onto a row of sinks. She talked about washdays, the slack for heating the water, how early we had to start and where to hang the clothes. Once again, she looked at me, not Lizzie. I should never have shown her that I knew about the Borax. She was going to train me as a maid, and Lizzie would scarper as soon as she'd got her money.

More rooms. More boring talk. We climbed the stairs towards our bedroom, turned left, not right, at the top and stopped before the corner. 'Now, remember,' Mrs Arbiter said to me, 'you never come this way without express permission.' Panting a little, she stooped to undo her laces. 'Servants' shoes wear out the carpets,' she said.

To me, it looked faded and worn enough already but Lizzie was already unlacing the shoes she must have been given that morning.

'I'm waiting, Jacqueline,' said Mrs Arbiter.

We tracked in stocking soles between the rows of dingy pictures then stopped in front of Master Oliver's door.

'Upstairs, you always knock. Downstairs, you never do. Have you understood me, Jacqueline?'

Mrs Arbiter opened the door onto a stink of Friar's Balsam and under it the pong of rotten eggs. Hoping to spot Llywelyn, I peered through the bars on the window. Below me lay the flagstones where I'd stood with Lizzie. On the grass below the terrace grew a monkey puzzle tree. Halfway down the lawn, leaves choked a big stone fountain beneath a pop-eyed fish gaping drily at the sky. Beyond the garden lay what had to be the major's country. Tidy farms. Coppiced coverts. Hedges neatly laid. My heart ached for the mountains and tangled, untamed forests, for a country that challenged the hounds and tested their huntsman's soul.

'Leave that window, Jacqueline,' said Mrs Arbiter.

Shelves lined the walls on either side, each with a row of eggs, white, blue, pale green or buff with large black blotches. They sat in upturned boxes lined with cotton wool, the small ones near the ceiling, the large ones by the floor. The writing on the labels might have been scrawled by an elf. Curlew. *Numenius arquata.* Mapple Fell 53,6. 4th April, 1944.

'Did he collect all these?' asked Lizzie, gone all sugary.

Mrs Arbiter frowned at the splatters on the carpet. 'He spends his Easter holidays trailing round the hedgerows then comes up here and blows the eggs all over the Persian rug.'

She opened a second door onto a smaller room with a wardrobe at the foot of a bed and a giant chest of drawers. A sketch pad lay on a wicker chair by a pile of magazines. What sort of boy read *Vogue*? On the bedside locker by a bottle of Lucozade stood a photograph of a woman smiling in front of the fountain, not dry, like now, but spilling water through the fish's mouth. Her hair looked straight and dark, like Master Oliver's, and her eyes, like his, were fringed with thick black lashes.

Lizzie ran her fingertip along the curly frame. 'Was she really as beautiful as that?'

'Handsome is as handsome does,' Mrs Arbiter said. 'If you ask me, they should have patched things up. Say what you like, but he's sensitive and schoolboys can be cruel.'

'Poor lad,' said Lizzie. 'No wonder he got sick.'

'The major telephoned this morning,' Mrs Arbiter said. 'The usual pay, he told me, and your Wednesday afternoons free, and anything broke I'll take it from your wages. I was surprised, I have to say, him taking you on unseen.'

Lizzie puffed her cheeks. 'When will he be home?'

'He? You mean Major Wetheral? That's nowt to do with you. It's his chauffeur, Alan Rumney, that fetches him from the station and me that bangs the gong when he arrives. More to the point is the work to be done beforehand. The major says to put you in charge of Master Oliver's room. Polly's a good enough girl but she's getting too familiar, sitting up here chatting the night away.'

I caught a whiff of stale fat from Lizzie's baggy dress. 'He'll be missing his mother,' she said.

'Maybe so but staff should keep their distance. You'll light his bedroom fire early every morning, run his bath, lay out his clothes, put yesterday's in the wash and change his sheets once a week or more. The major says he's got to get out hunting, so Jacqueline can help you clean his boots, wash and starch his stock and check his riding clothes.' Stern-faced, Mrs Arbiter glanced from Lizzie to me. 'Above all else, remember: he'll want to draw you in so you mustn't let him get too close. If you do, he'll try to get you on his side.'

Lizzie cocked her head. 'You mean against his father?'

'Aye. Or anyone who thwarts him.'

Lizzie and Mrs Arbiter clattered downstairs without me, even though they knew I'd never find my way. White, large as a lemon and lightly smeared with blood, the largest egg lay on the topmost shelf, alone, in pride of place, and too high for me to read the label. On tiptoe, I stretched out my fingertips, rolled the egg off the shelf and caught it lightly in my waiting hand. It warmed my skin as if the chick was still inside it. I moved towards the window, egg balanced on my palm, not white, I now saw, but palest blue, like milk skimmed of its cream. I puffed my cheeks and blew until it rolled from side to side, to and fro until I spied the pinhole under—neath.

Steps pounded down the passage. The egg jumped in palm. I curled my fingers as it rolled towards the edge.

'Jacqueline!' called Lizzie. 'Jacqueline! Where are you?'

I felt the eggshell crack beneath my fingers. 'I'm coming now,' I said.

'Don't be long,' she called as her footsteps thumped away.

My stomach pitched in fright. The egg was dented down one side. Best put it back and hope that no one noticed.

But Oliver had stole it from its nest, not caring that the mother bird would miss it, and blown the chick onto his nursery carpet.

'Chop chop,' I said, and jabbed my thumb into the shell.

Chapter Five

TURNING left this time, I made my way down to the kitchen, where smells of steak and kidney lay heavy on the air. Already men were seated in the servants' hall, heads bent over slabs of suet. I slithered between the plump boy and Mr Hoad. The boy turned and smiled, showing small white teeth.

'I'm Danny,' he said, jabbing his knife towards Mr Hoad. 'His son, for me sins, and Major Wetheral's groom.'

As the boy got back to his suet, I looked at him sideways on. Young, but not too young to have a faint moustache, and with plump, pink ears set tight against his head.

'Have they found Llywelyn yet?' I whispered.

'Nee, lass. Not a sign.'

I poked my fork into my cooling suet. 'Does the major know he's gone?'

'Not likely, lass, and nor will he be told until we have to.'

I felt hollow inside, like Master Oliver's egg. Hollow but not hungry, as if somebody had smashed me.

Mr Hoad looked up and down the table. 'They say in The Arms the major's off to gay Paree.'

A man with a lazy eye looked up from his plate. 'And all the while we're slaving here for nowt?'

Mrs Arbiter clattered down her knife. 'Major Wetheral's doing his best.'

The skin on the huntsman's face looked like tack in need of soap. 'And meanwhile that damn fox is killing all the geese.'

'Aye,' said Danny, 'and none of us will catch 'un – unless we find that bugger who unblocks his earths.'

Iolo never blocked an earth, but he'd have caught the vixen, lifting his pack from on top of his bright little cob.

'Tea, Polly,' Mrs Arbiter said.

Lizzie stood and brushed crumbs from her skirt. 'I'll see to the tea.'

'Can I go and look for Llywelyn?' I called as she left the room.

'Not so fast,' Mrs Arbiter said. 'You've got school this afternoon. I warned you I'd be phoning Mr Gonegal.'

'Can't I see him tomorrow?'

'He wants you straightaway.'

School, where beefy farm boys would call me Dirty Scouser. 'I can't go in this dress.'

'It'll have to do till we get you some sensible clothes.'

'I don't know where school is,' I lied.

Mrs Arbiter nodded towards the outer passage. 'You saw it as you came here from the station. Besides, you'll see the kiddies in the playground. Your mam's hung your raincoat by the door.'

The raincoat was what you'd expect: mauve with shiny buttons. I left it on the peg and climbed the kitchen steps. Ears out for Llywelyn, I trailed through the drizzle, past three hunters rugged-up in a paddock, then opened the rusty gates at the foot of the drive. Each gate held a shield I'd seen the day before, with a flimsy-looking hound prancing in the centre.

A knot of stumpy women waited at the bus stop, all wearing plastic rain hats tied beneath their chins. Their belted gabardines hung halfway down stout calves that rose like lisle tubes from zippered black galoshes. They glared at me. I guessed the thoughts behind their pebble glasses: how dare a girl like this walk down our street? The bus swished up and soaked my shoes and socks. The women soothed their snoods into rows of plastic pleats and snapped open leather purses they'd pulled from wicker baskets.

I crossed towards high wooden gates I'd missed the day before. Behind them, someone scraped a besom over concrete, rousing a smell of Jeyes Fluid mixed with tripe and dog shit. Hounds yelped. An ache swelled in my throat. Aneurin. Eleri. Caradog. I'd lost them for good.

A few yards down the street, small boys kicked an empty tin on tarmac and big lads lobbed a football at a netball post. A man in a donkey jacket over his dungarees crossed the playground towards the gates where I stood.

'Who are you looking for?' he asked in a foreign-sounding voice.

I tried to think of what to say in English. Nothing came. He called me in and closed the gate behind me. 'This way,' he said, and walked into the school. He stopped beside an open door with a name plate saying Headmaster. Inside, a Sir in a baggy suit sat over a sprawl of books.

'So this is Jacqueline,' he said, 'soaking wet, I see. Now tell me, child, have you got no raincoat?'

I said it was at home.

'Home? You mean the Hall? How are they doing up there?'

'They've lost a hound,' I said.

'A sorry business, all that gossip in the papers. Any sign of the major?'

'Not so far,' I said.

'And your mother's a widow, Mrs Arbiter told me.'

I curled my nails in my palms to hide the dirt.

'Well,' he said, 'she'll have plenty to keep her busy.' He sighed, picked up a pen and asked for my date of birth, the school I'd been to last and what form they'd put me in.

'I'm not quite sure,' I said. There'd only been one classroom, and one teacher taught the girls from five years old to twelve.

Sir wrote down my answers in letters too small for me to read them upside down. All the same, I could guess what he'd put from the deepening lines in his brow. *Jacqueline's not right. She thinks that she's a hound. She'd rather sleep in a kennel than a proper bed. They say she uses her nose too much and then forgets to blow it.* Then, on the line below: *she should have been left in Wales.*

He screwed the cap back on his pen and hobbled round the desk. 'How's Polly?'

I told him she was fine.

'That fellow should be made to marry her.'

I stared at the stains on Sir's tie and wondered which fellow he meant.

'I wish she could have stayed on,' Sir said. 'We might have got her reading.'

Swinging his gammy leg stiffly to one side, Sir limped ahead of me down a corridor, then opened the door to a classroom at the end. A young, plump Miss in horn-rims sat at the teacher's desk facing rows of boys and girls in home-made jumpers, grey skirts or shorts, with scabby knees above hand-knitted socks. I smiled. They didn't smile back, just stared, potato-faced, at my stupid tartan dress.

Sir propped his fists on Miss's desk and whispered in her ear. She pointed at a place beside a girl with corkscrew curls pinned to her scalp with fat pink kirby grips. Miss told the class I'd come from Liverpool and she knew they'd show me how friendly Westmorland children were.

'Is Liverpool still being bombed?' asked a boy at the back.

'Don't be silly, Robert.'

'Then what's she doing here?'

'Ask her yourself at break.'

Miss gave me a pencil with its tip already chewed, a sharpener, a ruler and an exercise book. A girl called Mary Molloy had already filled half the book. She must have been a vackie and gone home. Miss wrote a line of figures on the board: *pump, pedwar, wyth* and *deg*, and told us what to do.

'Do you understand me, Jacqueline?' she asked.

I nodded, but the hand of Gwyn the god lay heavy on my shoulders. Not only had I failed to find the hound: I hadn't even looked, just done what I was told. Miss turned back to the board, wrote another string of figures then sat at her desk. Brenda clamped her fingertips round a pencil, their four pink bulbs of flesh bulging over bitten nails.

'What do we do with the numbers?' I whispered in her ear.

She wrinkled her small snub nose. Perhaps she'd caught the smell of the ointment on my scabs. Sick and out-of-place, I stared at my exercise book till Miss shooed us to the playground.

Girls with fat pink knees began a skipping game:

When that man is dead and gone
We'll go dancing down the street
Kissing every boy we meet.

The rope whacked the tarmac, inviting me to jump. Brenda shoved me to one side.

Go back home, Stinky-Pooh, she sang, *dirty, stupid Scouser,*
Come to steal our sweeties and stone our little cats.

The other girls joined in, plaits bobbing as they skipped. *Stinky-pooh, stinky-pooh.* I bit my lip and wandered to the far edge of the playground, gripped the rails and stared towards the park. No sign of Llywelyn, not even a far-off whimper. But the major's hounds were babbling in their kennels: I saw the roofs, two doors away, and caught the smell of tripe.

'Gan yam! Gan yam!' yelled Brenda at the end of the afternoon.

I bolted across the playground then halted by the gates. Nowhere to go but the Hall. I dawdled past shops I hadn't noticed yesterday: one window stacked with empty chocolate boxes, and one with piles of offal slumped on imitation grass. After passing the row of cottages I crossed to the wall of the park, as high as the one at the docks but built of pale stone.

The big old house was glooming down the drive, its rows of windows watching as I tried to dodge the potholes. Halfway up, a soldier was loading a jeep with rusting wire. He stopped as I drew near. Had he come to look me over? Eyes on the ground, I walked on. An officer paced the gravel, short, with flabby jowls that bulged around his chinstrap.

'It's Jacqueline, isn't it?' he asked.

Someone had told him my name. Lizzie, still hoping to sell me.

His twinkling eyes grew smaller as he smiled. 'I've got a surprise for you.'

I started to run. I'd had enough surprises. Skirting the man and his stick, I tore round the side of the house.

'Watch out!' said a voice as I swerved onto the terrace.

A hound lunged towards me, towing Mr Hoad. Mud draggled his stern and streaked his milk-white coat.

'Llywelyn, *bach!*' I cried.

'The daftie had got himself stuck inside a trench. He was found by that officer feller on the drive. He hadn't even tried to get himself back out.'

I dropped to my knees. 'He must of done. Look! He's lost a dew claw and the other one is broke.'

'Broke or not, another night and he'd have been a goner and God knows what the major would have said. We're waiting for the vet to come and check him over so why not let him stretch his legs? I'd do it meself but I've got the pack to feed.'

Lizzie would want to quiz me: had I managed to speak English? Been polite to the headmaster? Remembered not to sniff? But Mr Hoad was handing me the leash.

'When you've finished,' he added, 'just bring him to his lodge.' He nodded at the roofs across the grass.

'I'm not allowed in there.'

'Just this once,' said Mr Hoad.

Squaddies were filling the trenches by the drive, each ditch a ten-foot drop to a claggy bed.

'Out the road, lassie,' said a sergeant, levering a clod with a horrible sucking sound.

Behind him lay a row of mounds like new-dug graves. Ears flat, favouring a forepaw, Llywelyn towed me away, onto the terrace and down the steps to the lawn. Now we were alone, I looked him over. For all his grimy coat, he was still a handsome hound with a sizeable knowledge box between his well-set ears, strong, muscled loins and a galloping arch to his back. We reached the grass. He sniffed in short, excited bursts. I breathed in. Smelt nothing. Impossible. For a hound, there's no such thing as empty air. I closed my eyes and tried again. Still nothing. Just a dull patch in my big and useless brain.

Llywelyn tugged me into a square of scraggy privet and pressed his chest against the fountain's lowest basin close to the spot where Oliver's mam had stood. Two smaller basins dribbled overhead. Muddy water trickled from the fish's lips. Llywelyn dipped his muzzle among the lilies, fleshy and green like Mr Jeremy Fisher's. In the murk beneath their leaves, large, speckled fishes flickered.

When the hound had finished drinking we strolled down to the stream. A windowless brick cube squatted on the bank, no taller than me, with a sagging wooden door. Llywelyn nosed it open and towed me down some steps into a chilly room. I knew what it was from the nearby *plas* in Capel: the place where they'd once stored the ice brought down from the mountains. Glad of Llywelyn's weight against my shin, I sat on the ledge where the ice had been packed in straw. The hound would never forget the night he'd spent in the trench, its oozing sides, his sense of being abandoned.

Shivering, I climbed the steps to what was left of the daylight. Llywelyn towed me back towards the house. Thick with smells of slack and mouldy wood, smoke shilly-shallied down from what must be the kitchen chimney. The pack set up a clamour as we trailed along the drive and kept it going till we reached the kennels. I turned the latch. Llywelyn balked. I dragged him through the gates as Mr Hoad crossed the yard towards us.

'Give us him,' he said.

Llywelyn pressed his belly to the concrete. The huntsman tugged his lead. The hound refused to budge.

'You'd mebbe better take him to his lodge,' said Mr Hoad.

A kennelman opened a door on our right, the lad with a lazy eye I'd seen at breakfast. I stepped inside. Beef and liver simmered in a copper. We crossed a concrete yard with troughs on either side, entered a second, covered yard and pushed through a door on the left. At last a chance to meet the major's hounds.

His dog pack sprawled on the benches that lined three sides of the room.

'They're a bonny lot,' the kennelman said.

My eye roved round the hounds. Each one was black and tan, with not so much as a spot of any other colour, in itself a remarkable feat of breeding. And each was sleek of shape and glossy-coated, clearly fed with butcher's cuts, not stuffed with dodgy offal or broken bourbons sloshed in gravy. I saw shapely heads and shoulders well set back. But what about the narrow skulls, the bland, unquestioning faces, shallow chests and slender loins? Well-fed but not well-bred, I thought, for all their matching coats.

I unbuckled Llywelyn's collar. Ears pricked, he stared through knowledgeable eyes at hounds who'd never cope with switchback mountains or track a fox through towering peaks and crags.

The major was right. His men were wrong. His pack should be outcrossed.

Chapter Six

'HOT water hurts my hands,' said Lizzie after supper. She didn't seem to know about the egg. Keen to get her on my side, just in case, I poured a heap of crystals in the sink.

The hot tap juddered on its long brass pipe. Polly knelt with a grunt, opened the Aga door, riddled the stove and raised her voice above the grating iron. 'Last night I saw a soldier,' she said. 'On crutches he was and tapped right past me door.'

So I hadn't heard him pass our bedroom. What if I'd woke to see him by my bed, his nose blown off and eyes dripping down his face?

'There was no soldiers on crutches,' Mrs Arbiter said, turning the pantry key on a dish of leftover herrings. 'Most of 'em were wrong in the head or cowards or deserters, sitting up all night playing cards.'

'Alan told me they was shell-shocked,' Polly said.

Mrs Arbiter dropped the key in her pocket. 'Except that Alan Rumney has never seen a shell.' She stalked into the corridor.

'Where's she gone?' asked Lizzie. A door slammed in the passage.

'Her sitting-room,' said Polly, pulling off her cap. 'She begged her hubby not to go to war but off he went to be the major's batman and now she can't forgive the major for surviving. His tank went up and threw him onto the sand. Meanwhile Mr Arbiter fried like a chop inside.'

'Poor old trout,' said Lizzie. 'Is that why she's gone bald?'

Polly lugged a hod of coke towards the Aga. 'It all fell out the day she got the news and her eyebrows too. That same night I seen him in his snow-white gloves carry a silver salver straight through his pantry door.'

46

'Don't go lifting that,' said Lizzie, reaching for the hod. 'At six and a half months gone, you should be putting your feet up.'

'Glad of the chance,' said Polly, patting her bump. 'Take that prong thing from the rail, and lever up the lid – go easy now, in case the gas jumps out – then slot that metal funnel in the hole.'

Lizzie hoicked the hod over the funnel's rim and tilted a shower of coke into the stove. 'Honest to God, it's a job for man,' she said.

'You're telling me,' said Polly, pulling out a chair.

'So where's this feller now?' Lizzie's voice had dropped. I stayed with my back to the room, splashing cutlery in the sink.

'AWOL,' said Polly, 'just the other day. Roared off in the major's motor car when he'd dropped him at the station.'

Lizzie pulled a pack of Woodies from her pocket. She'd said she had no money left for Kensitas. 'Men! Don't you hate the lot of 'em?'

In Bootle, she'd always seemed to take the uncles' side. Men will be men, I'd heard her say, and clever girls take precautions. But here she was, sat beside Polly, nodding and stroking her hair.

'For all he's so handsome,' said Polly, 'I wish I'd never met him.'

The ash on Lizzie's cigarette was drooping. 'Never mind,' she said. 'There's plenty of fish in the sea.'

'Not round here there's not. Half of 'em didn't come home and most that did came back without their marbles. Sometimes you think you're in a loony bin. Besides, it's not every feller will take on another man's brat.'

Lizzie handed her a lacy hanky. 'He's a local man, you said?'

Polly nodded and blew her nose.

The ash on Lizzie's cigarette drooped like an elephant's trunk, and still no sign she'd seen it or was looking for an ashtray. 'So he's not some hunting feller, Poll?'

Polly guffawed. 'Not on your life. They're all red-faced and ugly. Alan Rumney is the major's chauffeur.'

'Jackie,' said Lizzie, swivelling round to face me, 'you can run upstairs and get my Compound.'

I grabbed the torch from its hook by the door and trotted up to our bedroom. The little green bottle stood in its usual place. Less than half full. By the time I got back to the kitchen, Lizzie had fetched two glasses and Polly was dabbing her eyes with the cap she'd pulled from her pocket. 'But I still love him, you know, honest to God I do.'

The ash had fell and drifted on the table. 'He'll be back with the major, you'll see,' said Lizzie, pouring a tot.

Polly grabbed the glass and took a greedy gulp, as if sure she'd be cured of her Weakness and Painful Complaints. 'But the major might be gone for weeks. Master Oliver says he's scrounging for money in London.'

'Master Oliver, eh?' said Lizzie. 'What a funny boy.'

Polly took another gulp and lowered her voice to a whisper. 'They say in The Arms he's not the major's son. That his mother had a fling in France.'

'Who knows?' said Lizzie, twiddling her glass. 'And, by the way, I've got to do his rooms.'

'Rather you than me,' said Polly, 'changing sheets like that. No one's ever told him to sneeze into his hanky.' Big red blotches sprang up on her cheeks. 'And now he says I broke a bloody egg. I was there when he saw it was smashed and he practically burst into tears. A heron's egg, he said, and that's his favourite bird.'

I kept my face blank and busied myself with a towel. Polly was bigger than me and wouldn't get hit.

Lizzie sloshed more Compound into Polly's glass. 'When your man comes back,' she said, 'the major will make him marry you.'

Polly shook her head. 'You've never met the major.'

'Even so.' Lying again. Unless she'd lied to me. 'We could just explain,' she said to Polly.

'The major won't do owt.' Polly twirled her empty glass. 'Not while he's got that rattletrap of a Wolseley. Alan's the only one can get it on the road. And besides the major's gone so strange. He's got them burns - you'll see for yourself - his fingers are like claws. And he gives such screams at night they turn your blood to ice. I wish he'd get some treatment down in London.'

Lizzie started to talk about all the ex-soldiers she knew, the ones who took to the roads or couldn't remember their names. I hung the damp tea towels on the Aga rail and pulled out a chair beside her.

'Bed, Jacqueline,' she said.

'But tomorrow's a Saturday!'

'All the same,' she said.

I took the torch and tracked along the passage, close to the opposite wall as I passed the butler's pantry. Soon the twisty stairs were rising through the gloom. I climbed them as fast as I could. Jumped the last two steps. Caught my toe. Tripped. Let go of the torch. It crashed downstairs. I groped my way back to the landing, dropped to my knees and, fingers outspread, felt around for the torch. The air grew thick with the pong of burning chops. I jumped to my feet and dashed upstairs again.

A row of ghost-Lizzies rustled in the wardrobe, all her pretty dresses waiting to be worn. After undressing, I felt beneath her bed. Nothing. She'd forgot to bring up the po. Wanting a pee, I hovered by the door. The smell of burnt chops came creeping past the hinges: Mr Arbiter waiting with his raw red foot on the torch. I climbed into bed and recited the names of Iolo's pack – Bryn, Blodwen, Aelwen, Ynysfor - but the pee grew bigger and hotter till I could think of nothing else, not even the moan of the wind in the poky little chimney. I tugged at my knickers and pulled them tight between my legs. The pee swelled. I gasped and moved my hand. Water scalded my thighs. I clenched my muscles. It stopped. I let it go again. What was the point of trying when the bed was already soaked? I lay on the warm, wet sheet, hoping it would dry. Instead, it turned cold. The smell of pee grew stronger. I rolled out of bed and reached to open the window. Lizzie barged into the room, po in one hand and Tilley lamp in the other. Eyes glinting in its light, she ripped off the sheet and the blanket underneath it. A big yellow stain blurred the stripes on the mattress.

'No wonder he made you sleep with them filthy hounds.'

'I was scared of Mr Arbiter,' I said.

'So you were listening in again, Miss Snoop.' She yanked my hair. 'Was it you that smashed that egg?'

'No. I didn't do it.'

'Don't lie to me. You waited until I'd left the room.'

Blood pulsed behind my eyes. 'It was an accident.'

'The devil it was. You did it out of malice.' This time she yanked my hair so hard I tumbled to the ground. 'Stop it!' she said as I whimpered and yelped. 'Stop them stupid noises.'

I whimpered again. She tumbled on top of me, saying I was mental and how would she wash the mattress and she must have been mad not to leave me with that man. My nose banged the lino each time she whacked my head and blubbering wails came choking from my mouth.

'If Ma Arbiter gets wind of this she'll send us back to Bootle.'

She stood, arms folded, waiting. For what? I didn't know. For me to say sorry? I'd never do it again?

'I should never have come here.' Tears dripped down her cheeks. 'If only I'd known the shock I had in store. I tell you this,' she said, wiping her nose on her sleeve, 'in Polly's shoes I'd bloody well know what to do.' She sloshed water from the ewer onto the sheet and didn't even bother wringing it out. Then she blew her nose and nudged my bottom with her foot.

'Take off them dirty pyjamas, you stupid baby, and get yourself back into bed.'

I lay on the damp smelly mattress and jammed my fist into my mouth. Iolo had told me the truth. My mam was dead. No real mam could ever be so cruel.

Chapter Seven

NEXT morning, Lizzie's alarm was broke. 'Rise and shine!' called Polly through the wall.

Lizzie washed and dressed without a word to me. Tying on her apron, she darted through the door. Her footsteps thumped along the passage towards Master Oliver's room.

Mr Hoad was late for breakfast: he'd been seeing to the hounds. That morning, the meet was at Rosely, four or five miles away, and Colonel Tunnicliffe was standing in for the major. The major himself had telephoned: Oliver had to hunt so Danny had been grooming Oliver's pony. Billy, the whip, said they may as well not bother: they'd never catch that fox with old Tunnicliffe in charge.

Though I'd done my best to wash in scummy water, the pee smell hung around me while I ate. Trapped in my bubble of stink, I chewed on a fatty rasher. Men were wiping their mouths with the backs of their hands. 'Can I have some tea?' I asked, holding out my cup.

Lizzie cut me dead. Anger throbbed inside me. Iolo had never hit me, yet she'd called him cruel. Besides, the fault was hers for not bringing up the po. The men stumped off to kennels, farm or stables. Left prodding at my bacon with no tea to wash it down, I ached at the thought of everyone hunting without me.

Llywelyn started to howl as the pack left the village. Not stopping to ask permission, I pelted down the drive. Mr Hoad had left the gates to the kennels unbolted. I stuck my head inside the yard to check it was empty, then easily found a lead by the door to Llywelyn's pen.

'Druan â ti,' I said to him. Poor hound.

He ducked his head as I stooped to buckle his collar, knowing I hadn't struggled hard enough to find him. Your life is going to change, I whispered in his ear. As soon as the major returns you'll be part of a pack again, astounding them all with your speed and phenomenal fox sense.

Still limping a little, he trotted placidly beside me. At the top of the drive the double doors swung open. To my surprise, Master Oliver stood on the step. Instead of hunting gear, he wore a big tweed coat.

'Come over here!' he called.

Ignoring him, I let Llywelyn tow me sideways, heading for the path around the house.

'Hey! You! I've forgotten your name.'

Checked by the bossy voice, Llewelyn turned to look. I tugged him on. He balked.

'Well?' said Master Oliver. 'Aren't you going to answer?' He held a chunky-looking urn and a bunch of tatty chrysanths.

'It's Jacqueline,' I said.

He picked his way towards me down the steps. 'Zhackleen? That's French. It's my youngest cousin's name. And my brother was called Zhack.' He stood and faced me on the gravel. 'You're still wearing that same frock.'

Could he smell the pee? I backed away. His Adam's apple bobbed above his scarf. 'So, Zhackleen,' he said, 'it was you who broke my egg.'

So Lizzie had snitched. Cheeks hot, I smoothed the gravel with my toe.

'As you've just found out,' he said, 'blown eggs are fragile things. And so,' he added with a grown-up smile, 'it would probably be better if you left my shelves alone.'

As if I didn't know that a shell was easily cracked. 'I meant to break your egg,' I said and watched his smile fade. 'I meant to. I poked it with my thumb.'

He blinked and rubbed his eyes like a younger, shyer boy – the one who'd nearly cried in front of Polly. 'You smashed my favourite egg on purpose? Why did you do that?'

I stroked Llywelyn's head. *Please don't let the* Sais *cry.* 'I just don't know,' I said. 'Will you please not tell your dad?'

'I never snitch.'

Except he'd snitched the very first time we met.

His bony fingers ripped a tawny petal. 'In any case, my father wouldn't care. He'd tell me to grow up and take it like a man.'

A few chrysanths dropped onto the gravel. 'Oh, Lord,' said Master Oliver. 'Can you pick them up?'

I caught a whiff of Friar's Balsam, Vapour Rub and eggs, and waited till he picked the flowers up himself.

'What are you doing with that hound?' he asked.

'Taking him for a walk.'

He shifted the urn from hip to hip. 'I thought you were a townie.'

'I hunted in Wales during the war.'

'So you were Zhackee the Vackee.' He laughed at his silly joke. 'Maman says that only the English are stupid enough to hunt foxes. But it seems the Welsh are stupid, too.'

'No! They breed great hounds. The best in all the world.'

'Dogs that rip small animals to bits?'

The same old sissy stuff – and him a Master's son. 'Foxes aren't small, they're big,' I said, 'and hunting's part of nature.'

'That's what Father says plus lots of other stupid things.'

Llywelyn grew alert at a clamour across the fields.

'They're after my vixen,' said Oliver, 'but they'll never catch her.

My vixen! No fox can belong to a human. But at least, I thought as I turned away, he knew which fox the hounds were chasing.

'I say,' he called, 'would you come back here?'

I glanced at the rows of windows, trained on us where we stood. Don't let him get over-familiar, Mrs Arbiter had said.

'Take this.'

The urn was so heavy that I almost let it drop. Not checking that I could manage it and Llywelyn,, he slouched across the gravel, still clutching the chrysanths. I glanced at the windows. Empty, as far as I could see. Halfway down the drive, we climbed a style on the right and landed on a path I'd never noticed. It led us out of earshot of the pack, past the back of the kennels and onto a cinder track.

Ahead of us sprawled a graveyard in the dull November light. Beyond it stood a row of yews, six spreading masts of darkness. We opened the gate and trailed past mounds of ivy that clung with knees and elbows to ancient box-like tombs. Closer to the church the grass turned into velvet, and shiny marble headstones edged the gravel path. Opposite the porch stood a tablet of dark stone with a picture of a rosebud at the top.

Golden letters marched right down the centre. Oliver said them aloud, as if I couldn't read.

Mabel Eleanor Thwaites 1914-1943

Beloved Sister Of Joshua Michael Thwaites 1918-1941

Forever Grateful And Faithful

'She was my nanny,' he added. 'My father paid for the headstone. She died of palsy and her brother was gored by a bull.'

'What sort of bull?'

Oliver laid the flowers beside the headstone. 'What does it matter? All bulls are vicious beasts.'

The urn had made my arms ache. I dumped it beside the chrysanths. In a field beyond the yews, Sir was playing football with the Scouts. 'It must be nice,' I said, 'not having to go to school.'

Master Oliver picked up a trowel behind the headstone. 'Nice? Are you joking? I wish I could go back.'

'You mean you like it there?'

He gave a queer little jerk of his shoulders. 'When it comes to blood sports I'm a conchie.'

'Foxes will kill a whole flock of hens and only take one to their lair.'

'They panic inside a henhouse. It's a reflex. They can't help it.'

'All the same, I'd like to hunt again.'

He stared at me, trowel in hand. *Servants' kids don't hunt.*

Humming the tune of *Now thank we all our God,* he dug up a dandelion and chucked it on the path. Then raised his head. Stopped humming. 'Look over there,' he whispered.

Hands behind their backs, magpies minced through the gloom beside the church. One for sorrow, two for joy, three for a letter, maybe from Iolo.

'*Pica pica,*' Oliver said. 'What handsome birds they are. I took an egg from their nest at the foot of the lawn. It's a beautiful glossy blue with khaki spots.'

'Don't you think the mother bird will miss it?'

Oliver filled the urn from a standpipe by the path. 'Unlikely, Zhackie the Vackie. She'd laid a clutch of seven.' He knelt by the grave to fuss with the chrysanths, frowning as he placed them in the urn, the smallest round the outside and the tallest in the centre. 'And besides,' he added, placing the urn in front of the headstone, 'magpies scoff the eggs of smaller, weaker species.'

The shaggy bronze petals swam against the marble. 'Where's Mr Arbiter's grave?' My second gormless question.

'He doesn't have a grave and neither does my brother. They both have plaques on the wall beside our vault.' Oliver opened a door in the side of the church. 'Come with me and I'll show you, if you like.'

He stepped aside. A tunnel plunged into darkness, paved in slippery-looking stone. Dry-mouthed, I stroked Llywelyn's head. Heat flowed from his bump.

'Go on,' said Oliver. 'You can take your bloody hound.'

What if he pushed us down and turned the key? *Serve you right for smashing my heron's egg.* Llywelyn would be buried for the second time, trapped with me among the Wetheral dead. Was that the sort of thing Mrs Arbiter had meant? I wavered at the top. The door clicked shut behind us. Llywelyn seemed quite trusting, so I let myself be towed, head bent beneath the roof and right hand stretched towards the invisible wall. As we reached the foot of the ramp, Master Oliver flicked on a light and followed us down to a room of liver-coloured marble streaked with sago like you got in school. Llywelyn waved his stern, no more scared than in the icehouse. I pressed my knees against the heat of his ribs.

Two plaques were nailed to the opposite wall.

Captain John de Vere Wetheral 1920-1945
The paths of duty lead the way to glory.

Corporal George Arbiter 1896-1942
Faithful unto death.

Oliver pointed at a door beside the plaques. 'My family lies in there on shelves like in a tuck shop, the mouldiest on the bottom and the new ones higher up. I see their coffins every time another of us dies.' He crossed towards the door and turned to face me, his face thin and pale in the light from the single bulb. 'There are only two spaces left, one for me and one for Father.'

'What about your children?'

'I'm never going to marry. Here's where they'll bury me, Zhackie, stuck up at the top with my nose against the ceiling.'

I shuffled my feet, not liking the thought of his face pressed to the marble. He waited till I looked at him again.

'Zhackie,' he said in a solemn voice, 'will you come and see me?'

'What if I die before you?'

'Oh no,' he said, 'you won't.'

He reached for the big brass handle. I'd thought he was namby-pamby, but here he was, wanting to see a roomful of dead people. Before he'd stepped inside, Llywelyn's hackles rose. I clenched his lead. The upper door clacked open. Black against the light, a man stood on the threshold. Llywelyn growled. The man ducked through the doorway.

'Is that you, Oliver?' called a voice from the top of the slope.

The Reverend Beale. I'd seen him feed the cob he kept in a

paddock next to the garden. Though brave after hounds, said Danny, he was heavy on his horse: last week he'd lamed the cob along the Brampton Road.

'Is that you?' he called again. 'You'd better come up here.'

In Capel, when the minister spoke, everyone jumped to attention. Hands in his overcoat pockets, Oliver lounged against the marble. The clergyman inched himself downwards, fingers spread against the wall, narrow-shouldered, heavy-bottomed like a hippo.

'Is that the drafted hound?' He peered at Llywelyn through the gloom. 'And who has brought him here? The new maid's child?'

'Meet Zhackie the Vackie,' said Oliver, laying his hand on my arm.

The Reverend Beale pursed his moist, plump lips. 'You should be out hunting, not hanging round the crypt. That's what your father wants and so does Dr Madden. You need fresh air and plenty of exercise. And you, child,' he said to me, 'had better get back to your mother. A crypt's no place for girls, nor foxhounds, come to that. No, Oliver, you can stay. I want a little word.'

Chapter Eight

ON Monday, as I tramped across the gravel, puffs of cold jumped up and bit my ankles. In school, everyone was coughing, sniffing, sneezing, accompanied by long dirges from the hounds. On Saturday, they'd failed once again, slinking home, sterns low, without their fox. And once again, said Mr Hoad, the earths had been unblocked, and all the stakes and barriers shattered into splinters and stamped into the mud or flung into a stream. A madman's work, he said. A madman with an axe who must have -

'Jacqueline,' said Mr Marlozzi, 'you must move your desk.'

The caretaker rolled in a heater and stood it by the windows. Pale blue flames wavered in a ring. Mrs Arbiter had given me a set of cast-off clothes, bought, she'd said, at a village bring and buy. Their smell of mothballs, damp and cooking fat mingled in a fug of paraffin with other smells of unwashed liberty bodices, carbolic soap and sweaty farm boys' socks.

By three o'clock even Miss was yawning. 'Switch on the light,' she said to Gilbert Bell, a podgy boy whose mother worked in the sweetshop. 'I want you all to take out your *Gulliver's Travels* and read from chapter three to chapter six.'

Desk lids rose and chilblained fingers rummaged. Miss took an envelope from her handbag and shut it with a click. Soon she was deep in her letter. Nobody flicked ink pellets or flew paper darts, just sat, their big round faces looming at their books.

As the dirges from the hounds wound through my brain, I started to think in Welsh again, like I did when left alone. *Pwy oedd wedi dod â mi yma?* Who'd brought me here? Lizzie or mighty Gwyn? If it was

Lizzie, the most I'd ever do was trail Llywelyn round the village till the major sent him home.

Outside, in the darkening playground, a man spoke to Mr Marlozzi, a middle-aged Scouser, as far as I could tell.

'Jacqueline,' I heard him say. A spider crawled over my spine. 'Jacqueline Mary Elton is her name.'

'No. Eempossible,' the caretaker replied. 'It is lesson time. You will have to wait.'

Might the Scouser be my dad, home from the war at last? I couldn't see above the frosted lower panes. Maybe he'd suffered from shell-shock, like a boy in Capel's dad, who'd wandered the roads for months before remembering his name. Book shut, I watched the clock. If he had to wait too long, he might wander off again.

Mr Marlozzi jangled the bell at last. Miss came to and popped her letter in her handbag. 'I'm going to test you on that book tomorrow. Now file out in silence and don't forget your homework.'

I didn't have a satchel so I crammed my books into my shoebag. Smelling of damp from the boot room at the Hall, Master Oliver's cast-off duffle coat hung on my cloakroom peg. I was shoving my feet in my outdoors when Miss sat down beside me.

The class gawped at us both as they trailed out to the yard.

'Is something wrong?' I asked.

Miss's plump, pink face shone up at mine. 'Certainly not! There's a gentleman to see you.'

My heart gave a jittery thud. 'Is he a soldier?'

'No knowing. He's in civvies. Let's go to the playground and see.'

Mr Marlozzi stood beside a thin man in a trilby. A drizzle ran down my spine. Not my dad. Uncle Eric, with his grabby eyes and smells of Chesterfields and Brylcreem.

'Do you know this gentleman?' I heard Miss ask behind me.

'Yes. I met him in Liverpool. He's an uncle.'

'Oh! I didn't know he was a relation. Then I see no reason why you shouldn't have a chat. I'll ring the Hall and tell them you'll be late.'

I followed Uncle Eric to the pavement by the sweetshop where a single bulb shone through yellow Cellophane.

'Would you like some sweeties?' Uncle Eric asked.

Behind a sagging pyramid of empty chocolate boxes, Gilbert Bell was staring at us both. 'Cat got your tongue?' Uncle Eric asked.

'Sorry. No thanks.'

'So what about me question?'

'What question?'

His face hung yellow in the sweetshop light. 'Didn't you read me letter?'

My calves itched under my long woollen socks. 'I don't think I got it,' I said.

Uncle Eric tugged the points of his moustache. 'What do you mean, you don't think? Did you or didn't you?'

I felt stuck in a story I didn't understand.

'Somebody's kept it from you,' Uncle Eric said. 'That Eye-ti told me the way to the Hall but they wouldn't let me in. A big bald feller said your mam was busy and when I said I'd wait he slammed the door.'

'They've given her lots of work to do.'

Uncle Eric's eyebrows rose. 'So what about that feller?'

'What feller?'

'The one she's come here for.'

I slid my hand inside the wool and scratched my calf.

'There must be someone,' Uncle Eric said.

'You mean another uncle?'

Uncle Eric gave a downturned smile. 'Yes, in a way. Yes, I suppose I do.'

Sir. Mr Marlozzi. Mr Hoad. The Reverend Beale. Not one of them seemed the least bit like an uncle. 'There's nobody,' I said.

Uncle Eric stayed in front of the window, his face sad and

unhealthy in its light. 'Then why did she have to go? That's what I can't fathom. Giving up her business to work as someone's skivvy.'

'She thought that I needed to live in the country again.'

'Poor kid. Is that what she told you?' Uncle Eric said, pulling a snapshot from his wallet.

A woman was laughing and waving her furry black gloves at the camera. Although the snap was old, brown and curled around the edges, it fizzed and shone in the sallow sweetshop light.

'Mam! My real mam!' I shouted out.

'Before the war,' said Uncle Eric. 'Even before she had you.'

I grabbed the snap. 'Where is she now?'

He nodded at the Hall.

'Are they really the same?'

'Of course they are. Can't you see? It's just that she's gone blonde.'

I stared at the snap again. Could this be the woman who'd hit me? 'She's changed a lot,' I said.

'Her way of life's not easy and she's made a few mistakes.' He took the photograph and tucked it back in his wallet. 'I still want to marry her, Jacqueline. Has she told you that?'

'She's already married,' I said.

'In a manner of speaking,' he said with a long and thoughtful stare, like a teacher weighing up how bright you are. 'And she'll learn that a manner of speaking doesn't take you far. She ought to come back home and let me be your dad.'

I stared at his thin yellow face. I already had a dad. Must of done, or how did I get born?

A hound howled in the darkness down the street.

'Greyhounds!' said Uncle Eric who liked to go to the dogs.

'No. That's the bitch pack, saying they want to hunt.'

'A nice young girl like you shouldn't say words like bitch.'

'It's the name for lady hounds. Iolo told me so.'

'Your mam should never have sent you there. You should have

stayed at home. There's plenty of people in Bootle hung onto their kiddies.'

'I liked it in Wales,' I said.

Uncle Eric fumbled in a deep breast pocket. 'Now, Jackie, I've brought you a present,' he said, and pulled out a flat red case. 'Look at this. It's real leatherette.'

He unzipped it on three sides. It opened it like a book with a pale blue notepad on the left. On the right I saw a set of matching envelopes and three stamps in a little plastic pocket. I grabbed at the case: a chance to write to Iolo.

Uncle Eric snatched it back. 'Manners!'

'Thank you.'

He held it out again. 'It's for sending me regular news.' He winked, an uncle's wink, filled with hidden meaning. 'You don't have to tell her you're writing, just do it on the QT.' He pointed at the pillar box on the kerb.

I shoved the case in my shoebag.

'I want you to tell me how she is, when she gets fed up and especially if a man comes on the scene.'

'What if it's my dad?'

'Even if it is, your Uncle Eric won't surrender. Next time I'll be taking you both home.'

Home! The word pushed the air from my chest. For me it meant Capel y Bont with Iolo and the pack.

'Do you promise?' asked Uncle Eric.

A key turned in the sweetshop door and the light went out. Uncle Eric bent and gripped his knees. I jumped away just as he puckered his lips. He straightened and tilted his trilby over his eyes.

'Make sure you drop me a line if anything changes.'

He walked towards the station steps, not turning back to wave, his narrow shoulders looking hurt but proud. When he'd dipped below the street I sat on the ledge of the cenotaph and stared through the trees at the shivering lights of the Hall. A train chuffed. Doors slammed.

A whistle blew. I let my finger track the grooved-in names. George Arbiter. Ronald Threlkeld. Captain Wetheral. My dad hadn't died but may as well have done.

A train tooted far across the fields. Part of me sat on board with Uncle Eric. He was staring at the darkened countryside with here and there the cosy lighted windows of homes he'd never, ever get inside. And part of me stayed on the ledge until damp from the stone struck my bottom.

The wind started up like an engine as I reached the kitchen steps. Polly had slung a carpet over the railing.

I'll be seeing you in all the old familiar places WHACK
That this heart of mine embraces all day through WHACK

She sang in time to the whacks of the beater in her big strong hand.

'Why are you working in the dark?' I asked.

'Why d'you think? The major's coming home. Seems there's a meet in the village next weekend.'

My heart bumped. In the village? With luck I'd see a hunt.

'He's caught us on the hop,' said Polly. 'Hardly any warning. He'll be landing at the station on Friday afternoon.'

I suddenly knew why she sang: The chauffeur would be home.

That this heart of mine embraces WHACK
All day through WHACK WHACK.

In that small café
The park across the way

I left her singing and whacking. The notepad bumped my legs. Somebody coughed as I climbed the servants' stairs, a lingering, dried-out wheeze that died in a croak. Mr Arbiter. I lunged for the door at the top and fell into a hall.

Walls of marble rose on every side, semolina-white like the marble in the crypt, with the same liver-coloured streaks. A bell on a wire hung on the right beside the double doors. On my left, a flight of stairs led to a shadowy landing. Overhead, rain pattered on a dome of grubby glass with plaster goats prancing round its base. A grandfather clock in the corner wheezed as if it had bronchitis. No wonder. Gusts of cold air flew out of the empty fireplace and a draft whistled through a gap in the panes of the dome.

How to get out? I crossed to the opposite side. A vacuum cleaner grumbled overhead. Probably Mrs Arbiter cleaning the major's bedroom. He slept at the back of the house, just below our attic because, said Mr Hoad, he liked to listen to his country. If I followed the sound I might find my way to our room. I opened a door onto a corridor with a carpet. I shouldn't be here. And wearing my outdoor shoes! I dashed up another flight. Pictures lined the walls. The snarl grew even louder as I climbed. The notepad's corner poking through my shoebag, I tracked along a passage towards what looked like servants' stairs. A door swung back. I spun away. The roaring stopped.

'Come back here,' I heard Mrs Arbiter call.

I turned. She was standing in the doorway. She'd rolled her lisle stockings round her ankles and her Electrolux curled behind her like an obedient snake.

'Off with those muddy shoes,' she said, 'and get yourself in here.' She pointed at an orange rug just inside the room.

More rugs sprawled around an easy chair. Gripping its arms, Mrs Arbiter lowered herself to its seat. The Electrolux ponged: time to change its bag.

'Now who was that feller?' she asked.

'Uncle Eric.'

'Oh. He should have said he was your uncle.' She looked me up and down. 'So what have you got in that bag?'

I emptied my mind before she could see inside it. 'Just shoes and stuff,' I said.

She held out her hand. I gave her the bag and watched her pull out the case. She unzipped it and saw the stamps. 'So he wants you to keep in touch.'

I stared at the case, scared she was going to keep it.

'I've told you before: you use the servants' stairs. What if the major sees you roaming round the place?'

I let my eyes drift sideways to the high four poster. A nightie sprawled across the eiderdown and a skinny pipe lay on the bedside table.

'Do you hear me?' Mrs Arbiter asked. Her gumboil hat had risen an inch above her hairline, showing a ring of white skin. She zipped it up the case and gave it back. 'Now out of my way,' she said. 'I've got work to do.'

A draught whooshed past, slamming a door out of sight. I tracked along another passage lit by dingy wall lights until the servants' stairs heaved up ahead. Though our lamp wasn't meant to be lit before nine at night, light shone into the passage at the top. Eyes closed like a hound's, I sifted the air outside our room. Perm. Veet. Bleach. Robin starch, all overlaid with the pong of nail varnish.

'Jacqueline?' called Lizzie.

Foot propped on an open drawer, with cotton wool between her toes, she was painting her nails with her favourite Crimson Poppy. I hovered in the passage, wanting to turn back.

'Come in,' she said. 'Oh, Jackie, pet, I'm sorry that I hit you.' It must have been her bath day because her cheeks shone pink.

I walked into the room, pleased that she'd said sorry, though the fist of anger still throbbed inside my chest.

She smiled. I saw the woman in the snapshot, older now and lined, with her hair gone blonde. 'Uncle Eric said you should never have come here.'

'Is that why you're late back? He caught you outside school?' She screwed the brush into its little bottle, not even throwing a glance towards my shoebag. 'Barmy blighter, coming up here to make mischief.'

'I wouldn't have wet the bed,' I said, 'if you'd brought up the po.'

She pulled me towards her and nuzzled her face in my neck. I smelt Nivea and Veet from the time before the war. Mam. Could it be her? After all these years?

'Oh, pet,' she said, 'if only you knew what I do.' She pulled the cotton wool from in between her toes.

'Mam,' I said, trying out the word.

'That's better,' she said with a smile. 'And everything else is going to get better now the major is coming home.'

'Mrs Arbiter says I've got to keep out of his way.'

'Did she indeed? She's in for a shock or two.'

'Mam,' I said again, 'do you think he'll let me hunt?'

'I'm not quite sure about that. We'll have to wait and see.' She rummaged beneath her pillow and pulled out a doll. 'Look, love, I remembered.' She waggled its arms and legs. The blank blue eyes clicked open: a present from my dad. I'd unwrapped it on the pavement beside his motor car.

'You must have forgot her,' said Mam, 'all those years ago.'

Wrong. The day I'd left, I'd pulled her out of my pillowcase. Now I grabbed her by her springy yellow curls, dropped to my knees and shoved her into my shoebag.

'Poor little dolly,' said Mam, pulling the cork from a fuzzy glass bottle.

'What's that?'

'Olive oil from the major's bathroom.' She rubbed the yellow goo into her hands, pulled on a pair of old gloves and fumbled with darned fingers for a Woodie. For once she didn't bother to open the window, just flopped onto her bed and leant against the headboard. I struck a match and held the flame to her cigarette. 'Oliver's mam's coming home,' I said, as the tip glowed red.

'Who told you that? Polly, I suppose?' Mam snorted out twin plumes of grey-blue smoke.

'She is! I saw her nightie on the bed.'

'Rubbish. They slept in different rooms. What you probably saw was the major's kaftan.'

'What's that?'

'A sort of frock men wear in Arab countries.' Mam flicked her ash into a jar of Ponds with smears of cold cream still on the inside. 'Be nice to the major, won't you, Jackie, pet, and show him what a lovely girl you are. He could do a lot for you, you know.'

Chapter Nine

FOR the rest of that week, Mam tried to make Polly look pretty, trimming her hair and lending her powder and lipstick. She also made her cups of tea and egged her on to talk. I was usually sent to bed before those talks got going, but I guessed that Mam would hear a lot about Mr Rumney.

On Thursday night, I pulled the writing–case from the dark beneath my bed. *Dear Iolo,* I wrote, *Llywelyn is full of* hiraeth, *a vackie in a place where no one speaks his language.* Although I was writing in Welsh, I could hardly find the words, as if all the *Saeson* had knocked it out of my head. *He'd feel better if he caught a fox, but on his first day out he lost the rest of the hunt, just because of a stupid* Sais *huntsman. The major gets home tomorrow, but he's a* Sais, *too, whose pack is too stupid to catch the local vixen. Mr Hoad is nice but speaks no Welsh and will never understand Llywelyn's inner gifts. So please could you ask Dai Meredith to fetch him?*

And when he does, could he fetch me too? Though I think the woman really is my mam (though now and again I'm not sure) I'd rather be with you. You know that I was born to hunt. You told me so yourself but here, because I'm a servant's kid, they're never going to let me.

I signed myself Jacqueline Elton in case he'd forgot who I was. How babyish my letter seemed. Would he take any notice? The envelope itself I addressed as best I could: Mr Evans, The Kennels, Capel y Bont, Nr Corwen, North Wales. Then I slid the writing-case back underneath my bed.

The door knob turned. I jammed the letter under my pillow.

'You've lit the lamp,' said Mam.

I sat on my pillow. The paper crackled.

'You should be in bed.'

The envelope crackled all night each time I turned my head. Next morning, after Mam had gone to light the nursery fire, I crunched the letter deep into my pocket. Not daring to leave it in the post bag in the hall, I dropped it in the box outside the sweetshop.

Miss let me out at two so I'd be back before the major. A smell of Jeyes Fluid was surging from the kennels. Besoms scraped the concrete in the yard. Llywelyn yelped excitedly as I passed, as if he knew the postman's bike was leant against the pillar box and Tommy Fell was pulling all our mail through its door.

The Hall sat square and watchful at the end of its bony tunnel, its windows newly shined and gravel freshly raked. In our room, Mam had squeezed into her beetle-black Kayser Bonder, strapless with an uplift and a plunge.

'Oh good,' she said. 'You're here. Fasten me up.'

I grabbed the zip below the long white V of her back and tugged till the corset met between her shoulder blades. She pulled on her frothy black pantelettes and wriggled into the dress she'd shortened and altered to fit around her waist and hips.

'So what do you think of your mam?' she asked in a shallow voice as if the corset had knocked the breath from her body.

'Why are you bothering with stuff that nobody's going to see?'

'Why?' She crooked one leg at the knee and checked her fancy seam. 'Good foundation garments help me look my best.' She tied on a starched white apron, arranged the bow and patted herself on the bottom. Then, before I could dodge, tore at my scalp with a brush.

'My God, I feel dizzy,' she said. 'I should never have had that fag.' She fluffed her hair round her cap, starched like her collar and cuffs. The gong rang somewhere deep below our floorboards, a run of muzzy taps then two enormous wallops, like the ones from the naked man at the start of a film.

'Oh pet,' said Mam in her breathy voice, hands pressed to her cheeks. 'Run downstairs and say I've got a headache.'

69

The echo from the gong churned round our ears.

'Please, Mam, please come with me.'

'You heard me. Tell them I'm sick – that I'm lying down. And if the major speaks to you, remember to call him Sir.'

A fire blazed in the big stone hearth in the hall, and the air smelt of the chrysanths on the nearby chest. The double doors stood open. Hands clasped behind his back, Master Oliver waited at the foot of the steps, with Mrs Arbiter on his right, next to Mr Hoad, then Billy Boustead, the whipper-in, and five kennelmen or farmhands, joshing each other and dragging on their rollies. Bright and out-of-place in a tight pink jumper, Polly stood next to Danny at the end of the row, her red-checked skirt straining round her waist.

Mrs Arbiter turned as I ran down the steps. 'Where's your ma?' she asked.

'Got a headache.'

An engine stuttered in the street. I tracked back up the steps.

'Not so fast,' Mrs Arbiter said. 'You can take you place over there.' She pointed at a gap between Danny and Polly.

Polly gripped my hand. She'd washed her hair and, instead of scraping it back, pinned her fringe with Mam's blue butterfly slide. The rest she'd left, like Mam had said, to hang silkily round her face. The wind clacked the trees. Master Oliver blew his nose, a namby-pamby in his thick tweed coat. The stuttering grew louder. A motor car turned through the gates. The kennelmen pulled off their caps. Danny pinched out his roll-up and jammed it behind his ear as the car jounced towards us over the potholes.

It halted at the steps. The driver's door swung back. Tanned and alert, a uniformed man sprang out. Squaring his shoulders, he opened the car's rear door then, keeping hold of the handle, stared straight ahead as if about to salute.

'Oh Lordy Lord,' whispered Polly.

A gingery man in tweeds unfolded himself from the back, straightened and looked around, as if unsure of where he was. Though tall, his shoulders were stooped. He wore a straggly red moustache, and his rain-grey eyes drooped downwards at the corners.

More like a master than the major, the chauffeur stood erect and ran his eye along the line of servants. Polly gripped my hand so tight she crunched the knuckles. Mr Rumney's green-grey eyes lingered on her for a second before he turned to pull two cases from the boot, both scuffed, one tied with twine and the other with leather straps. I caught a whiff of cinnamon, cloves and hot metal as he dumped them on the gravel by Mrs Arbiter.

Still looking wary and out-of-place, the major shambled towards us. Oliver clucked, an anxious noise deep inside his throat.

'Welcome home, Sir,' he said, straightening up as if before a teacher.

The major held out a bent red claw, crossed with purple scars. Oliver touched a shrivelled knuckle, then snatched away his hand.

The major turned to Mrs Arbiter. 'You say the reporter chappies have finally vamoosed?'

'Yes, Sir, they've all gone.'

'And no one making mischief round the village? Good, good. I knew it would all die down.' He turned back to Master Oliver. 'And have you seen much sport?'

'No, Sir. Doctor Madden says I might have swollen glands.'

'Really? He told me you're on the mend.'

Oliver clucked again. 'I've been hacking round the lanes.'

Mr Hoad hissed beneath his breath.

'You'll never get better like that,' the major said. 'Tomorrow the meet is going to be here in the village – just the place for you to start again.'

The skin above Oliver's nose grew pinched and tight. 'Yes, Sir,' he said. 'I look forward to it, Sir.'

The major turned to Mr Hoad. 'And have you caught that fox?'

'No, Sir,' said Mr Hoad from the leathery mask of his face.

'Well, I dare say we'll nab him tomorrow.'

71

The motor car hiccupped and bumped towards the stables as the major walked along the line of men, stopping here and there to ask about the farm, the stock, the coverts, the fences, the state of the fields.

'Ah, Polly,' the major said next. 'I thought that you'd be gone.'

Polly's face swelled. 'Yes but I've nowhere to go, Sir.'

I noticed the bags beneath the major's tired-looking eyes. 'What about your family?' he asked.

'They're Jehovahs, Sir.'

Bringing a whiff of pipe smoke and the coal smell of the train, the major turned from Polly and stopped in front of me. The blood pulsed in my ears. Did I dare mention Llywelyn?

Just as I opened my mouth, Mrs Arbiter spoke at his elbow. 'This is the new maid's child. Jacqueline Elton's her name.'

My mind still on Llywelyn, I stared at the major's brogues.

The major puffed up air into his gingery moustache. 'And where's her mother?' he asked.

I met his rain-grey eyes, sad, a little bloodshot and fringed with sparse red lashes.

'She's got a headache, Sir,' Mrs Arbiter said.

'A headache and a daughter,' he said, as if the two were linked. 'Why not send her up to see me later. Tonight, I think we'd better have a roast. Lady Susan is coming to dinner, and probably Beale and Tunnicliffe and a few of the hunt committee.'

Mrs Arbiter picked up his cases. 'I'll see what I can do, Sir.'

By the time I got back to our bedroom Mam's corset lay on her bed, the cones of its brassiere pointing at the ceiling. Mam herself was pulling on her dress over her white, everyday underwear.

'So how did he look?' she asked, fastening her cuffs.

'The major? He looked tired. Not very glad to be home.'

'And what did he say when he heard that I was here?'

'He said he'll see you later. He'll be hunting in the morning and the meet's right here in Foxleigh.'

'Really?' said Mam, lacing her sensible shoes.

I drew a shaky breath. 'Please could I follow the hunt on foot, just for a little while, just to the very first covert? Danny says I can go with him and I promise I won't get lost.'

'Yes,' said Mam to my surprise. 'Yes. Of course you can.' On reaching the doorway she looked at me over her shoulder. 'And Alan Rumney? Was he there?' she asked.

'Yes, he was.'

'So what did he say to Polly?'

'I don't think that he spoke to her at all.'

She tutted. 'You don't think? You should have kept your wits about you.'

She couldn't have guessed I was thinking of Llywelyn. But when she'd gone odd moments sprang to mind: how Oliver had lied about hacking round the lanes. How Mr Hoad had hissed: he'd inform the major later. How the pack had clamoured when they heard the major's voice, and how he hadn't seemed to hear them, just shambled up the steps.

Later on, I visited the kennels. For once, instead of talking to Llywelyn, I began by sitting with the leaders of the dog pack: friendly, grizzled Warlock; noble Churchill and Nimrod the deep-chested with his big, distinctive voice. After that, the bitches: Fable, easy to spot with her narrow head and shoulders, and comic little Quickly, her nervy, swine-chopped sister, so badly overshot that Billy Boustead, the whip, had wanted her drowned. Decent hounds all but *yn union yr un fath*. Too samey. Light of bone. Lacking depth of chest.

A gangling man, pin-headed, with sticky-out ears, Billy called me as I crossed the yard. 'You'll have to stay away, lass, now the major's home.'

We stepped into a dark, low-ceilinged room that stank of horse flesh, Jeyes Fluid and dried blood. I took the regular bucket of meat donated by the butcher. Foxes are killed in the kennels, Iolo always said. Billy fiddled with a blood-stained Rizla.

'Aha!' I'd found two cloven feet and a risky bone. 'Does the major never do this job himself?'

'A good pack lives for its Master, not for grub that lands in a trough.'

I checked a lump of sinews for dangerous, twanging windpipes. 'If they live for him, he should have come to see them.'

Billy poked inside his tin of Navy Cut. 'I dare say he's got other things to do.'

I stirred porridge through the offal and lugged it to a lodge. Billy tipped the mixture in a trough. The dog pack tumbled forward, dodging the long stick he used to prod the bullies off the weakest.

'Did the major mean to breed them all alike?'

''Course he did,' said Billy. 'He likes a matching pack, and they're full to the gills of beautiful stud book blood.' He knocked Brimstone back from the weedy Chamberlain. 'They're all of 'em descended from great Ranksborough, Sir Walter Wetheral's prize hound. They've got his portrait somewhere in the Hall.'

Was Ranksborough the source of their run of inborn flaws? I made up my mind to check. 'Do you think they'll catch that vixen?' I asked next.

'You mean that fox? With all his earths unblocked? Not unless we nab the scum who does it - a vicious sod who doesn't just remove the wood but smashes it to pieces for everyone to see.'

A shiver squeezed my spine. A local man for sure, lurking in the darkness with his hammer. When your quarry has outwitted you, according to the god, you dishonour its brave spirit if you kill it underground.

'And now,' said Billy as he hauled a bucket from a cooler, 'you can go and see your bloody hound.'

74

Chapter Ten

I RIFFLED through a book with tissue-paper pages and print too small and faint for me to read.

'Put that back,' said Polly. 'You know we're not allowed.'

I snapped it shut and sneezed into a cloud of dust. Dull green or brown with faded golden titles, boring-looking books lined every wall. Polly punched another cloud from a velvet cushion. At five o'clock that evening, she'd lit the library fire. The flames already springing up the chimney spangled in a line of bottles on the sideboard.

Now she spread a map on a table near the hearth. Her fingernail, bright crimson from Mam's bottle, traced a huddled row of oblongs by a road. 'Them's the cottages,' she said, 'and this here is the church, this black thing with a cross, and there's the green beside the pub where they'll be meeting.'

On the opposite edge of the village I saw a big black square. The Hall and there, three fields beyond the stream, the first covert to be drawn, marked with a flag on a pin. Other small flags lay beyond a blue line for the river, black lines for major roads and red for the railway track.

It didn't make sense. What good was a map to a huntsman? His country can't be fitted on a table, its gossiping streams shrunk down to lines and its coverts to little green circles. Besides, he holds his country's layout in his head, and sees no need to waste his time on plans. The hunted, not the hunter, is the one who takes charge of the hunt.

A smoky brown smell hit my nose, mingled with rotting grapes. Polly was refilling the decanters.

'Are people going to drink?'

'The hunt committee? You can bet they will.'

The night before a hunt Iolo stayed in the kennels. How can you ready yourself, he'd ask, while swigging port and brandy?

At six o'clock I stood at the sink, rinsing cut-glass tumblers while Mrs Arbiter basted roast potatoes. The door swung back. Though Mam had combed her hair and smeared her face with powder, a v-shaped vein showed blue in the whiteness of her brow.

Mrs Arbiter straightened and stared. 'So you're feeling better.'

The vein in Mam's forehead pulsed. Mrs Arbiter stared for a second longer then bent to slosh more grouse fat on the spuds.

At twenty to seven, I took up my post by the chest in the hall. Opposite the big front doors the staircase led up to a landing divided from the stairwell by a marble balustrade. Glancing through the struts I saw a row of Wetherals staring outwards from their golden frames: children clutching puppies, ladies with their pugs and gentlemen in wigs and velvet breeches.

As the grandfather clock wheezed quarter to, Mrs Arbiter appeared. 'Just in time,' she said, opening the doors.

A little green sports car bucketed over the potholes and slewed to a halt by the steps in a squirt of gravel. All smiles and rosy cheeks, a lady wriggled out.

'He's back at last!' she called, running up the steps.

'He certainly is, Your Ladyship,' said Mrs Arbiter.

I'd heard the kennelmen talk about Lady Susan: how she raced her sports car round the lanes and, when hunting, took her fences straight, flying five-barred gates on Lucy Glitters or another of her string of narrow mares.

'Bad frost,' she said, pulling off her headscarf, the kind with horses' heads and snaffles in each corner. Released, hair framed her forehead in thick blonde buffalo horns. 'And just this afternoon that fox has snatched a turkey. A damn good thing the meet will be at Foxleigh.'

'Take the headscarf, Jacqueline,' Mrs Arbiter said.

I caught a whiff of stables and a brisk gardenia perfume.

'Now, Your Ladyship, she's going to help you with your fur.'

'Sweet child,' said Lady Susan as I slid it off her shoulders. 'Are you the new maid's daughter? Yes? I thought you were. Where's your mummy?'

I smoothed a row of small animal skins joined by tiny stitches. 'Putting out the knives and forks, I think.'

Lady Susan rummaged in her bag. 'I suppose you'll be tucked up by the time that I go home.' She dropped a sixpenny piece into my hand: enough to buy more paper and a proper book of stamps.

'Say thank you, Your Ladyship,' Mrs Arbiter said.

'No need, no need,' called Lady Susan over her shoulder. Mrs Arbiter ushered her towards the drawing-room, leaving me to carry the fur to the cloakroom. One motor car, then another, came chugging up the drive. Engines died. Deep voices shouted greetings. The bell in the hall jangled on the end of its rickety wire. Mrs Arbiter hurried back to re-open the double doors. The fire jumped in the grate. A band of men marched in, broad-shouldered, ruddy-faced in their moving tunnel of cold: the Reverend Beale, who'd walked across from his rectory; one gentleman jingling his keys and one with a handlebar moustache, and three men who looked like farmers in rabbitskin hats, woollen scarves and coats that smelt of mothballs.

When everyone had arrived, I made my way downstairs. Mrs Arbiter served the major and his guests while Gilbert's mother from the sweetshop cooked our supper. That night we ate roast pork, a gift from Colonel Tunnicliffe, with taties, brussels sprouts and strips of crackling. The kennelmen asked for seconds and sometimes thirds and even Mam forgot about her figure.

Only Polly sat in silence, pushing taties round her plate, her plump, red face downcast beneath the jaunty slide.

'Buck up,' said Mrs Bell as she doled out apple sauce. 'It's just that he's busy angling for a dinner invitation. Sees himself cocked up among the gentlemen.'

Mr Hoad and Danny talked about the hunt. Though the horses had been fed, the hounds were going hungry. Major's instructions, said Mr Hoad, so they'd be keen on the scent. Now the major was back, the earths would all stay blocked. No coward scum would dare defy the proper Master.

'Is he taking Llywelyn?' I asked Mr Hoad.

'No, lass. He likes a tidy pack. Why would he want a woolly white feller among his black and tans?'

The kennelmen all laid bets on the outcome of the hunt – would the major catch his fox or not - except that neither side had money enough to pay. While Polly and Mam cleared the dining-room table, I watched Mrs Arbiter press the major's coat. She was prodding her iron between the shiny buttons, each one engraved with a tiny galloping fox designed, she said, by Sir Walter Wetheral.

'Why are bits of the coat blue instead of red?'

'My Lord! I thought you used to hunt.'

'In Wales we wore what we liked.'

Mrs Arbiter thumped down the iron as if to say: I might have guessed. 'The collar and cuffs are what you call facings,' she said with one last thump, 'and if they're pale blue like these it shows you belong to our hunt.' She hung the coat on the overhead rack and pulled down a pair of green cords. 'By the way, your teacher has mentioned your clothes. Put these on whenever you go to the stables.'

I took the trousers, worn old things with buttons down the front.

'Now run to the boot room and find me a brush for this topper.'

'What sort of brush?'

'A brim brush. Where's your common sense?'

A man in a lovat suit was lolling against the boot room table. A farmer who'd got himself lost while looking for the cloakroom? I hadn't taken his coat and yet he looked familiar with his olive skin and curving nose.

'We meet again, Jacqueline,' he said.

I closed my eyes. Caught smells of cinnamon and cloves. Bay Rum. An aftershave I'd never liked.

He snapped his fingers. 'Look at me,' he said.

And then it came. The chauffeur. Had he been speaking to Polly?

'So you've just arrived from Wales?' He spoke like Colonel Chinstrap, Mam's nickname for an uncle whose fillies ran at Ascot.

'Not really. I stayed for a month with my mam.'

'Your mother? And where was she this afternoon?'

I tried to remember which excuse she'd gave. 'She was sick,' I said. 'I think she had a headache.'

'You mean she's gone to bed?'

'No. She's clearing the dishes.'

'So she's got over her headache,' he said, as if the thought amused him. 'And what about your father? Where is he?'

I blinked. 'I think he's dead.'

'Dead, you say?' Mr Rumney gave a whistle. 'Now there's a thing. How did he die, might I ask?'

'Behind enemy lines,' I said, even less sure of my ground. 'Behind enemy lines in France.'

'And who told you that, I wonder?'

'My mam.'

'How old are you?' asked Mr Rumney, changing tack.

Bored of all his questions, I pretended not to hear, but stepped to one side to eye the table behind him. Rows of brushes marched across the wood, from small to big, with bristles stiff and floppy, long and short.

He too stepped sideways, blocking my view. 'If you won't answer, I'll have to guess.' He looked me up and down, taking his time, as bad as any uncle. I waited, glad he'd get it wrong. I'd grown so tall that nobody took me for twelve.

He cocked his head, closed his eyes then opened them again. 'Twelve years,' he said. 'Let's say twelve years, five months and a couple of weeks.'

Exactly right. I didn't reply. Somebody must have told him. But who round here knew how old I was?

'A fine age for a girl.' He gave a know-all's smile. 'Now what is it you're after, Jacqueline?'

'A brush to brush the major's hat.'

'A brush to brush the major's hat.' He made my words sound stupid. 'Did the old boiler send you?'

Old boiler? What was that? A hen too old and tough for roasting. Something in me didn't like his disrespectful words. Ignoring him, I craned my neck to see the table. Which of all those brushes did I need?

He picked one up and flopped its bristles on his palm. 'Make sure that Ma Arbiter follows the nap, going anti-clockwise. Do you know what anti-clockwise means?'

As if I was daft, I thought, grabbing the brush.

'And when she's done his topper, she can polish it with this.' He picked up the velvet pad that had lain beside the brush. 'The major's fussy when it comes to hats.'

I grasped the pad. His fingers tightened round the velvet, tugged it from my grip and held it out of reach.

'Little word!' he said.

'Thank you.'

I grabbed the pad again and dashed towards the kitchen. Mrs Arbiter sat in front of the open Aga door, legs apart and stockings rolled down to her ankles.

'You took your time,' she said as I handed her the brush. 'But never mind, you clever girl. You even brought the pinch pad.'

I swallowed, keen to take the credit but sensing that the chauffeur wouldn't let me, not for long. 'Mr Rumney gave it me.'

'So he's still hanging around. He thought he would eat with the gentry, all dressed up in the major's cast-off tweeds.'

'Does he hunt?'

Mrs Arbiter brushed the hat in clockwise strokes. 'Doesn't know one end of a horse from the other. His job is to block the earths the night before a meet, and take the terriers to covert in the morning, in case the major wants to dig the foxes out. A coward's way of hunting, it's always seemed to me.'

Chapter Eleven

I JAMMED on Master Oliver's cast-off wellies. Clenching my toes to keep the boots on my feet, I ran from the Hall towards the stables. The fields lay in early sunlight. A south-westerly ruffled the trees. A perfect scenting day. Ahead of me reared an archway in a high stone wall. Beyond it, lay a large, cobblestoned yard with a pump in the middle and looseboxes on three of its four sides. Through a doorway on the right, a leggy, gingery gelding stood in the first of a row of stalls. Arching its neck, it leered at me as I entered, showing the whites of its eyes: Fives or Better, the major's testy hunter. I'd already seen the bruise from a kick on Danny's knee.

Danny himself stood balanced on an upturned bucket, a darning needle in his thick red fingers, his free hand resting on the horse's withers. Flat-eared, the hunter's head snaked sideways, baring two clenched rows of yellow teeth.

'Stop gawping at me, Jack,' said Danny. 'Start on Micah's mane.'

Master Oliver's pony stood in the next-door stall. What had he done to deserve this gentle, barrel-chested grey?

'I don't know what to do.'

'Did they learn you nothing at that place?' He parted a carroty hank of mane and waved a double length of yarn. 'Plait it like a girl's then twist it round.'

I threaded a needle and fumbled Micah's mane into a row of clumsy-looking knobs.

'Why can't Oliver do this job himself?'

'Cut the clattin', Jack. It's time we was tacked up.'

'When will they be here?'

'What d'you mean? They don't come to us.'

Fives or Better's hooves struck sparks as Danny led him to the archway. The mean hindquarters jigged beneath the plaited stump of tail. I waited till they'd cleared the yard then trudged behind with Micah, glad the gentlemanly pony couldn't see his plaits. Danny halted Fives or Better on the carriage sweep. I hung back ten yards or so away.

The double doors swung open. The hunter pawed the air. Face stern beneath his topper, a man ran down the steps. The major. Not drab and uncertain, like when he arrived. He paused, erect in his scarlet coat with its facings and bright buttons.

'Who did Micah's mane?' he asked with a scowl. The folds of his stock swept up to the confident tilt of his chin.

'Me, Sir,' said Danny, hanging onto the hunter.

The major sprang into the saddle. 'You're lying, m'boy,' he said. His lobster claws hidden by his gloves, he fumbled in his pocket for his watch. 'Ring the bell,' he said.

Danny tugged the pull beside the open doors so long and loud the clang bounced round the gravel. The pack began to yelp as if they'd heard it, too, and hooves clattered in the lane beyond the gates.

'Again,' the major said.

As Danny touched the pull, Mrs Arbiter appeared, her gumboil hat set low.

'I'm sorry, Sir, but Master Oliver don't feel well.'

A nerve jumped in the pouch beneath the major's eye. 'Where is he? In his nursery, I suppose?'

'Yes, Sir, and he says that he feels dizzy. I think his fever might be back again.'

Fives or Better rolled his eyes and pranced across the gravel. 'Send him down at once,' the major said.

The clock in the hall struck quarter to the hour. Its chimes had barely died when Oliver wavered through the doorway, not feverish-looking but yellow above the black of his jacket.

'Sir,' he said, leaning against the wall.

'For Pete's sake stand up straight and don't you think it's time you learnt to tie your stock? No, boy, no, don't bother with it now. Can't you hear that hounds have left the kennels?'

Master Oliver fiddled with his gloves.

'Chop chop,' the major said.

I pulled down Micah's stirrups and stood at his nearside. Oliver caught my eye and gave a sheepish smile. Not wanting the major to think that I approved, I kept my face blank as I angled the stirrup. Oliver swallowed like you do when your mouth has filled with salt.

'He needs a leg-up,' Danny said.

I sighed like Mrs Arbiter when Polly slopped the tea. Oliver raised his left foot to the cup I'd made of my hands. His right knee shook at the job of bearing his weight. I hoisted him into the saddle. Though he landed with a thud, Micah didn't budge, just stood, head down, till Oliver's toes had fumbled their way to the stirrups.

I held out his crop.

'Keep it,' he said with a ghostly grin. 'I'd only get it tangled.'

As his horse curvetted, the major swayed in the saddle, joined to it at the spine. Fives or Better settled as he reached the gates, head up, ears lightly pricked, reins stretched along his neck. Ten yards behind, Oliver clung to his pommel, his cap on the back of his head, knees and elbows out.

'Off we go,' said Danny to me.

I wrapped the thong round the crop and tucked it besides the steps. I was going to watch the major work his hounds. Danny plunged ahead of me down the lawn. We braced ourselves to jump the stream at its foot. Beyond the wood lay the smug-looking farmland, its fields well-drained, its spinneys carefully coppiced.

We reached the covert just as hounds arrived. Panting and prick-eared, they milled round the horses' hocks, The major gave his last instructions to his whipper-in. Lady Susan waved from on top of her peppy mare, and a farmer whose coat I'd taken in the hall winked at me and pulled a pasty from his pocket. Little groups arranged themselves nearby: a bunch of loud young gentleman on roans, young, wasp-waisted ladies, faces daubed with pan stick make-up, a band of farmers sitting well back in their saddles, and solid-looking children in blue and purple ties, with sheepskin numnahs under their Toptanis. All of them yakking instead of watching hounds.

Danny and I took our places beside the covert. Mr Rumney strolled up, a spade on his shoulder and a pair of Jack Russells on leashes. I pretended not to see him. Master Oliver reined in Micah near the group of ladies. The pony was tossing his head and his bit was flecked with foam. Slacken your reins, I said to Oliver under my breath. Lady Susan offered him a piece of Toblerone. He shook his head, as yellow as when he'd left the Hall.

Danny climbed onto the fence and peered into the spinney. As far as I could see it was free of brush and saplings and orderly little paths wound between the trees. Last night, the major had posted a man to guard the blocked-up earth, so the vixen had already spent a night outside her den. Had she scarpered when she heard the pack or was she still close by, holding in her scent?

The major was sending his hounds into covert. Mulberry, Scorcher, Accurate, Airy, Jafferman and Curate flung themselves at the fence. The rest of the pack went tumbling after the leaders, ears flapping as they landed, to spread out and disappear. How Iolo would have hated this wild flurry. He used to whisper his hounds into the wood, tufting or fanning them out at will. *Leu in, Bronwen, leu in, Myfanwy, leu in, Geraint and Rhodri.* The wind round his head would murmur through the trees. No, not the wind. Iolo, head flung back, giving his pack the time to learn the wood. *Leu in, leu in.* His crop would dangle as he sang, seemingly unaware of all around him, even of those hounds still bunched around his heels. *Leu in,* he'd sing again as his call wound through the leaves. *Leu in, Ifor and leu in, Ynysfor.* The Master, the brains of the pack. The pack, the brains of the covert.

The major dismounted and gave his reins to Mr Hoad. Fives or Better, now fully absorbed in the business of being a hunter, stood still as a kitchen chair with the huntsmen's matching greys. A blackbird piped on a nearby branch, a cautious, fluting sound. Below it, Danny sat and stared into the covert. Cattle mooed nearby. A lady's hunter whinnied. The young men dropped their voices like in chapel.

'The fox has scarpered long ago,' Mr Rumney said. 'I saw him leg it when I blocked his earth.'

A hound gave tongue on the east side, less of a yelp than a caw: Airy contradicting Mr Rumney. I slowed my breath, took counsel from the god. With the field on the north side, cattle to the west and yet more hounds speaking on the east, the vixen would almost certainly break to the south, upwind of the stock and well away from the pack. Alone, I slid round the edge of the covert. The god led me to a spot where claw marks pricked the mud, fine red hair fluttered on the fence's upper strut and clay from once-wet brushes caked the lower bar.

I took up my post away from the rest, on the opposite side of the covert. Wind twiddled the branches and loosened their gaudy leaves. Deep in the covert, Sacristan spoke, then Jafferman. A clump of high grass rustled beyond the rails. Its stems bent as a shape launched itself at the fence, flowed between the bars and headed straight towards me. The vixen, slender and low slung. I spread my arms, trying to drive her back. She halted and stared a couple of yards away, as orange as if she'd selected her coat to match the fallen leaves. Canny and composed after months of dodging hounds, she stood so still I saw the blonde tips of her pelt, glossy after all her goosey feasts, and the tender whiteness of the fur inside her ears.

I filled my lungs to shout the View Halloah. Deep inside the covert, hounds began to whimper. The vixen didn't seem to hear them, just stared through golden eyes. Not yet, they said. My time is not quite yet.

The breath died in my throat. The hand of Gwyn was on me. A pigeon flew out of an oak with a noise like a football rattle. The vixen's ears swivelled towards the cause of its alarm: Oliver steering Micah round the covert side, eyes on me then noticing the vixen.

'Oh! Well done,' he breathed.

Somewhere in the spinney the hounds were drawing closer.

'Scram,' Oliver hissed, and waved his arms.

No need. The vixen knew what she was doing.

'Scram,' hissed Master Oliver again.

Danny was pelting round the covert side. The vixen turned to eye the opposite side of the field.

'View halloah!' yelled Danny, plucking off his cap.

The vixen ducked her head and dashed across the grass, an animal protecting the specialness of her death. The major crashed out of the wood, followed by Jafferman, Warlock and Churchill. He raked Oliver and me with his angry, bloodshot gaze 'What are you two doing, loitering round here?'

'Not loitering, Sir,' said Oliver. 'Waiting for the fox.'

Hoofbeats thundered round the covert side: Mr Hoad on top of his dapple grey, then Billy, on her sister, leading Fives or Better.

The major jumped into the saddle as hounds picked up the scent. The vixen had already reached the opposite hedge, her brush an orange smudge against the brown. The huntsmen bucketed over the paddock behind the major, followed by the Reverend Beale, clutching the brim of his topper, the gentlemen kicking up clarts in the ladies' faces, then Oliver, hands high, sawing on the reins.

Plump face blazing, Danny swung towards me. 'You'll get me into trouble, Jack. I shouldna have brought you here.'

He walked away. The wind turned clammy on my skin. A pair of eyes at man height was peering from the wood, sly eyes, tilted slightly upwards. Somebody was spying. Then a figure detached itself from the trees, a spade in one hand and two terriers on a leash.

'So you've annoyed the major,' Mr Rumney said. 'What will your mam have to say?'

'She doesn't care about the hunt.'

'But she cares about the major.'

I saw her pale face and anxious eyes.

'Cheer up,' said Mr Rumney, 'I'll try and put things right. She's a reasonable woman, all in all.'

Sez him. A man she barely knew.

'We should get acquainted, you and me,' he said. 'You know my flat in the stableyard?'

I'd seen the corner byre where the major kept his Wolseley and the flight of steps beside it leading upwards a door.

'If you come to see me, we can talk about your dad. I knew him well, you see, and could tell you lots of things.' He pulled a bar of Five Boys from his pocket, the same kind of chocolate brought me by my dad. 'And I'll put in a word for you with the major. We don't want your mam to get sacked, do we, Jacqueline?'

Questions tumbled through my mind: where had he met my dad? Did he live nearby? Or want to see me? But, not liking Mr Rumney's know-all air, I shut my trap and grabbed the bar of Five Boys.

'Little word,' said Mr Rumney.

'Thank you.' I plunged after Dan who was marching to the Hall, hands deep in his windcheater pockets. On either side, the major's country clenched itself against me, its hard, unfriendly ground thumping the soles of my gumboots, now caked with mud from hurtling through the fields.

'I'll help you with the mucking out,' I called to Danny's back.

He barely spoke while we cleaned the stables, laid fresh straw and filled the water buckets. When he left to square the midden, I ran to fetch Oliver's whip. It felt solid and easy to hold, with a leather-bound shaft, supple plaited thong, stag horn handle and twin silver collars. Round the top one ran the words: *Oliver de Vere Walter Wetheral* and underneath a date: 13.11.1931. Fourteen years ago. Probably the day that he was born.

Danny had disappeared and Flintlock's box stood empty: the grooms on second horses would meet at Linnets Wood. Throat aching and sore-eyed, I climbed up to the hay loft. Its window looked across the yard to Mr Rumney's flat. I opened his bar of chocolate and bit into a smiling boy. A mystified babble wove through a light south-westerly. For all the good conditions, the pack had lost the scent.

Just as I finished munching, hooves clopped under the arch. I glanced through the window: Oliver on Micah. The pony's plaits had come undone and his head was hanging low, as if he knew about his rider's flapping stock, missing gloves and breeches patched with mud. What a useless boy. I'd thought I might stay put, but already my feet were rushing me onto the steps.

'Bravo, Zhackie the vackie,' he called, looking up.

I ran across the cobbles and reached to take the reins. He punched me on the arm as if I was a boy. 'We did so well,' he said, 'shooing her like that.'

An icy feeling drizzled inside my chest. He was giving me false credit and I should have told him so, but words were tumbling from his mouth in a fast, excitable flow.

'The stupid old hounds couldn't get anywhere near her. She led them a merry dance along the Appleby road, over Clitheroe's Bog, across the River Braithwaite then she doubled back downstream. I think she went to ground in Linnets Wood. The usual chappie had unblocked her earth and Rumney didn't arrive in time to dig her out.' Oliver grinned and punched my arm again. 'I knew the moment I saw you that you were good at heart.'

'I've made your father angry.'

A cloud scudded over the face of a smaller, younger boy. 'Don't worry, Zhackie the Vackie. It's me he'll take it out on. He'll never be content until he's turned me into my brother.'

Yarico, Jack's hunter, still lived in the box next to Micah's, a tired old horse with spavins and fractured elbows. Master Jack, said Danny, had broken Yarico's wind.

'We Wetherals love to hunt,' continued Oliver. 'It's in our blood, says Father. Until I came along and spoilt it all.' He slithered out of the saddle, handed me the reins and, head low, plodded from the yard.

Chapter Twelve

THAT night, a blubbering wail floated through the wall: Polly crying, like she did each night. I drifted off to the sound of her snuffles and sobs, then jerked awake at the creak of a floorboard. An icy draft curled round my bed. Someone was in the room.

A match struck. Mam flared into sight. As she fiddled with the lamp, I glanced at the clock on her locker. Twenty-five past twelve. 'Where've you been?'

'Ssshhh.' She nodded at the wall.

'Where've you been?' I asked, more loudly than before.

'Jackie, will you keep your bloody voice down?'

I caught a sour tang. 'You've been to The Arms!'

Mam glared at me, her face a cold white mask. 'Yes. I was talking to the huntsman.'

I reared up on one elbow. 'Did he mention me?'

Mam stood, stiff-backed, in an icy column of cold. 'Of course. The major's furious,' she said, frowning at the buttons on her satin blouse. 'Whenever will you learn that you mustn't interfere?'

A clammy feeling settled in my chest. Mr Rumney hadn't fixed things after all.

Mam kicked off her high heels and rubbed her toes.

'Next time I'll keep out of the way,' I said into the silence.

'There mightn't be a next time,' she said, still rubbing her toes. 'Carry on like this and we'll be back in Bootle.'

'But Mam! I want to hunt.'

'Then you should have done what you were told.' She slid a heavy jumper over her corset, the black one with an uplift and a plunge, and pulled a cigarette tin from her handbag: not Woodies or No 6 but pricey Craven A with their scarlet lid that matched her lips and nails.

'Where did you get that?'

'It was a present.'

She fiddled with the wheel of a new brass Zippo lighter. A flame shot up and lit the crease between her brows.

'From someone in the pub?'

'No. It came by post. And for God's sake keep your voice down.' She lit the cigarette and stared into my eyes. 'From now on, you must learn to keep your trap shut.'

'What? All the time?'

'Yes. Starting this Friday. The major will be talking to your school.'

Miss had already told us he was coming, like he did at this time every year. 'He'll be speaking to the big boys, not to us,' I said to Mam, 'so we're supposed to sit at the back and listen.'

Mam grabbed an empty jar of Ponds and blew two dragon plumes. 'Then make sure you do.'

She stood a long time at the window, smoking her luxury cigarettes. Then she sat on the edge of her bed and buffed her nails. Polly was sleeping in silence on the other side of the wall, but now and again I heard a warbling scream below the floorboards: the major having a nightmare, like Polly had said he did. At last Mam blew out the lamp and climbed into bed. The old house creaked and settled its limbs around us.

On Thursday night I watched Mrs Arbiter iron the major's coat, the lightweight one he wore for hunt balls and committees. Later, she showed me how to polish his boots, made to measure, she said, with mahogany-coloured tops. I shoved my arm into a long black leg, wiped off the mud with a cloth dipped in warm water, dried the leather and rubbed in two colours of Kiwi. As I shined each boot I prayed that Gwyn would put things right. Then I jammed in the trees and left them in the boot room for Mrs Arbiter to carry to the major's dressing-room.

Sir slapped each of us on the shoulder as we filed in. 'No horsing around, if you please, and big boys in the front. This talk is meant for you so you'd better have some decent questions at the end.'

I slid onto a bench near the back. His booted legs outstretched and his hands in his breeches' pockets, the major was already seated on the stage. Seemingly deaf to the hubbub in the body of the hall, he was gazing at the row of steamed-up windows, his topper perched like a conjuror's hat on the table by his side.

Sir pinned a map to the wall behind the major's chair: the one that Polly had laid on the library table, with the same little flags now joined together by string.

Brenda slid into the space beside me. 'So he's home again,' she said.

'Oh yes,' I replied. 'I see him every day.' A lie. I'd not seen him since the hunt. But I'd helped to lay his early morning tray. While his Darjeeling brewed for four and three-quarter minutes, Mam laid wafers of lemon on a silver dish and I arranged three Marie biscuits on a gold-rimmed plate with pink and yellow rosebuds sprawling round the centre. But she, not me, carried it up to his bedroom.

Swinging his gammy leg, Sir walked across the stage and said it was good of the major to give up his valuable time. Without a doubt, he said, the boys would be full of questions but must put up their hands and wait till asked to speak.

'Now then,' said the major. He stood and surveyed the front rows. 'Mr Gonegal here has told me you're going to leave the village for jobs at the base and The Metal Box.'

The boys bent their heads.

'And I've come to tell you not to,' the major said to their partings. 'Our hunt provides great chances for honest, hard-working lads.'

The boys all stared at the floor while he read out a list of jobs: huntsmen, whippers-in, fence-menders, vets, earth stoppers, blacksmiths, terrier men, hay merchants, kennel men, grooms, the lads in the flesh house, the men who made the saddle sandwich boxes and all the publicans grateful for the extra trade.

'So,' said the major, 'there's some of the things that you could do.'

Gilbert Bell put up his hand and asked what the huntsman did. An older boy sniggered. Gilbert was so fat from stuffing himself with sherbets that his mam had had to make a patch for the seat of his shorts.

'Modern man hunts by sight,' the major said, 'like we did in the war, but your hound is a sensitive chappie who mainly goes by his nose. Mr Hoad and Mr Boustead help the pack to pick up the scent.'

The major's lobster claw grappled Sir's cane from the table and pointed it at the map. 'We are lucky enough to live at the heart of a famous hunting country which we can, roughly speaking, divide into four.' He quartered the map with his stick, and pointed to Foxleigh, Rosely, Sebergham and Calthwaite, each with their small white marker surrounded by green for woods, thin blue lines for rivers and dark brown squares for fields.

Brenda's fingers rummaged among her corkscrew curls. The nit nurse had told her last week that she'd better get them cut but her dad wouldn't let her chop her pretty hair.

The major held up a photograph. 'Ranksborough,' he said, 'the founder of our famous line.'

The photo was too small and faraway for me to see.

'My great-great-grandfather even had Ranksborough's portrait painted. It hangs today in our gallery in the Hall.'

While the major talked about the lineage of his hounds, I made up my mind to inspect the portrait: did Ranksborough look as flimsy as the modern pack? The major began to talk about the job of Master: how arduous it was, how many hunt balls he had to host, coverts to maintain and committees to chair. And then he had to foster good relations with the farmers, pay for any damage incurred by the hunt and ensure they all kept their fences free of barbarous wire.

He paused after the joke. Nobody laughed. Serve him right. Brenda's freckled hands were tearing at her scalp and Gilbert was prodding an undershot boy with a ruler. On the chairs at the back, Miss was whispering to Sir. Not seeming to hear the kerfuffle, the major stared at the windows.

At last he pulled his attention back to the hall. 'And now,' he said, his lobster claws dangling at his sides, 'can any boy tell me the names of some modern-day hounds?' He smiled at the lads in the front, who looked at the floorboards again. 'Starting with A,' he said.

Silence filled the hall.

'Or any hound at all,' said the major.

The boys continued to fidget and jab each other's ribs. The major raised his eyes towards the teachers at the back. Miss looked annoyed. Sir stroked his chin. The boys bent their heads again, apart from Gilbert Bell who was poking the neck of the boy in front with his compass. Meanwhile the major was fumbling for his watch.

'Anyone?' he asked.

My eyebrows twitched. My ears pricked up. A chance to put things right. I waved my hand. The major didn't seem to see me. I sprang to my feet. He scanned the back of the hall. Nobody budged. I waved my hand again. 'Oh, it's you,' he said.

'Bryn, Caradog and Eleri,' I called out, pleased I'd got their names in alphabetical order.

'Those are Welsh. Besides, I asked for names beginning with A.'

'Accurate, Airy and Alphabet. Abbot, Astronaut, Auditor.'

He held up his hands, palm outwards, as if I was charging him down.

'Bombshell, Buckshot and Bugle,' I added, getting into my stride. 'Captious, Cauldron and Chatterbox. Dedalus, Diphthong and – '

'Whoa there! Enough!'

A big girl swung round and looked at me down her nose. The

major turned to a boy who said his mam had walked a pup called Catchword. I started to tell him that Catchword had been stifled but Sir was saying he thought we might call it a day. The major backed to his chair and lifted the skirts of his coat. Before he could sit Miss stood up and said that it was cruel, so many people and hounds chasing a poor dumb animal.

Still clutching his skirts, the major spoke to the steamed-up glass. 'Charlie – that is, the fox – is hunted *as a gentleman* and, as such, lives under my patronage. You must have heard how good he is at breaking into hen coops, how strong and cunning when it comes to killing geese – crimes that would land a commoner before the magistrate. In Charlie's case, his extravagant tastes are indulged. But, like any gentleman, he has his obligations and his, first and foremost, is to show the huntsmen sport on any day from November to the beginning of March.'

'But wouldn't it be kinder just to shoot him?'

'What if he were wounded but not killed, and dragged out his days with a bullet festering in his eye?'

Miss opened her mouth but before she could speak Sir hobbled up to the platform and said that Major Wetheral had kindly given us all a holiday on Monday. The boys cheered. Sir said thank you to the major. Now he'd take him for a slap-up tea.

I was trudging across the playground when Gilbert stepped into my path. Despite the ice on the tarmac his jacket hung unbuttoned, showing tartan braces stretched over rolls of fat.

'Eh! You!'

I jumped. He'd never spoken to me before.

'Eh! You!' He jagged my hair so hard it burnt the roots. 'What are you doing in our school? You're just a stupid vackie. You should have gone back home to Liverpool.'

Iolo used to say that bullies were chicken but Gilbert was two years older than me and didn't look chicken at all.

'Yer made us look reet thick,' he said, 'shouting out them names.'

'I didn't mean to.'

'D'you know what the women that come to our shop are saying? They're saying your mam's a tart and her fancy men come to see her.'

Tart. A gooey blob of strawberry jam, sticky and red in a case of frilly pastry. A treat you crammed in your mouth and longed to eat two of, even three, to gorge yourself on its sugary, gummy fruit. A treat that made you sick. 'She hasn't got any fancy men,' I said.

'Then who was that skinny feller hanging around?' Gilbert stuck his thumbs in his braces. 'They're saying he's her fancy man and yer dad.'

Tears jumped into my eyes. 'He's not my dad. My dad was a soldier – an officer - who … died behind enemy lines – along with lots of other people's dads.'

Gilbert breathed his Liquorice All Sorts in my face. 'Then where's his name on the memorial?'

'It's on a different memorial. One in Liverpool.'

'Liar, liar, pants on fire. Everyone knows you're a by-blow.'

The pack was behind me, belling across the playground: wise Aneurin, loyal Caradog and clever little Eleri. I lifted my lip and snarled, baring all my teeth.

'Stop!' Gilbert shouted. 'Stop!'

I shoved my face in his and snarled again.

Gilbert stuck up his hands and backed away. 'You shouldn't be doing that!' he said with a fat white smile.

I growled even louder.

'Stop it!' he said, squinting over my shoulder. 'Stop it! I've got a bad heart.'

I turned. Mr Marlozzi was crossing the playground towards us. 'What are you doing?' he asked, spreading his hands. 'Jackee, I am surprised at you.'

Not knowing what to say, I fingered my red-hot scalp.

'Go home, both of you,' he said, shooing us over the tarmac. 'It is four o'clock. I need to lock the school.'

Gilbert crossed towards the shop, moaning and clutching his chest. My shoebag bumping awkwardly on my ankles, I tumbled through the women lumbering down from the bus. Not stopping to say sorry, I tore on towards the Hall.

Danny was leading Flintlock down the drive to his paddock. The day before, the major had summoned him to the gunroom: what had he thought he was doing, charging around on foot and, worse, letting a girl wreck his sport? But at breakfast that morning Danny had been his usual friendly self.

'Steady on, Jackie. You're making him jib,' he said to me now.

My breath came in panicky gasps. 'Has Gilbert got a weak heart?'

'Gilbert Bell? Not as I've heard of. Has he had an attack?' Danny lowered his big red face to mine. 'What's the matter? Did he say summat wrong?'

I stared at Flintlock's hooves, each ringed with seven nails and all their nerves and muscles safe inside the bone. 'Not wrong. Just mean and rude.'

'What was it, Jack?'

I tried to speak but choked on the lump in my throat.

'Spit it out,' said Danny.

'Gilbert said I didn't have a dad.'

'That's rubbish and he knows it. Everyone has a dad.'

'Except mine's dead,' I said, knowing I lied again.

'Mebbe he is but so is old Flintlock's here and what do he care about that?'

Flintlock stared at me down his blaze. 'But he's got a pedigree.'

'Not him!' Danny slapped the gelding's rump. 'Take a look at his backside, big as a ruddy cook's, and them feathers on his hooves where I forgot to trim 'em. Fives or Better's the pedigree nag and think of the fuss he makes, flinching at each puff of cold and balking at the mud. Flintlock's the boyo you rely on to take his fences straight.'

I looked into the centre of Flintlock's inky pupils. Who could ever know the hurt he'd felt? 'If I was king, I'd make sure every animal had a pedigree and if they didn't their owners could make one up.'

'A made-up pedigree? You're daft, Jack, proper daft. Now cut the clattin' and get yersen back to the Hall.'

Chapter Thirteen

FOR once, the front doors stood ajar.

Go on, whispered Eleri, the cleverest of the bitches. Now, while you have a chance. Take a look at that famous hound the major boasts about. He may not be as great as the major thinks he is.

Although I knew the major was at tea, my heart thumped in time with the rowdily ticking clock. I kicked off my shoes by the newel post and climbed towards the landing. Halfway up, I glimpsed the row of pictures on my left: snub-nosed spaniels; small boys whipping Shetlands; gentlemen smirking at heaps of dying pheasants and, first in line, a woman and a slim young man together on the terrace. The woman's brows showed dark against white skin well-protected from the sunlight by a broad-brimmed hat. Her magenta mouth drooped in a pout. The major's wife. I knew her from her photo. The man was younger, laughing, head flung back, his Adam's apple bare above an open collar.

But where was Ranksborough?

In the last and biggest picture on the left a plump, bewigged gentleman in acid yellow breeches sat on a bench beneath a lime green tree. Chin resting on his owner's silken knee, a handsome, black and tan hound stood sideways on, ears back, eyes moist with adoration. *Sir Walter Wetheral* said the label on the frame, *with Ranksborough, founder of the Westmorland Foxhounds.*

Ranksborough looked well-made, his outline clean, his head and neck refined. All in all, a stylish stallion hound. But where was breadth of loin, strength of bone and muscled back? Not a hound to take you through the rough stuff.

A woman laughed outside, confident and horsy. I swivelled as the double doors swung back. The major crossed the threshold, arm crooked for Lady Susan, and saw my shoes kicked off at ten to two.

'What's this? What's this?' he asked.

Keeping to the marble, I edged my way back down.

'There she is,' the major said to Lady Susan. 'That's the very girl who wrecked our sport.'

'Ah! Jacqueline,' said Lady Susan, pulling off her headscarf.

Hot and clumsy-feeling, I hovered on the stairs.

The major set his trilby on the chest inside the door. 'And in the school just now I couldn't shut her up. The village lads could hardly get a word in.'

'I dare say they'll get over it and Ollie seems to like her.'

'An odd boy,' said the major as if I wasn't there. 'I really don't know what to do with him. I thought things would get better when I bought him Micah.'

'Thing is,' said Lady Susan, 'he thinks that hunting's cruel.'

'Did he tell you that?' the major asked.

'Yes – and other things,' said Lady Susan, her forehead framed as usual in thick blonde buffalo horns.

The major rang the little bell that waited by his hat.

'Where's your mother, dear?' Lady Susan asked me.

The major helped her shrug off her fur coat. 'Her mother should be here,' he said, 'and she should be downstairs.'

I searched for an excuse but couldn't find one. 'I went to look at Ranksborough,' I said.

'Ranksborough?' echoed Lady Susan.

The major gave the bell a second, more energetic ring 'It's a painting, Now, for heaven's sake, let's have a cup of tea. I dodged the invitation from old Gonegal.'

'Oh do let's take a look. I've never seen your portraits.' Lady Susan climbed the stairs towards me, her cream silk headscarf trailing from her hand. I continued downwards, heading for my shoes.

100

'Aren't you coming with me, Jacqueline?' she called. 'We can take a look at – whatshisname.'

'I'm not meant to be here in case I bump into the major.'

'You can't bump into him now because you've already seen him.'

The fur still on his arm, the major passed me on the stairs, his long, booted legs taking them two at a time. 'She may as well come, too,' he said. 'Why else are we trekking up here?'

Down in the hall, the door from the passage opened.

'Mrs Arbiter?' called the major as he reached the landing. 'Could you ask Elizabeth for tea? For Lady Susan and myself, that is. Oh, and by the way - ' The door slammed shut. 'Do you know,' he added, 'I sometimes think she hates me.'

'Rubbish! She adores you. It's obvious, you know.' Lady Susan rubbed her pink angora arms. 'Don't you want to put your shoes on, Jacqueline?'

I crammed my feet into my outdoors, their laces still done up. Lady Susan smiled as I climbed back up towards her, following her trail of stables and gardenia. 'And, child, for heaven's sake stop clinging to the edge.'

'If I don't my shoes will wear out the carpet.'

'I suppose they will but not for ages yet.'

'Mrs Arbiter says that servants' shoes wear out the carpet quicker.'

Lady Susan whinnied at the major's back. 'William! Did you hear about the servants' shoes? Can that really be your Mrs Arbiter?'

Ignoring her, the major turned along the left-hand balcony, past the portrait of his wife and elder son.

'Oh! The artist flattered her!' Lady Susan said.

I saw it in the major's face: he wasn't going to answer.

'William? Don't you think the artist flattered her? But what a lovely picture of dear Jack.'

I caught the major up and stood two paces back. He was staring at Sir Walter in his acid yellow breeches and double chin above his silk cravat.

'Poor, poor Ollie,' Lady Susan said. When the major took no notice, she trailed along towards us. 'Oh,' she said, 'so Ranksborough's a hound.'

The major's claw hovered by the picture. Had he seen that Mam had forgot to dust the frame? His knuckle, like a little skull beneath the raw red skin, almost stroked the W branded on Ranksborough's shoulder then dropped again as if afraid to touch it.

'His dam was put to stud at the Duke of Rutland's. A shrewd decision, Susan, wouldn't you agree?'

Lady Susan cocked her head. 'Oh, I most certainly do.'

Could neither of them see what I'd begun to see? That Ranksborough, though good-looking, had sown the seeds of weakness? That most of his descendants had long been bred too close?

'Don't you think so, Jacqueline?' Lady Susan asked.

A perfect chance to talk about Llywelyn, a hound whose get was valued throughout Wales, descended from none other than the Gelli.

'Jacqueline?' Lady Susan said, her kind, broad face creasing in a smile.

I smiled back. Chickened out 'He's got a curly tail.'

'That's right!' said Lady Susan.

I swallowed and ploughed on. 'I think the artist might have got it wrong. The major's hounds don't have curly tails.'

Impatient but amused, the major glanced at Lady Susan. 'She's right,' he said, then turned to me as if I'd just appeared. 'Right, that is, but only to a point. In those days they admired what they called a gay stern. My grandfather bred it out back in the 1920s.'

Better to have bred out the spindle-shaped hindquarters. But already the major was pointing across the stairwell.

'Oh! Susan! Take a look at Lady Laetitia.'

A middle-aged lady sat by an urn with a fluffy brown dog on a leash, its blue eyes dazed as if from staring at a ghost.

'Now, Jacqueline,' said the major, 'what breed of dog is that?'

A hairy dog? A lap dog? A dog with frilly ears? *Eleu in, Eleri. Leu in, Taliesin.* But their answer kept dashing away like a wily afternoon fox. I shook my head. My pack had failed to find. Lady Laetitia lifted her lip in a sneer.

'You should know by now,' the major said, sounding like a schoolboy glad to get his own back. 'That's the breed on the Wetheral family crest. It's actually a gazehound, Jacqueline.'

'What on earth's a gazehound?' Lady Susan asked.

'It's an old-fashioned name for a dog that hunts by sight. That one is most probably a saluki.'

I put up my hand. The major didn't see me till Lady Susan nudged him with her elbow.

I dropped my hand. 'You said in school that hounds hunt by smell.'

'She's got you there,' said Lady Susan, nudging him again.

'True enough.' For once, the major looked at me and smiled. 'But then I meant our foxhounds. Greyhounds go by sight and so do Afghans and Borzois and lots of other breeds.'

'When I grow up I'm going to be a lady huntsman,' I told him, encouraged by his friendlier tone.

'That's one job that I forgot to mention.' I caught the major's wink at Lady Susan. 'But I'm not really sure that such a thing exists.'

'I think there was one in Wales in the First World War.'

'Ah! Wales!' Again, the major turned to Lady Susan. 'Have you seen that brute they sent on loan? So coarse and white among our little beauties! As if we'd breed from that. I'm going to send him back.'

My insides swirled. How dare the major call Llywelyn coarse?

'What's the matter, Jacqueline?' Lady Susan asked.

I spoke directly to the major. 'Llywelyn's needed by your pack.'

'Humph! That's what Dai Meredith said.' The major shot another grown-up glance at Lady Susan. 'Whimsical, like all the Taffs, you know.'

'Welsh people know their hounds,' I said, 'more than people here.'

103

The major stared at me through tired, bloodshot eyes. 'Oh, child, what shall we do with you?' he asked.

'Remember,' Lady Susan said, 'we need to think of Ollie. It might help him to go hunting with a friend, and Pixie's got too fat from being out at grass.'

The major's Adam's apple skittered up and down.

'And she'll look good on horseback,' Lady Susan said, and glanced down at her solid hips and legs. 'Skinny, with long thighs that sit flat against the saddle.'

'Good in the saddle or not,' said the major, 'I don't want them getting too close.'

What a snob. As if I wanted to.

'I don't see too much danger,' Lady Susan said. 'After all, their paths are very different.'

'Perhaps you're right. Anything to get him to a meet. We'll try her out and see how she behaves.'

A second chance! Thanks be to Gwyn ap Nudd and Lady Susan.

'She can start at the Pony Club meet,' the major said. 'It's only a week away, and at Kellaway this year.'

Kellaway Castle: the home of Lady Susan and her sisters. I'd seen a picture in the servants' hall. The major fixed me with his rain-grey eyes. 'Above all else, you'll stick with Master Oliver. For all his silly views, he knows the ropes.'

'Yes,' I said. How else could I have answered? The major couldn't know how fast I'd pick things up.

'You don't know as much as you think you do,' he said. He kept his eyes on mine. Could he read my mind? 'You'll find things pretty different from your little hunt in Wales.'

Full Cry

Chapter Fourteen

MRS Arbiter settled her Sunday hat above her brows. It was exactly like her weekday one, but black. 'Where's your ma, Jacqueline?' she asked, jabbing a pin in the felt. Why, I wondered, when she had no hair?

'Upstairs getting ready.'

The day before, Mam had caught the early bus. At tea-time she came home with bulging carrier bags, hurried straight upstairs and unpacked them on the bed: hairy tweeds just like Lady Susan's, a pair of leather lace-ups and a pale blue cashmere twinset.

'She's going to be late,' Mrs Arbiter said, jabbing a second pin, 'so I don't suppose she'll mind if I give you this.'

The letter was addressed to me in forward-sloping writing, hurled down in the way that teachers didn't like, with the tails of its ps and qs entangled in the words below. And the envelope was ripped open.

'I had to check,' Mrs Arbiter said. 'Not that I understood a single word.'

Sitting by the Raeburn in his stocking feet, Iolo updated his journal after every hunt. Date; country; pack; conditions; length of runs; number of kills, page after page on the feats of every hound, which one first to speak, which hottest on the scent, which boldest through the thickets and bravest in trapping the fox.

But now his words seemed stern enough to rip the flimsy paper. *If only I'd known to warn you*, he'd wrote in Welsh. *My cousin Dai has told me all about the major, and rues the day that his Llywelyn was drafted to that pack. The night before a hunt the major sits and drinks and, worse, he chases foxes whose hour has not yet come. The souls of animals wrongly killed wreak vengeance on the hunter. The major has already lost his wife and elder son. Don't hunt with him,* cariad. *It will lead to nothing good.*

The letters throbbed. Iolo seemed to know so much. Could it all be right? Before I could think of an answer, heels clopped in the passage. I shoved the letter in my pocket as Mam walked into the room, wearing her new tweed coat and silky headscarf. The church bell started to toll. Polly appeared behind her, bosoms flopping, her blurry skirt gaping at the zip.

'O Lord!' she said. 'I look a holy show.'

Mam glanced at Polly's tear-stained face and greasy, uncombed hair. 'Poor Pol. Don't let him get you down.'

Polly looked away. She'd stopped sitting with Mam in the kitchen and sometimes ignored me if we happened to meet in a passage.

'Here, Pol,' said Mam, handing her a comb.

Polly shook her head. 'Keep it. I don't want it.'

'You're taking things too hard,' said Mam. 'Best go and put your feet up.'

'I'm in charge, not you, Elizabeth.' Mrs Arbiter pinned a poppy on her collar. 'And, besides, the major wants us there.'

Mam snapped her handbag shut. 'The major don't know how you feel when you're six months gone.'

Polly flopped down at the table and sat with her head in her hands. 'Go on,' she said, 'and leave me here. I'll be fine, I swear.'

Mrs Arbiter opened the outside door. One hand on the letter in my pocket, I followed Mam and her up the outside steps.

'Where's your poppy, Elizabeth?' Mrs Arbiter asked.

'I'd no money for the tin.'

'But money enough to buy new clothes, it seems.'

'I meant I had no change.'

Mrs Arbiter ran her eye over Mam's bulky coat. 'And you came here with your widow rigmarole.' Mrs Arbiter must have been listening to the women in the sweetshop. 'And there was poor Polly, thinking you're so good.'

'You're jumping to false conclusions.'

'I can conclude what I like but I wouldn't upset a kiddie.'

Mam clopped on, blank-faced, across the carriage sweep. Under clouds as flat and grey as porridge, the three of us marched in silence down the drive. Halfway, Mrs Arbiter heaved herself over the stile. Mam and me trailed behind her through the graveyard and joined the flock of parishioners dawdling through the porch in sheepy scarves, mitts and bobble hats.

Inside the church, a feeble light peered through narrow windows at row after row of heavily varnished pews. In winter the chapel in Wales smelt of Michaelmas daisies, gorse and tubs of shaggy chrysanthemums. Here, the pong of Barbours dangled in the air, bulked out by damp tweed, beaver lamb and the chemical reek of mothballs.

The major sat in the front pew on the left, the long flat back of his head tapering into a scarf. Master Oliver sat beside him, close to the paraffin heater at the foot of the altar steps. Lady Susan sat across the aisle, in a row of what I guessed were sisters, all wearing matching scarves patterned with horses' heads.

Mrs Arbiter led us into a pew near the back. A draught swept round our feet as men from the farm trooped in, their chapped red faces strangled by their collars, cheeks nicked from their Saturday visits to the barber. Ahead of us, the church was filling up, my view of the altar blocked by solid backs. Three pews in front, Gilbert knelt beside his mam and fidgeted with the patch on the seat of his shorts. Over his shoulder, I glimpsed the Reverend Beale, his sack-coloured face balanced weightily on his cassock, lumbering from the vestry onto the altar.

A door whumphed shut behind us. No need to turn my head. I'd caught a waft of hot metal and Bay Rum. We shuffled up to make a space. The chauffeur sauntered past us and knelt beside a red-haired girl from school. Sit. Stand. Kneel. Cough. Sing. I wished I could take the letter out of my pocket, smoothe it and tuck it safely in its envelope. We warbled O God our help in ages past, not loud and joyful, heads flung back, like in Capel, but in a sickly wail. God had never helped us much at all. Then, faces numb with cold, everyone mumbled the Creed.

Out in the kennels a hound started to sing, a shivery sound winding through my ears: Llywelyn, for once, giving the note to the bitches. Three dog hounds crooned in a baritone, then three more soared above them, echoey and sweet, the kind Iolo used to call the counter-tenors. Spitfire took the note, then Accurate and Airy, and then more dog hounds, deep and forceful, led by Jafferman.

A wind swept round the church. It brought a tang of mud and moss and wagged the stone leaves wreathing the tops of the pillars. Iolo's letter crackled in my pocket. What had brought Gwyn ap Nudd to the major's church? Not seeming to notice the sudden green spring light, everyone watched the Reverend Beale climb up to the pulpit. A ring of stone lilies stirring overhead, he gripped the wingtips of the bird that held the Bible. Everyone sat down, coughed or sniffed.

'St Paul to the Corinthians,' he said, sounding as if he'd popped a hot potato in his mouth. Each time he came to 'charity' he swapped the word for 'huntsman', lifting his head and staring to make sure we understood. The *huntsman* suffereth long, and is kind. The *huntsman* envieth not. The *huntsman* vaunteth not himself. The *huntsman* is not puffed up. The *huntsman* doth not behave himself unseemly.

The Reverend was wrong. A huntsman is nothing like *Charity*. I bit my cheeks so as not to laugh. A huntsman is crafty, rough, aggressive, surly, devious, sly. He forgets about other people. Never thinks twice about breaking the law. A snort escaped from my nose. Mrs Arbiter tutted. I groped for a hanky, found nothing except the letter. O Gwyn ap Nudd tell me what to do. When I looked up, the light had died. The wind had gone, leaving only smells of moss and mud. The Reverend made the sign of the cross. The major walked down the aisle. How pale he looked, and scraggy, with his thinning red moustache, especially now with pink-cheeked Lady Susan on his arm, her solid calves in chunky sheepskin boots. Master Oliver slouched behind them among her lumpy sisters. The rest of us followed them out and down the street to gather round the soldier on his pillar.

A mean little wind fidgeting with his cassock, the Reverend Beale spoke about his days as an army padre. How loyal and good the men had been, how brave their officers. Mr Reginald Arbiter. Eight men from nearby farms. The Reverend Beale recited the names on the memorial, on and on, as if most of the village had died. Archibald Laidlaw who ran the pub. Three brave lads from the flesh house. Grand soldiers all, while working for the hunt, they'd learnt about English loyalty and service. And the bravest of them all was Captain Jack, as famous for his courage on the field of battle as for his daring in the hunting field.

Master Oliver turned up his collar against the drizzle, glanced at me and smiled. Instead of smiling back I stared at the ground by my feet. I wanted to make it look as if my dad had really died. I needn't have bothered. Gilbert had gone home. Mrs Arbiter stood, eyes shut, her handbag pressed to her tummy, tears rolling down the creases in her cheeks. Everyone else was staring at their shoes, apart from Mr Marlozzi, who'd fought on the other side, and Mam, who watched the major as he stood head bare in the drizzle, his medals like new pennies on his chest.

Billy pulled his horn from between his jacket buttons, his scar a thin white ladder on his cheek. It bulged as he blew the Last Post. The drizzle grew worse as if someone had turned on a tap. We shivered for two minutes then Billy played the Rouse.

The Reverend Beale mouthed words into the downpour:

At the going down of the sun and in the morning
We shall remember them.

The major propped a wreath of poppies against the pillar. The moment the service was done everyone started gabbing. The major clamped his lobster claw on Lady Susan's elbow and steered her to her little green MG.

'Off to drinks at Kellaway,' Mrs Arbiter said. 'We'll be waiting lunch again.'

The major settled Lady Susan in the passenger seat then folded himself behind the steering wheel. The hunt staff and the kennel men marched in a gang to The Arms and cottagers trudged, heads bent, up their garden paths. Everyone else stayed clustered on the pavement apart from Mam who turned and walked towards the drive.

'So she's left you on your own,' a voice behind me said.

I swung round. Mr Rumney pointed at the cenotaph. 'You mustn't go pretending that your dad is dead.'

My tongue gone stiff as a hoof, I stared at my shoes.

'He's brave, your dad,' he said. 'I know him pretty well. Him and me are real pals, you see.'

'What's he like?' I asked, not sure I was doing right.

'Like you, he is. Tall. Quite determined.' Mr Rumney paused, lit a Craven A and squinted at me through the curls of smoke. 'You never came to see me like I asked.'

Mam would never have let me. I fiddled with my gloves.

'Don't worry,' said Mr Rumney. 'She doesn't have to know.'

'Where is he now?' I asked, drawn in against my will.

Mam appeared as if she'd jumped up through a trap door.

'Lizzie,' said Mr Rumney, 'you and I need to talk.'

Mam grabbed my wrist and pulled me down the street. 'Not now,' she called over her shoulder. 'It's neither the time nor the place.'

'I can explain it all,' said Mr Rumney.

She yanked the gates at the foot of the drive so hard that flakes of rust dropped off the flimsy hounds. 'What was he saying?' she asked.

'That he knows my dad.'

'That's nonsense. He's busy making mischief.'

'So he's never met him?'

'I wouldn't say that, exactly, but he doesn't know him well.'

Still holding my wrist, she strode towards the gloomy old box of a house with the pile of clouds still pressing on its lid. At the kitchen steps she gave my wrist a shake. 'It's good that you're learning all the hunting fol-de-rol but you've got to keep away from Alan Rumney.'

'I'll do my best.'

'Promise?'

'Cross my heart and hope to die.'

'And if he tries to get pally, don't take any notice. Just come to me and tell me what he said.'

Chapter Fifteen

THE doll lay in the dust beneath my bed, the only real present my dad had ever brought me. I dragged her out. Her wide blue eyes clicked open in alarm. One hand round her neck, I wrenched off her arms and legs then let her limbless body tumble backwards on the counterpane.

Her eyes clicked shut. 'Serve you right,' I whispered, and yanked her hard blonde hair out strand by strand. Then I hid the pieces in my shoebag.

The bins stood in a row of four outside the kitchen, tucked behind the steps that led from the garden down to its door. I raised the nearest lid, looked round for lurking rats, then tipped the doll's remains onto a pile of bones. The bald pink head rolled to the side then lay face up and stared. I pulled a piece of cardboard from underneath the scraps, hid the furious eyes and slammed the dustbin lid.

Mrs Arbiter was sitting by the Aga, reading last week's *Westmorland Gazette*. 'Polly's cleaning the gunroom, Jacqueline,' she said. 'Tell her to look out Master Oliver's old ratcatcher. You'll need something decent to wear if you're going to the meet.'

The usual spiteful draft sneaked down the gunroom passage. Dusty prints lined the red flock walls. Gentlemen in toppers, coattails flying, long, thin feet crammed downwards into stirrups, spurred low-bellied horses over rows of matching hills.

I knocked. 'Come in,' called Polly.

Though out of the draft from the outside door, the air in the room struck cold. The fire's single bar seemed barely strong enough to warm the gumboots in a row beneath the window. Their rubbery stink mingled with traces of pipe smoke. Farther in, I caught the pong of sweaty socks and the tang of oil from the gun rack in a glass-doored cabinet against the right-hand wall. Mam had said the major sat here every night, drinking, paying bills or writing in some book. At all other times he kept the gunroom locked, apart from the hour each Monday when Polly was meant to clean it.

Instead, she was lolling in his desk chair, the swivelling sort the secretary sat in at school. A photograph hung on the dark green wall above the desk. Thumbs hooked in the pockets of his army coveralls, a thin, sunburnt man lolled against a tank, his face beneath his panama creased in laughter. It took me a couple of seconds to recognise the major. He was gazing at a stouter, grey-haired man crouched in the sand by the tracks of the battered Matilda. The older man was pouring what might have been tea from a kerosene can into a dented mug. Curly letters squirmed along the sand below their feet. *'From mud, through blood to the green fields beyond.'*

'Who's he?' I asked, pointing at the grey-haired man.

'Who d'you think?' said Polly. 'Mr Arbiter.' She'd stopped crying by the time we got back from church, and I hadn't heard her sob last night in bed. But her eyelids still looked swollen and her hair hung lank.

'Does the major ever see his ghost?'

'If he does he never says owt about him.'

She yanked a handful of papers out of a pigeon-hole. 'Final demands,' she said. 'You can tell from all the red. The silly old dobby spends it all on the hunt. No wonder we none of us ever get our wages.' She riffled through the bills then shoved them back again. 'What's this I hear about you and Gilbert Bell?'

Trapped in a high glass case on the wall above her head, a big grey fish gaped down in angry surprise. My knees started to shake. I looked for a second chair. Not finding one, I stood beside the desk.

'What were you playing at,' asked Polly, 'growling like a dog?'

Despite the chilly air, the heat swept into my cheeks. 'He said that Mam was a tart.'

Polly twirled round to fix me with her big blue stare, harder and stonier than it used to be. 'Now I wonder what might have given him that idea?'

Still hot-cheeked, I heard Mam's girlish laugh and saw her silly hats and peep-toe shoes. 'She's not a tart,' I said. 'It's just that my dad is dead.'

'Is that what you really think?'

A row of books stood on the shelf above the desk, all of identical size, wider than they were long, and each with a year written in gold on its spine. Hunt Journals. The kind Iolo used. Avoiding Polly's gaze, I pulled down 1931. The usual stuff. Dates. Location of meets and coverts drawn. Which hounds quickest to find. Length of runs. Number of foxes killed, all in the major's small, pernickety hand. And then my eye fell on a longer than usual entry.

13th November 1931. *An excellent day,* the major had written in navy ink, *despite an early snowfall during the night. Creditor found in Thornton and owned the line on top of a drystone wall. We kept after our fox – a vixen with only half a brush - along the railway track, over Wiley Marshes, two miles south along the Appleby road and through Thurston ford. Queensbury and Triton tumbled her over at twenty-five to four in among Cowan's Belted Galloways. A seven-mile run in all. The longest of the season.*

The major dropped a line then wrote: *My beloved wife, Félice, delivered of my second son at home at precisely twenty-five to four. Oliver de Vere Walter Wetheral. 6 lbs, 11 oz. Dr Madden and Mrs Bell in attendance.*

So Oliver had been born at the moment of the kill. I opened my mouth to tell Polly. She was tugging the topmost edge of the open desk, carved in a row of pointy flowers and leaves. Behind the carving lay a shallow drawer of envelopes. She grabbed the nearest, pulled out the letter and waved it up and down.

'Guess who this is from.'

I smelt Lily of the Valley, a familiar, sickly smell. 'She wrote to him about a job,' I said.

'What? Out of the blue?'

The air in the dank little hutch turned even colder. 'She'd met him before, in a pub in Liverpool.'

'Is that what she told you?' asked Polly, holding out the letter. 'Here. You can read it if you want.'

Dear William, I read at the top of a page. My thoughts shot out of control. 'I don't want to. I can't. I think it's all in English.'

'Try,' said Polly, waving the letter in front of my face. 'I want to know what she said.'

I caught sight of myself in the shiny glass doors of the cabinet: a frightened ghost of a girl. At her back, the guns stood, shoulders stiff.

'No,' I said. 'I can't.'

Polly sighed as she bundled the letters back into their drawer. 'You're useless, you.'

'I'm meant to try on Master Oliver's old ratcatcher.'

Polly heaved herself from the chair, locked the door behind us and dropped the key in her apron pocket. 'Now don't go telling anyone what I've showed you.'

She walked ahead of me down the gunroom passage. Up the servants' stairs. Along the passage past our bedrooms. Her big black shoes flopped off the darns in the heels of her socks. At Oliver's nursery door she stopped, tapped, then pushed into the room. A grubby light struggled through the monkey puzzle tree, showing new eggs on the shelves beside the door. I squinted at a label. *Falco tinnunculus.* A sketchbook lay open on the windowsill.

Llywelyn was climbing the slope up from the garden, head bent, ears cocked, a forepaw slightly raised. Oliver must have drawn him from above - I knew from the cushions of muscle he'd caught on both sides of his spine - maybe from this very windowsill.

'So what do you make of it?' asked Polly.

'He looks in good condition.'

'Not the dog. I'm looking at the lass.'

Serious and tall, with hair chopped short, a skinny girl had looped

Llywelyn's lead around her wrist. More than just walking together, the pair was moving as one, left legs raised a little from the grass. Shoulders back, the girl was looking ahead, eyes out for whatever might concern the hound who walked with his muzzle inclined towards her knee. My stomach pitched. Oliver had seen my crooked parting, a sock half-fallen down and the scabs on my knobbly knees.

'Quite the artist,' Polly said. Hitching up her skirt, she knelt to rummage through the wardrobe's bottom drawer.

'I'd rather wear the clothes I wore in Wales.'

Polly heaved herself upright. 'What? Them shabby trousers. You can't wear them, not on a Wetheral pony.'

She handed me some jodhpurs with the mouldy smell that came from months or years in a crowded drawer. I unzipped my skirt and dropped it on the carpet. Her face an extra head above my shoulder, Polly stood behind me, staring at the glass.

'Did you ever wonder where you got them from?' she asked.

I met her round blue eyes. She pointed at the mirror.

'Them long white legs of yours.'

I pulled on the jodhpurs and fumbled with the buttons down the front.

'I mean,' said Polly, 'with your mam so small.'

Still staring at my legs, she handed me a jacket, then stood in silence as I tried it on. It looked baggy, like the jodhpurs, and like them smelt of mould.

'Why d'you think the major's saying you can hunt?'

'Dunno. I haven't thought. Because of Lady Susan.'

Polly moved so close I caught the smell of her dinner. 'If I was in your shoes I'd be asking questions.'

My mind snapped shut against her. 'Go away,' I said. Her red face crumpled. 'Go away,' I said again. 'I don't want you here.'

'I was only trying to help you.' She waddled to the door. 'The thing with you is that you know nowt about owt.'

I waited till she'd clopped off down the passage, then swapped the jodhpurs for my old cord trousers. Like the doorbell on its wire in the hall, a bell was jangling somewhere deep inside me. To try and shut it out, I pressed my face against the window. The sky grew dark and raindrops spat against the glass. Although the bell inside me jangled on, I knew I wouldn't - couldn't - ever answer, no matter who or what was waiting on the step.

Chapter Sixteen

THE night before the hunt, I lost all hope of sleep. Earlier that week, Danny had tried me out on Pixie, a pony descended from the oldest line in Europe, its presence recorded on Exmoor in the Domesday book. My breath had caught in my throat when he led her from her box. Her mane and tail flared glossy black. Her coat shone berry bright. A powerful build. Fine legs in long black stockings. Cream dapples on her belly. A large, intelligent head. A mushroom-coloured muzzle, velvet-black inside her nostrils. The mushroom shading round her black-lashed eyes made her look as if she wore expensive make-up.

My head throbbed. Hot air ballooned in my chest. Tomorrow Llywelyn was joining the pack. The major had agreed. Although Iolo's warning had been clear, I felt sure – almost sure – that he'd want me to watch Llywelyn, and report on him if need be. Pictures of the chase went fizzing through my brain: Llywelyn the first to pick up the scent, Llywelyn the first to speak, Llywelyn leading the pack in pursuit of a wily fox. And me galloping after him on Pixie.

The clock struck eleven. Mam not back from The Arms. I climbed out of bed and opened our window. The rain that had fallen all day had stopped an hour before. The night air soothed my skin like friendly paws. Ears out, I caught the gossipy splash of the stream, the snort of the Reverend's cob from his shed in the nearby field and the whirring of some bird in the trees beyond the lawn.

Gusty and fresh with the tang of dying leaves, a wind swished up from the wood, making a lamp swing crazily past the fountain. As it drew nearer, I caught sight of the figure holding the lamp. Doubtless Mr Rumney, back from blocking earths: the Kellaway coverts were

120

riddled with tunnels and dens. As he reached the terrace, the moon sailed out of a cloud. Not Mr Rumney. Master Oliver. He'd probably been visiting his hides. My elbows on the sill, I watched him blow out the flame then, pale and open-mouthed, duck into the house.

Next morning, I woke to the thump of feet on the lino.

'Damn, damn, damn,' said Mam. 'Polly forgot to wake us.'

Not forgetfulness. Spite. Now I'd be late at the stables. When Mam had dashed along the passage, I swabbed my face with my flannel and struggled with numb fingers to button my shirt and trousers. Down in the kitchen, Mam was scrabbling clinker from the Aga onto a newspaper spread on the floor.

'Has the stove gone out?' I asked.

She raised a cross white face. On the table, fine dust had aleady coated the major's plate of lemon slices. White-knuckled, as if she was wringing its neck, Mam twisted a sheet of paper into a spill, jammed it in the Aga and struck a match. I opened the door to the passage. The draft killed the flame.

'Get out of here,' said Mam.

From the fields beyond the garden, darkness watched, prick-eared. I should have woken early, breathed slowly in and out, let the day take shape around me like I'd been taught by Iolo, sensing its temperature, wind direction and moistness of the soil. Instead, I felt twitchy, rushed and out of sorts.

A whinny rang out as I slithered towards the stables. I followed it through the open door on the right. Each stall had a horse or pony tethered by its manger.

Bucket in hand, Danny was dunking Flintlock's tail. 'You're late,' he said, not looking round.

'I'm sorry. Shall I do Pixie?

'Pixie don't matter. You'd best get on wid Micah.'

Lumps of dung matted Micah's belly. He flinched at my sopping sponge. I told him his master was lazy, lying in bed while the rest of us did the work.

'Cut the clattin', Jack.'

'The yellow's not coming out.'

'Put some shampoo on your sponge and dab it straight on him.'

I soaped the yellowed coat, rinsed and soaped again. I'd meant to spend a good half-hour on Pixie. But here I was, fussing with Oliver's pony. Like as not he'd skulk in bed, pretending he had a headache.

Though the sky was turning turquoise in the east, scraps of night still lingered overhead. I swirled the scummy water down the drain and ran to the pump over cobblestones still slick with last night's rain. Just as I reached Micah's stall with a bucket of clean water, he lifted his tail and dribbled green dung down his hocks.

'I'll fix him with chalk,' called Danny from the gangway. 'You'd best get yerself a bit of breakfast.'

Though Mam had got the Aga lit, the porridge was cold and lumpy. Men sat over half-finished bowls, smoking and slurping their tea.

Mr Hoad pushed his dish aside. 'Them posh kids and their ponies will be slithering in mud.' He grabbed a plate of sausage, egg and bacon. 'None of 'em will jump – they'll all on 'em look for yats.'

Yats? He meant gates. I grabbed a slice of cold toast and dashed into the boot room. Tearing the bread with my teeth, I pulled on my hand-me-down clothes. Mrs Arbiter had shown me how to knot the tie but the knack had seeped away from me overnight.

Half-choked by the lumpy knot, I jammed on a crash cap then squelched back to the yard. I'd only just started on Pixie when boots clacked on the cobbles.

'Morning, Dan,' called Oliver from the doorway.

No reply. Oliver should be waiting in the Hall, not peering at Danny while he fiddled a red ribbon through the glossy plait of Fives or Better's tail.

'Morning, Zhackie the Vackie,' Oliver called into the silence.

That stupid name again. I hissed between my teeth, a habit I'd caught from Danny and Mr Hoad. Tapping his crop on his boot, Oliver wandered down the gangway and hovered just outside Micah's stall. Though Danny had daubed the pony's flank with chalk, the yellow still showed on his coat, now clumped with damp. Expecting a finicky comment, I glanced at Oliver. He caught my eye and gave a wobbly smile.

'I think my jods look nice on you,' he said.

Body brush in hand, I kept on hissing. The night before, I'd helped lay out his clothes: black jacket, narrow, neat-collared and scarlet-lined, a stock which now rose in silky white folds to his chin and buff-coloured breeches, close-fitting and cut to slide into the tall black boots I'd polished. So he must have known how I felt in the tweedy bulk of my jacket and the embarrassing bulge of the buttons on my jodhpurs.

He hooked his crop over the wooden partition. Eyes fixed on my chin, he walked into the stall. Startled, I stopped brushing. He stood so close behind me I caught his smell of Coal Tar soap mixed with Robin Starch. His thin white hands fluttered in front of my face.

'Your tie's not right,' he said.

Hoping he wouldn't catch my musty pong, I felt his fingers fidget at the knot. It slackened. He tied it again – over, under and through - then smoothly slid the knot up to my collar. 'There now!' he said, moving to face me. 'You look quite the proper Reptonian.'

Not knowing what he meant, I turned away. Master Oliver clack-clacked down the gangway. By the time I'd saddled Pixie, he was mounted and Danny was clinging to Fives or Better's reins. I jumped onto Pixie and followed them round to the front.

Master Oliver waggled his crop at the lid of dark grey cloud. 'What a vile day!' Micah ducked his head, a gallant, handsome pony who'd bravely jump whatever he was asked to. On this damp and muddy morning, could he trust his rider not to steer him at north-facing fences with steep and slippery landings?

A clamour rose from the kennels across the field, followed by the clatter of hooves in the street: Mr Hoad and Billy taking the pack to Kellaway. No sign of the major. Fives or Better shivered and pawed the gravel. The babble and clatter faded into the distance. Danny said the major had never been late before. Even sensible Pixie whinnied and champed her bit. A minute ticked by and then another. The double doors swung back. The major stood on the step, stern-faced beneath his topper.

'Oh! There you are!' he said. 'Where were you at breakfast?'

'Didn't feel much like it, Sir,' said Master Oliver, 'so I thought I'd take a wander to the stables.'

Straight-backed, the major ran down the steps. Danny gave him the reins and stumped towards the kitchen, not even turning to wave as we rode away. The major led us at a steady trot, past the shut-up school and empty playground. We swung down a path that skirted the spinney where, Danny had told me, a Land Girl hanged herself. The major urged Fives or Better into a trot so fast that Pixie had to canter to keep up, and Micah was fighting Oliver for his head. Slacken your reins, I thought. Tuck your elbows in. Jabbed by low branches, we charged down a rutted track until we reached a shrubbery of bushes trimmed like poodles. I was starting to think we'd missed our way when hoof beats chimed ahead. The horses pricked their ears. Fives or Better whinnied. Ahead of us, Lady Susan trotted round a bend, bobbing up and down on her nippy little mare.

The major reined in and doffed his topper.

'You look half-frozen,' she said. 'You've time for a glass of Cherry Heering? Yes! Of course you have! And you, too, Oliver – if you're allowed, that is.'

Lady Susan wheeled towards a sweep of lawn. Behind it stood a house of rosy brick, its windows lit and wood smoke floating from the chimneys. Hounds waited on the grass outside the nearby stable block, milling round the hocks of the huntsmen's matching greys. For a second, I saw the pack through the major's eyes: handsome, I had to admit, with their uniform black and tan. And there, on the edge of the pack, looking gawky and uncertain, woolly, white Llywelyn stood farthest from the huntsmen.

Lady Susan clapped at a man in tails. A tray of drinks at shoulder height, he dodged his way towards us through a group of riders. The major fumbled at a glass, grasped it by its rim and slopped a drop of crimson on his yellow gloves.

'Can you manage, William?' Lady Susan asked.

A dull red stain crept up the major's cheeks. He dropped his reins and crop on Fives or Better's neck and bent again to take the glass two-handed.

'Oh, well done,' Lady Susan said.

A gentleman rode past on a weight-bearing bay roan with a Roman nose that matched his own.

'That's Colonel Tunnicliffe, the Field Master,' the major said to me on a breath of bitter cherries, 'and you must do exactly as he tells you. And Oliver,' he added, 'the same applies to you. No clever remarks or thinking you know better.'

The Reverend Beale clopped up on his lanky, cow-hocked cob. Green with age, his jacket skirt was spread around his saddle. As the major talked to him and Lady Susan, Oliver edged his pony close to me and Pixie. If only he'd slacken his reins and tuck his elbows in.

'Do you really like this sort of thing?' he asked.

Porky gentlemen, cheeks flushed beneath their toppers, patrolled the grass on big-boned, muscled hunters. A cut of the whip here, a job in the mouth there: strapping children bullied well-groomed ponies; haughty ladies, faces daubed in panstick, wore sharply-angled bowlers that nodded as they talked.

'No,' I said. 'I don't.'

He brightened. 'I knew you didn't, underneath! People risk their lives in fancy dress just to catch a frightened little fox.'

Mr Hoad was tooting on his horn. I tensed my calves, felt Pixie's furry warmth. Iolo would agree about the fancy dress and probably with the other things that Oliver had said. But for now I had no time to think. Already the major was spurring down the track. Pixie fizzed with excitement. Cantering after the massive hindquarters of the Field Master's roan, red- and black-coated riders surged ahead of us, followed by Pony Club children and farmers wearing tweeds. I cut in front of a lady on a ewe-necked palomino.

'Wait!' Oliver shouted. 'We're meant to stick together.'

'But I want to watch Llywelyn.'

'Our place is at the back,' called Oliver in a bossy voice.

I wheeled Pixie round and waited beside him.

'Now!' Oliver slackened Micah's reins.

At the end of the lane we tore across a quaggy field, the horses ahead of us flinging up clarts in our faces. I glimpsed Lady Susan crouched over the neck of her mare, her bottom two bobbing eggs encased in cavalry twill. Twigs lashed my face as we butted through a hedge. Soon we were pulling up outside a covert, waiting dark and secret in the rain-drenched light. A wave of damp jumped up from the grass. Hounds dashed into the spinney. Llywelyn wavered behind them, glancing at Mr Hoad.

'Go on, Llywelyn *bach*,' I whispered. 'Show them what to do.'

Mr Rumney sauntered up with a haversack on his back, two shovels over his shoulder and his terriers on a lead. Dumping the shovels, he leaned on the fence and chatted to Mr Marlozzi. Unnoticed by Mr Hoad, Llywelyn wriggled at last under the bottom bar. The major and Lady Susan handed their reins to the huntsmen, climbed the fence and vanished into the wood.

A lady raised her veil and lit a cigarette. Didn't she know that smoking wrecked the scent? I waited for Colonel Tunnicliffe to make her put it out, but he was too busy prising the lid off his saddle sandwich box. Three men in army uniform were laughing and fooling about, prodding each other in the ribs with their crops. Not that they'd disturb the pack, to judge from the random yelping.

'I'm cold,' Oliver said, unwrapping a bar of Whole Nut. 'Cold and rather bored.' He divided the chocolate in two and gave me half.

'Oh ho,' he said and popped a square into his mouth. Tight-lipped, the major was climbing out of the wood.

'Rumney,' he said. 'You forgot to block the earths.'

Mr Rumney stood up from the fence as if ready to salute. 'Certainly not, Sir. I blocked every one.'

'Then we can thank the bloody saboteurs,' the major said. 'Panty-waisted, sandal-wearing sissies. And you, Rumney, should have obeyed instructions. If you'd done what I'd told you and waited till after dark, they'd all have been on the bloody train back to bloody Carnforth.'

'But I did wait, Sir. I waited till eight o'clock.'

Oliver ate another square of chocolate.

The major treated Rumney to a savage glare. 'I wouldn't want to think that you're trying to deceive me.'

The Reverend Beale steered his cob towards us, his face a meaty red beneath his battered topper. 'Odd business with these earths, Oliver, don't you think?'

Oliver sat with an animal's tense and troubled stillness.

'Wouldn't you agree?' asked the Reverend Beale.

Sheep baaed nearby. 'Most certainly,' Oliver said.

With a last long look at Master Oliver, the Reverend Beale turned his cob away. Behind us, the army men were grumbling to each other. Bloody sabs. They wreck other people's sport. The gentlemen swigged from their hip flasks. A couple of children on Shetlands headed homewards. The woman with a veil was lighting a second cigarette when the Field Master walloped round the covertside on his roan.

'Follow me. We're off to Parson's Spinney.'

We clattered down a narrow lane, through a run-down farmyard and cantered across two fields. The riders ahead of us slowed. I pulled up beside them, stood in my stirrups and stared.

I'd known the Powmaughan crossed the fields a mile away from the Hall. Now I saw why I'd never managed to spot it. Swollen by the recent heavy rain, it cut broad and deep at the spot where the pack had checked. Its Bisto-coloured water raced beneath a bank that fell away in a steep and slithery drop. The major spoke to Mr Hoad and Billy while scanning the fields that stretched beyond the river. Oliver bounced up to him on Micah, hands chest high and the thong of his crop tangled in his reins.

'I want to go home.' His voice rang out, as if he didn't care who heard.

'I'm taking the young 'uns up to the ford,' called a stringy woman. 'Oliver, you can come too, if you like.'

Warlock was already plunging over the edge, followed by Sacristan and Jasper, then more hounds surging so fast I couldn't tell them apart.

'Oliver stays with me,' the major said, his eyes still on the fields across the river.

A chunk fell off the bank and splashed into the water. Mr Hoad and Billy urged their horses at the drop. Oliver's face turned Omowhite under the peak of his cap.

'If I can't go home,' he said, 'I'll go with the Pony Club.'

'Give into fear,' replied the major, 'and fear will be your master.'

'Except I'm not afraid.'

A startled gust of wind bounced off the water.

'Then you'll cross the river,' said the major.

Once I'd stood on the diving-board at school, sickened by the chlorine pong mixed with sweaty feet and the cat calls of the bullies zinging round my head.

The matching greys were plunging through the river. The major gathered his reins.

'You'll be all right,' he called to Oliver, 'as long as you sit well back.' He jammed down his topper and drove Fives or Better at the drop.

Though Oliver yanked his reins, Micah kept pace with the bigger horse, clearly preferring the crunch of the bit to the thought of falling behind. Fives or Better crouched like a cat as he tilted over the edge. Micah followed, head down, with Oliver flopping like a doll.

'For Pete's sake sit back!' shouted the major over his shoulder.

The pony tried to brake as he hurtled downwards but Oliver knocked him off-balance by slumping forward. Micah fought to steady himself on the brink but a slab of soil broke off beneath his hooves. He teetered a second then plunged into the river.

'Papa!' Oliver cried as he bounced onto Micah's neck. He tried to grab his plaits then flopped face down in the water. The major jumped out of the saddle. Oliver struggled to his feet. The major pointed at a glint beneath the surface.

'You've dropped your crop,' he said.

Oliver looked at his father. His father looked at him. The muddy brown water churned over the tops of their boots. A bubble had formed around the man and the boy.

'You've dropped your crop,' the major said again.

Oliver mopped the wet that dribbled from his fringe, then scrambled up the opposite, shallower bank, leaving the major midstream. A huic halloah floated through the air: a fox had been sighted a field or two away. The major jerked to life and followed with the horses.

A group of grooms was trotting through the field. I recognised Danny, a bowler jammed down on his fat little ears. The major shook his head. They'd arrived too soon.

'You'd better go straight home,' he said to Master Oliver. 'Follow the river until you reach the ford. And make sure you give your pony a hot bran mash.'

Micah whinnied to Pixie from deep inside his chest. Head down, Oliver took the reins.

'I'd better go with him,' I said to Danny.

'Go with him? You're barking mad.'

Not even attempting to climb into the saddle, Oliver plodded along the bank, followed by Micah, head low and dripping mud.

I looked up at Danny, towering above me on Flintlock. 'The major said we had to stick together.'

Danny's eyes turned ferret-sharp above his fat red cheeks. 'You think he cares about Oliver now? A son who's just disgraced him? Use your loaf and stick with **me**.'

Chapter Seventeen

I CAUGHT a babble on the wind. Lost. Caught again. It faded in seconds. Hounds were hot on the scent. Guessing they'd already run a mile or more, I gathered my reins and pointed Pixie at the bank. In the water below, I caught a glint of silver: Master Oliver's crop. I'd collect it as I crossed.

'Whoah there, Jack!' said Danny. 'Where d'you think you're going?'

'I thought we could follow the hunt!'

'Not like that we can't.'

'We grooms need brains, not speed,' said Lady Susan's groom, a bony woman with bright grey eyes and thin lips she kept curved in a smile. 'It's our job to find the quickest way to the covert. No owner's going to thank us for a tired second horse.'

The grooms spoke, heads together, as we followed a path round a field. Carruther's Wood or Joey's Copse? Probably the copse. We swung onto a track through an avenue of beeches. Silence, apart from hoof beats on dead leaves. Yelps scratched the circle of daylight at the end of the trail.

'So we were right!' said Danny. 'Charlie's doubled back.'

We crossed a field and passed through an open gate. I pinched my nose at the pong. Slurry! The fox had likely rolled in it to throw hounds off his scent. But Llywelyn, at the head of the pack, was tearing round the grass.

Their horses blowing steam through flaring fairground nostrils, the riders checked to watch the pack still racing round in circles. Llywelyn started to bell and headed for a gate, then Musselman and

Tubman. We followed the slowest of the riders into a narrow lane, then swerved over a ditch and into plough.

'Headlands! Headlands!' the Field Master cried, waving us onto the grass around the edge.

Llywelyn held the lead, followed by Truculent and Warlock. I scanned the clarts. A lump of earth moved, halted then moved again. Not earth, but a muddy creature scraping the clods with his nose. A dog fox with a tattered ear. Pixie and I pounded alongside the hedge, close to the pack now streaming across the furrows. Dragging his waterlogged brush, the fox broke into a run. Stopped for a second. Limped towards a copse. Air scraped my throat as we bumped through a channel of clods. The fox put on a sprint but he was sinking fast. Hounds were bobbing twenty yards behind him. Free of the furrows at last, he reached the shadow of the trees. Llywelyn surged, with more hounds in his wake. A muddy blob scrabbled at the fence. Dropped back. Turned, remembering his youthful steel and staunchness. He glared and snarled, ears flat, an animal at bay. Llywelyn faltered a second, then was on him. The fox gave the scream a wild thing gives when unready to give up its spirit.

As he screamed, the major blew the kill, a wavering note that rang eerily round the trees. We'd reached the point to honour the fox's passing, when he leaves his earthly shape to join the Spirit Fox. Heads bowed, the riders wait until the Master has dismounted. His task is to appease the fox's soul by marking the spot where he died with a coin or a gift of tobacco.

Instead, the gentlemen stood in the stirrups, eyes and faces bulging, toppers black amidst the steam from their horses' necks. The ladies sat on the edge of the group and watched: only three of them left, including Lady Susan.

'Go in and tear 'im,' bellowed the major, cupping his hands. 'Get yourselves in, boys and girls, and tear 'im.'

A shiver tightened my spine. Iolo had already warned me. The major was offending mighty Gwyn. Sterns up, the black and tans pulsed on top of the vixen. Only Llywelyn hung back, head low, not sure this was allowed. Cracking his whip, Mr Hoad waded through the pack, braying them off the body with the handle. Scorcher, Warlock and Sacristan hung on longest, jaws clamped on the fox's legs. The huntsman tugged the body by the scruff, hacked off the brush and gave it to the major. Everyone cheered and said what a gallant fox he'd been, and what a fine run he'd given them for their money.

'The major did well,' said Danny, his face alight with pride.

Mr Hoad threw the fox back to the hounds. His paws flailed mid-air, as if he was still alive, and then the pack was on him again, ripping him apart.

'I sort of wish he'd made it to the copse,' I said to Danny. It was all I could think of to say.

'If he had, he'd have probably got away, what with that same bugger unblocking all the earths.'

Lady Susan manoeuvred Lucy Glitters alongside Fives or Better. 'This is the Pony Club meet,' she said. 'Shouldn't we be blooding one of the children?'

'We should indeed,' the major said, 'but Maudie led 'em off.'

The Reverend Beale chipped in through a mouthful of corned beef sandwich. 'Where's Oliver? I seem to recall he hasn't been blooded yet.'

Nobody replied.

'What about little Jacqueline?' Lady Susan asked.

No! Not daubed with the blood of a fox disrespectfully killed.

'After all,' added her Ladyship, 'she is on a family pony.'

'She was told to stick with Oliver,' said the major.

'Perhaps he didn't want her to,' Lady Susan said.

Colonel Tunnicliffe's mottles tightened on his nose. 'She isn't even in the Pony Club,' he said.

The major sighed and beckoned me towards him. I held back. Might I bring down the wrath of Gwyn?

'Don't be shy, dear,' Lady Susan called.

Half-aware of knee-length boots and muddy martingales, I steered Pixie through a group of giant hunters and reined her in beside the major's knee. He bent. I glimpsed raw stump and draggled fur. Smelt blood and shit as he dragged it down my cheek.

He jumped off Fives or Better. 'Now get yourself back home.' He took Flintlock's reins from Danny and gave two sharp pips of his horn. The pack began to gather, their coats so thick with mud I couldn't spot Llywelyn. Then I saw him trotting towards Flintlock, stern up, ears cocked and eyes fixed on the major. As horses and hounds set off across the field, I followed the grooms' tweed backs down a lane towards the village. Yarrow, cuckoo pint, willowherb, priest's pintle: wild men and women of the hedgerows watched me as we passed: what will Iolo say? they seemed to whisper in my ear. Lady Susan's groom took the Kellaway turn-off. Fives or Better lengthened his stride for home. The clouds had darkened by the time we reached the stables. Though the clock said only half-past three, rooks scudded to their rookery as if night had come too soon. After seeing to Pixie and checking Micah's hay net, I stumped towards the house on aching legs.

Mam was crossing the kitchen, holding a tray laden with slices of bread, a jam dish, cakes and a china teapot. 'You've got mud on your cheek,' she said as I shut the outside door.

'Not mud. It's blood. From the fox.'

She stared at me, her mouth a small round o. 'You mean you're smeared with an animal's blood? You're savages, you lot.'

'The major did it, because I was in at the kill.'

The crockery on the tray rattled a rebuke. 'And what about poor Master Oliver?' she asked.

Oliver. I'd forgotten all about him. My eyes roved back towards the bread and jam.

'At least,' said Mam, 'you could have seen him home.'

'But I'd have lost the hunt.'

'And what would that have mattered, you nowty, selfish girl? He's laying on his bed, not eating, hardly speaking.'

Cold from the flagstones swept into my ankles.

'Mrs Arbiter's already sent for the doctor. It'll be next door to a miracle if he's not caught his death.'

Chapter Eighteen

THE doorbell jangled. Mam set the tray high on a larder shelf, untied her apron and flung it on a chair. Clammy twill clung to my knees. Hunger gnawed my stomach. When she'd run into the passage, I tried the larder door. Locked, and the key not on its hook. I felt inside her apron pocket. Empty, too.

The wind was getting up, half-drowning the clatter of hooves: the major and hunt servants coming through the village. I heard voices on the gravel, then a whicker. Tired old Yarico calling to Fives or Better. The major shouted for Danny and then the front door slammed.

Hoping for something to eat, I hung around the kitchen. A row of pipes was rustling in the ceiling: the house announcing that someone was running a bath. Hot and deep, with Epsom salts to soothe the major's muscles. Afterwards, wearing his slippers and kaftan, he'd settle in the drawing-room, light his skinny pipe, ring for gin and salted nuts then take an early supper, the same as after every other hunt. Oxtail soup. A fine old Burgundy. Mushroom omelette. Grilled tomatoes. Queen of Puddings. Cream instead of custard. Port and Stilton. Celery. Bath Olivers fanned on a napkin in a basket.

No singing from the kennels, just a wind that moaned and sobbed. Mam banged in, found a bowl and started cracking eggs. My stomach cramped.

'Can I have the leftover bread and jam?'

'Not with your face plastered with blood and muck.'

She cracked another egg. The inner door swung back. Mrs Arbiter, hat low. 'Where's Master Oliver?'

Mam scooped a piece of eggshell from the bowl. 'No idea. He was in his bedroom when I left to show the doctor to his motor car.'

'Well, the major wants him and he's nowhere to be found. You'd better come and help me search the house.'

The Aga roared, a hungry beast waiting to be fed. Mam turned her angry sewn-up face on me: all your fault, you selfish, stupid girl. A row of torches hung beside the outer kitchen door. The grown-ups took one each and left the room. If I followed them, they'd tell me not to bother. If I stayed behind they'd think I didn't care.

My mind a snarl of jagged, clashing thoughts, I waited till I heard them overhead. Once the chase was on you had to follow, and nothing should distract you from the pack. But another voice was speaking as I trailed upstairs, a crabby little voice that said I should have stayed with Oliver; that thanks to me he'd disappeared and no one knew where to.

Mam and Mrs Arbiter were combing every passage. The square set of their shoulders and disapproving backs led me up a second flight of stairs. We tracked through rooms I'd never seen before: a schoolroom with a row of high oak desks. A sitting-room with curtains flapping in the draught. A room with broken furniture piled against the walls and cabbage shapes of damp across the ceiling. Our footsteps heavy on the floorboards, we reached the final room. Inside the door, Mam fumbled at the light switch.

'The army lifted all the bulbs,' said Mrs Arbiter.

The torchlight wobbled over rows of iron bedsteads, and at the end a stack of padlocked chests, each marked with a cross the colour of dried blood. A row of gas masks goggled on their pegs. Crutches leant deserted on the wall, as if the men who'd needed them had died.

'Tsk,' said Mrs Arbiter. 'What did we expect? I told the major that he'd never hide up here.'

A tide of panic rose inside the house. I felt it in the clenched air of the room, saw it in the jitter of the torchlight and heard it in the buzzing round my ears. A motor car churned up the gravel. Mrs Arbiter walked to the window. Tail lights were jouncing down the drive.

'That'll be Rumney gone to fetch the farm lads. We'd better take a last look in the nursery.'

We walked in single file down a passage then another. Not stopping to knock on Master Oliver's door, Mrs Arbiter stepped inside and crossed into his bedroom. Empty. I knew from her face as she turned away.

Mam followed Mrs Arbiter into the passage. Two stiff backs and not one glance at me. My boots pinched. The heavy tweed sat damply on my shoulders. My bones ached as if I'd caught the flu. Wind scratched around the gutters and whimpered in the chimney. Glared at by the lumps of coke still burning in the hearth, I caught the frowsty smell of Oliver's sheets. Not his fault. Mam had forgot to change them. Not minding my muddy boots, I settled myself on his counterpane and fitted my head into the shape left on his pillow. The photograph on the locker was turned towards me: Oliver's mother who'd run away to France.

I jumped up from the bed and tore downstairs, grabbing a torch as I passed the kitchen door. A top-heavy figure was pedalling up to the Hall, steering his clunky black bicycle between the rain-filled potholes: Constable Coulthard, unsmiling, solemn-eyed, jowls bulging round the chinstrap of his helmet.

'Good evening,' I whispered.

He stared at my face, not speaking or even blinking. Had he been told what I'd done? And then I remembered my cheek. I pulled my sleeve over my knuckles and scraped the rough tweed over my skin until I felt sure the blood and muck had gone. Then, skimming the puddles, I pelted towards the street.

Villagers were coming home from work, the men in boots and clogs, the women wearing headscarves. Normal people in a normal day. No yelps came from the kennels as I crossed the empty yard.

I was met by the brackish breath of hounds who've caught their fox. I shone my torch. Full-bellied, they sprawled on their benches, legs outstretched. Llywelyn was easy to spot. He lay, spine pressed against

Sacristan and paws entangled with Scorcher's. He thumped his stern as I approached. Ignoring the rest of the pack, I crouched beside his bench. *'Helpa fi, fachgen,'* I whispered in his ear. Boy, I need your help.

He raised his head an inch then let it drop. I touched his neck and spoke a little louder. *'Helpa fi.'*

This time, he didn't seem to hear me. I dipped my face to his. He gave a rumbling growl. Leave me alone. No point in keeping on. He was acting as he had to. Llywelyn of the valleys had become the major's hound.

I ran past the lighted pub and down the station steps. A whistle blew a field or two away, and a sign with ghostly letters was peering through its whitewash. _OX_EI_H. A keen east wind had scraped away the clouds and a small moon lit the bridge above the tracks. My jodhpurs still clinging clammily to my knees, I halted on the bridge and scanned the left-hand platform. The signal dropped its arm. I jumped. The whistle shrilled again. The lines ticked. A train huffed round the corner, the one you'd catch if you were heading south. A gentleman and lady left the lighted waiting-room. The clatter slowed. They crossed the platform to a carriage. The guard jumped down and beckoned to the gentleman, whose hand was resting on the lady's back. Small and slight, she wore her collar up, Russian boots and black fur hat pulled down. Maybe guests of Lady Susan's leaving early: I'd seen a group of strangers on her lawn. They walked together to an open door. A whistle blew. Doors slammed. The train chuffed from the platform.

O Eleri. O Caradog. If only they could hear me. I dawdled up the drive towards the Hall. A big black bicycle lay slumped against the steps and above it, at the top, the double doors gaped open. Not sure what else to do, I drifted round the back. Shoulders hunched, his lobster claws buried in his pockets, the major stared into the darkness beyond the terrace steps.

'No sign of him so far, Sir,' called a hoarse voice from the lawn.

Mr Rumney lit a row of naphtha flares and stuck one in each urn. Beyond the balustrade, the garden trembled into life. Two policemen dragged a bundle down the terrace. 'The dragnet, Sir.' They dumped it at the major's feet.

More men ran down the lawn with flares held shoulder-high. Shrubs sprang out of darkness. Disappeared again. Behind me, knuckles rapped on glass. I swung. A slim black shape stood in a lighted downstairs window. Mam beckoned. *Don't go acting like a bloody dog.* I swung back towards the garden. The smell jumped up to meet me. Cigarette smoke. Trampled grass. Manure on hobnailed boots. And, beneath it all, the faintest scent of boy. The smells swam up the tunnels of my nose. Warming them, I cast around the lawn.

'What's that child doing?' cried the major.

I tore across the grass, caught the hint of boy again then lost it in the naphtha's petrol reek. A policeman ran towards me, his helmet tucked under his arm. I dodged him, clever, twisty, and dashed towards the fountain.

The major shouted something from the terrace. I caught a whiff of woollen socks, leather soles and fright. Help me, Gwyn and Dormach, Aneurin and Eleri. Riding high inside my knowledge box, I loped on down the lawn. Men were crying overhead. The gardens spun away. Lamps bobbed through the trees beyond the stream. The hot scent towed me downwards. Nostrils open wide, I followed it chest-high towards the wood.

The bank turned brown and dropped towards the water. Stern up, I cast again. The scent swerved to the right. Ahead of me, the icehouse wobbled in the torchlight. I snuffled at the gap beneath the door. Smelt footsteps, dirty sacking and a whiff of sour berries mingling with the pong of eggy sweat. My itchy hackles pushed against the wood. It gave. I tumbled down the steps. A shape lay on the bench.

'Help!' I cried, a girl again, my voice high-pitched and small.

Shouts came from the wood. The thump of boots. Splashing in the stream.

'There's something here,' I shouted.

Boots thundered down the steps. Before I could escape, hands

140

dug beneath my armpits. 'Out of here now, girlie. That's quite enough of that.'

A whistle blew. Two burly arms propelled me up the steps. Men with flares came crashing through the wood. I shook myself and stood, not knowing how I'd got there.

'We've found him, Sir,' a young policeman shouted.

A body lay unmoving on the grass, its arms outflung, its thin knees flopping sideways. The major hurtled down and knelt beside it.

'Oh, Oliver,' he said, face melting in the glare.

'We'll carry him for you, Sir,' the young policeman said.

The major clasped the body to his chest, staggered as he stood then marched towards the terrace, surrounded by the farm hands holding flares. A gaggle of lads from the flesh house stared at me and muttered, then vanished as I plodded up the lawn. On the terrace, Mr Hoad gathered burnt-out flares. I slunk past him without speaking, like a rated hound.

In the kitchen greasy pans were piled in the sink. Plates were clinking in the servants' hall and the hot-pee smell of kidneys hung thickly in the air. Although my stomach griped I couldn't face the frosty looks, so traipsed upstairs, too sick of heart to care about the ghost.

Wind moaned in the chimney and howled around the eaves. Hangers jittered in the wardrobe as I got undressed. A fox was barking up above the trees, too echoey and high to be a living fox. Three rasping yaps. Silence. Three more hollow yaps. I looked out as a car raced up the drive. Dr Madden dashed, too late, towards the steps. Inside the house, footsteps thumped upstairs. The major called for someone at the far end of the passage, in a high-pitched voice I'd never heard before. I dozed a bit, then woke inside the crypt. Master Oliver was standing beside the family tomb.

'You can visit me here,' he said with a greenish smile.

The door creaked back, showing a stack of coffins, the top one with an open lid beneath the marble ceiling. I screamed. A figure walked towards my bed, its eyes two round dark holes, its face white in the lamplight. I screamed again. Its small black mouth flapped open.

'For heaven's sake shut up,' said Mam, dumping the lamp on the chest.

'I thought you was Oliver's ghost.'

'Oh, Jacqueline.' Mam leant against the chest. 'How could you see his ghost when he isn't even dead?'

'He is. I saw his body in the icehouse.'

'Nonsense. He'd just passed out. What would you expect? He'd downed his dad's supply of gin then knocked back a bottle of aspirin. Dr Madden's made him drink a pint of mustard water.'

Poor Mam. She thought a doctor could frustrate a fox who'd laid its vengeance on its killer's shoulders. She fetched a tray from the passage and set it on my knees. Toast thinly smeared with marge and jam. A glass of Barley Water. Just to show she'd not forgotten what I'd done.

'Now try and get some sleep,' she said as she left the room. 'You're not going to help him by lying awake and fretting.'

But how could I not fret? Each time I closed my eyes, I saw a boy plod homewards, followed by his pony. I fell asleep at last but didn't dream of him. I saw an ancient fox pelting through the plough land, ears flat, a pack in mad pursuit, and blood on the stump where his tawny brush had been.

Chapter Nineteen

NEXT morning, I slept in. By the time I got down to the kitchen, the smell of the Sunday roast hung thickly in the air.

'How's Master Oliver?' I asked.

Mrs Arbiter glanced at the tray I'd carried from our bedroom. 'You didn't get much to eat last night,' she said.

'No,' I said. Mam was upstairs, changing out of her uniform.

Mrs Arbiter slid a plate from the bottom oven. I saw fried mushrooms, tomatoes, kedgeree and two kidneys on a gold-rimmed plate. 'Here,' she said. 'Eat this. The major didn't touch it.'

I picked up a knife and fork, almost as glad of her kinder-than-normal manner as I was of the food. 'But how is he?' I asked again.

'As well as can be expected, though he's still got a very bad head. Lucky that Dr Madden knew exactly what to do.'

She'd cooked the kidneys in a rush. I knew from the traces of red, and frills of white still hanging from their tips. Not even pepper and mustard could mask the tang of wee. But I'd bolted them down by the time that Mam walked into the room. The church bell tolled. Polly appeared. We all trooped down the path. In the porch, whispering people turned their sheepskin backs. Inside, the major's pew was empty. So was the Kellaway pew across the aisle. As we reached our place, faces turned towards us then swung away like rows of startled sheep. My insides chilled despite the extra food, I squeezed between Danny and Mam, liking the solid warmth of their arms. His face extra meaty and red above the white of his cassock, the Reverend Beale turned to us at the foot of the altar steps.

'Almighty God,' he droned, head bowed, 'vouchsafe to hear our prayers on behalf of Thy servant, Master Oliver, that he may soon be restored to health and strength.

'Hear us, O Lord,' murmured the people around us. Even Mam and Danny bowed their heads.

I didn't join in. No point. Their god knew nothing of the hunt. Besides, I'd seen the Reverend yesterday, standing in his stirrups like the rest, his hands cupped round his purple lips. *Go in and tear 'im, boys and girls.* The crime was ours. But if Oliver recovered it might just mean that Gwyn had something worse in store.

That afternoon, I made my way to the stables. All horses had a rest day after a hunt: the major's rule, said Danny, and a good one, too. But when he saw me grooming Micah, he told me to tack up and said I'd better take him for a ride. He hadn't covered many miles yesterday but after his tumble he should be checked for limps or sprains.

I grabbed the pommel and Danny boosted me into the saddle. Micah was taller and narrower than Pixie, with elegant ears alert on a graceful head. Dusk was falling by the time we reached the drive, drifting downwards through the park and hanging in the hedges. Though Micah didn't wince or limp, he stayed behind his bit, a generous mount who knew he'd failed to keep his master safe. The village air hung thick with smells of beef and Yorkshire pud, and everyone had drawn their bedroom curtains. Reins slack, I let the pony choose the route, not caring where we went or ended up.

Micah swung into a lane where stones poked through the tarmac. Pines marched through the dimness on each side. The tarmac turned to soil. Micah plodded on. The ground grew spongy, sucking at his hooves. He stopped. Beyond his ears, reeds shivered in a stretch of brackish water. I squeezed his sides and tried to steer him round the edge. For once he didn't budge or even crop the grass, but stood as if he knew it was expected.

Oliver had stared at this same view. Had he thought about his mother, and wondered if she missed him? Or prayed that his father would relent and send him back to school? Wind formed an icy skin around the reeds. Micah chomped his bit then headed back between the pines. Snow dithered down in thin, mean flakes as we reached the lane. A bell chimed five across the fields. I let Micah choose his pace past empty barns and farmyards. Hoof beats muffled, we tracked up the drive towards the carriage sweep where Lady Susan's sports car crouched, half-blanketed in snow.

The horses had been fed and settled for the night. After wisping Micah and giving him his oats, I said goodnight to Pixie then trudged along the terrace. Shreds of white spun round lighted windows as if the house was trapped inside a snow globe. I fumbled at the door and fell inside the household passage. My nose felt raw, toes numb inside my soaking socks.

'Oh, there you are,' said Mam, holding out a tray. A cup of Oxo steamed beside a plate of bread and butter, crusty and thick-cut.

My mam. She must have heard me coming home. 'I don't want it on a tray,' I said. 'I'd rather eat with you.'

She laughed: whatever next? I saw the silver napkin ring.

'You're just in time. I'm in a rush,' she said. 'I've got to make the bed in Lady Wetheral's room.'

'Is she coming home?'

'No, but Lazy Susan's staying overnight.' She held out the tray. 'Take this up to Master Oliver.'

She was asking for help. Did that mean I'd been forgiven? Though I was keen to say yes, my hands hung numbly by my sides. 'I'd rather not. He might not want to see me.'

The cup and saucer clattered. 'Of course he will. And so he should. You saved his life, you know.'

I flexed my aching hands. He might have lost his mind, have left it in the icehouse, freezing on the dusty shelves among the wisps of straw. A bell clacked in the kitchen.

'Look sharp!' said Mam. 'I'll bet that's her. She'll want a bedroom fire.'

I took the tray and plodded up the stairs. At the top, I dumped it on our chest of drawers, took three gulps of Oxo, then topped it up with water from the pitcher. My hand shot out and grabbed a slice of bread. Still chewing it, I reached the nursery door. Behind me, just an empty passage. Below, two empty floors of haunted rooms. I knocked and turned the knob. A sigh heaved through the air. A gasp of wind beyond the terrace. Or else a slide of snow from the monkey puzzle tree. I knocked again. A louder sigh. I entered. On my right, a yellow slice of carpet. Tray first, I pushed into the bedroom.

Thinner-faced than ever in blue and white pyjamas, Oliver lay propped against a stack of pillows. I gripped the tray. He stared through eyes as pale as heron's eggs. Not at me. At the wall behind me.

'It's me, Jackie. I've brought your tea.'

The fire that sputtered in the nearby hearth hadn't warmed the cube of freezing air around the bed. I dumped the tray half-crooked on his knees. He didn't even glance at it.

'Why not drink your Oxo?'

'Go away,' he said.

The cold clutched at my stomach. 'I'm sorry that I left you.'

'Don't worry about that. I knew what you were doing and trusted you to do your best to spoil the hunt.'

My right cheek scorched. My fingers rose, as if to check I'd washed it. Clean and smooth. He'd never know.

'But they won. I heard them blow the kill.' His breath caught in his throat. 'My vixen's dead.'

'That wasn't your vixen we – they – killed. It was one of the Kellaway foxes.'

'You're trying to protect me. I know it was my vixen.' He struck his chest. 'I feel it here.'

'It was a dog fox and you'd tried to save him. You found out where he lived and walked for miles at night.'

His bony fingers clenched the blankets round his chest. 'And then I joined the hunt.'

'Only when you had to.'

'Father could never have made me. Not if I'd stood firm. Whatever made you poke inside the icehouse?'

I stared out at the flakes spinning wildly through the night. 'Somebody had to,' I said after a while.

'Rubbish. No one else would have ever looked in there.'

I couldn't stop the words that tumbled from my mouth. 'Then I'm glad I did. They said you might have died.'

'How stupid can you be? That was what I wanted.' He shoved his tray aside. 'You may as well have this.' His fingers tapped the plate. 'Go on,' he said. 'It's yours.'

Coal settled in the hearth, a small, accepting sound. If he meant it, Mam would never know. I took a giant bite of fresh, white bread, savouring its crusty, doughy taste. Conscious of him watching, I took a smaller bite. Around his bed, the air was growing warmer. He tapped the cup. I scooped a lump of unstirred Oxo, swallowed it and licked my fingertip. *Manners, Jacqueline!*

Oliver pointed at the last half-slice. I spoke through a mouthful of bread. 'I'm eating all your food.'

'That's the point.'

I'd reached the final crust before I understood. 'You can't do that.'

'Why not?'

'Who will ride your ponies?'

'They'd be sent to Kelso, I should think.'

Micah with his barrel chest. Dogged little Pixie. As I chewed the bread, footsteps thumped along the passage. I forced down the gummy lump and swallowed hard.

'Here! Take this,' said Oliver, handing me his napkin.

I wiped my mouth and left a smear of Oxo. Someone knocked. If only I'd been farther from the bed.

'Come in,' he called and snatched the napkin back.

'Your father will be pleased, Master Oliver.' Although Mam smiled at him, her eyes were flat and hard. 'You've eaten all your bread and drunk all your Oxo, too.'

Chapter Twenty

IT snowed all during supper and as I climbed the stairs. Mam had left a towel on my bed. Bath night. I draped the towel round my neck, traipsed back down, past the row of servants' lavs and into a cubicle that ponged of sweaty feet. Half-lost among the shadows on the ceiling, a single light bulb dangled. Worn brown lino pinched my toes with cold.

Gas jets belched and scalding water dribbled from a pipe. The bath was ringed with grime you never could scrub clean. Three inches of hot water, Mrs Arbiter had said. If the door had had a lock, I'd have drawn four times as much. Why did I have to bath? I'd never bathed at Iolo's, and no one seemed to care if I smelt like one of his hounds. I added cold, peeled off my clothes and climbed over the rusty rim. Whichever way I turned I jutted above the surface, which stayed level with the bottom ring of dirt. A colicky feeling nipped me in the guts. Too chilled to move, I lay till Polly barged into the room.

'Hurry up,' she said. 'I haven't got all night.' Her bump had grown to twice the size since I arrived. How would she manage to wedge herself into the bath? And wash in three inches of water? Or would she disobey? She folded her arms, leant against the wall and stared at what she'd called my long white legs. I climbed out and patted my goose bumps with the threadbare towel, pulled on my pyjamas and climbed the stairs to bed, even colder than when I'd got back from my ride.

Next morning, I slept in. By the time I reached the kitchen, Mam was lugging coal in from the yard.

'Lucky for you that school is shut.' She handed me a scuttle. 'The major's sent down from the hall to say the fire's going out.'

He stood beside the chest, the telephone to his ear. 'Miss? Can you hear me?' he shouted down the line.

I lobbed a heap of slack onto the embers. A coil of smoke hung sulkily overhead. Not seeming to notice it or me the major stayed, back turned, jiggling the receiver with his lobster claw. 'Miss! I want a line now.'

I grabbed the empty scuttle. He slammed the telephone onto its hook. Back in the kitchen, Mrs Arbiter juggled an egg into a silver cup and set it on a tray complete with silver toast rack, butter pats and Tiptree marmalade.

'I'll take that up,' I said.

'So you can scoff the lot?'

'I promise I won't touch a thing.'

She picked up the tray and headed towards the door. 'I don't want you upsetting him with prattle about the hunt.'

Danny and Mr Hoad came in to warm themselves by the Aga. Ten minutes later Mrs Arbiter brought back the tray. I gave it a sideways glance. The food was untouched.

Mrs Arbiter nodded at the toast. 'You'd best have this,' she said to Danny and Mr Hoad.

Mr Hoad pointed at the teapot on the Aga. 'But with a proper brew, if you please, not that piss they drink upstairs.' He unscrewed a twist of paper from his pocket. 'I allus save me sugar for a Friday.'

He stirred it in, clink, clink, clink against the thick white china. Mrs Arbiter locked the rest of the food in the larder.

'Have you heard the news?' asked Mr Hoad. His thumb jammed the spoon in his cup as he took a noisy swig. 'About some feller on his way to see the major. They say his car's got stuck on Shap but nobody knows for sure.'

Danny smeared a butter pat on his toast. 'They're saying in The Arms that he's a special Lunnon doctor.'

'Then he'd best be quick,' Mrs Arbiter said. 'The lad's so thin he's like to waste away.'

A man ran down the steps outside the window, collar up, hands jammed deep in his pockets. Mr Rumney stamped into the kitchen and winked at Mam as if to say: you can't do owt about it, not now, with no one on your side.

'You're wet,' said Mr Hoad through a mouthful of cold toast.

'Bugger it. And sod the bloody major.' Mr Rumney squeezed his sopping trouser legs. 'He sent me all the way to bloody Kellaway to check that Lazy Susan had got home. For all I care, she could have waltzed there in her slippers.'

The snow spun down all week, blocked the nearby roads, muffled stamping hooves and singing from the pack. When no one was about, I'd climb the servants' stairs and tiptoe down the passage to the nursery. Not moving, scarcely breathing, I'd stand beside the door, ears out for a cough or even a creak of the bed. Nothing. Just a blackbird in the garden or a sigh from the wind in the monkey puzzle tree.

One day, heavy footsteps came clumping up the stairs.

'I'm defeated,' I heard the doctor say. 'It's almost as if he's shell-shocked. I wonder if there's something he's not saying?'

I scarpered round the corner in my stocking feet.

'You read all that stuff in the papers,' Mrs Arbiter said. 'About the uncle who liked to parley with the Krauts.'

'Yes, yes. But Oliver's English and goes to an English school.'

I crept down the servants' stairs.

Crispy, salty game chips on a flowered paper napkin. Half a pheasant, golden skinned and baked in honey. Slices of smoked salmon. Wild mushroom sauce. Stilton. Pears and walnuts. Queen of puddings. The patient's favourite foods, all cooked by Mrs Arbiter. She'd lay the tray herself and puff up to the attic. Each new day the food came down untouched. Grim-faced, her back erect, she locked it in the larder, then served it to the major for his dinner.

It stopped snowing on the Thursday of that week and Danny said the nags fair longed to sniff the air. We greased their hooves, rugged them up and led them to the paddock, filled their nets with hay and smashed the ice on their troughs. Ignoring the brown clouds bulging overhead, Danny greased the runners of a sledge, towed me to the lawn and pushed me down the slope. Though he wore no gloves and his hands and face shone purple, he didn't seem to care about the cold or the soaking patches on his jerkin. He jumped behind me as I picked up speed. We swooped towards the barbed wire fence between us and the brook. Ten yards off he dug his heel into the snow. We slewed towards the ice house and fell into a drift.

The second time, I towed the sledge to the steepest part of hill, hopped on before Danny could reach me and scooted down alone. Cold lashed my ears and blasted out my thoughts. I dropped the rope and pushed again. The garden skidded past. The icehouse raced towards me. The sledge slewed into the fence and tumbled me into the snow.

Danny ran downhill and pulled me to my feet. 'What did you think you were you doing? Look. You've bust the fence.'

I didn't care. Breaking was better than thinking.

'You're daft,' said Danny, driving a post back into the ground. 'Daft, Jack, proper daft.'

That night, as I drifted to sleep, Mam whispered in my ear.

'Get up, Jackie, pet. You're wanted.'

'Who by?'

'Shhh. You'll see.'

My heart bumped. 'What time is it?'

'Nearly midnight. Hurry.'

She watched me shove my feet into my indoors, then left me to follow her down the stairs, across the hall and into the gunroom passage with its usual whiff of socks and warming wellies. At the far end she tapped on the half-open door.

'Come in,' the major called.

Her knuckles dug into my back. 'For heaven's sake act normal.'

I stepped inside the room. The door clicked shut behind me. Back turned, the major scratched in a hunt journal. He'd propped more books on the shelf above his desk. *The Foxhound Kennel Studbook. A Gentleman and his Hounds.* He screwed the top on his thin black fountain pen and set it underneath his secret drawer. Eyes red, moustache unkempt, he swivelled round to face me,

'You're shivering,' he said. 'Where's your dressing-gown?'

I listened for Mam's footsteps in the passage. Silence. She might be outside, so I didn't like to say I'd never had one. 'I forgot to bring it, Sir. I think it's back in Bootle.'

The major jabbed his pipe stem at the carpet near the fire. I stepped towards a worn patch. A draft snaked round my ankles.

'Child, you've grown,' he said.

If I asked him how he knew, would I be acting normal? He rummaged in the ashtray and found a bendy brush.

'It's hard for Oliver round here. He's half-French, you know, and they don't like it much, and then of course he goes away to school.' I caught the major's breath: a mix of whisky and tobacco. Drunk, I thought, and watched his hand walk crab-wise to a glass. On the desk beside it, in its tarnished frame, his younger self grinned down at Mr Arbiter. The older major poked a dottle from his pipe and fished tobacco from a leather pouch.

'The truth is, Jacqueline. Well, never mind the truth. You have the qualities, you know. An eye for hounds. A good seat on a pony and brave enough to take your fences straight. You make me think of Jack – that is – that was – my elder son. He died by accident, you know, shot by one of his men fooling about with a gun. His mother never got over it. A week before VE day. Well, more's the pity. There it is.' Sucking on his pipe, the major fiddled with a match. 'Oliver's in a line of huntin' Wetherals, which means, Jacqueline, that huntin's in his blood, though, poor boy, he doesn't know it yet.' The major stuffed tobacco in his pipe. 'My son is not a coward. Do you understand me?'

'Yes, Sir. Yes, I do.' But did he understand his son? How he cared about his vixen and detested killing things?

The major struck the match. It sputtered out. 'Thing is, he won't be pushed. But he likes you, Jacqueline.'

Oliver. His sketch pad and his trig. The Latin labels underneath his eggs. His fashion magazines. The funny words he used. He'd never like a girl whose mother was a maid.

'We – that is m'self and Lady Susan – we've had a word and think that you might help him.' The major spoke through yellow, clamped-together teeth. 'That is – I mean – help him learn to hunt.'

He meant: to hunt like him. Impossible, I thought. Oliver would never see a fox dismembered.

'Well?' the major said. Smoke rolled upwards round his head, giving off a frowsty, sour smell.

I played for time. 'But, Sir, he isn't eating. He won't be strong enough.'

'That's my point. He cannot eat because he's in a funk. Poor chap, he wants to get over it but doesn't know where to begin. He needs your help to get his courage back.'

Did the major know what he was asking? That I, a chance-bred bitch, should help the tail male? And a male so fiercely guarded by Mrs Arbiter? The gunroom rolled around me with its smoke and smell of whisky. I struggled to explain but couldn't find the English.

'You're not answering,' the major said. 'Have you heard the rumours? Don't worry, Jacqueline. I'll never sell the kennels.' His voice crackled, as if coming from a wireless. 'Hoad is getting old and will soon be pensioned off. In a few years' time I'll need another huntsman. A lady huntsman, as you called it once.'

At his final word his pack began to sing, Churchill first, a low, excited moan, then Sprightly in a high A flat, Spitfire's baritone and Fable's yipping treble, harmonizing, climbing through the trees.

'Do you understand me?' asked the major.

So as not to cut across the long, ecstatic howls, I nodded, closed my eyes and listened to the hounds. They were spelling out Gwyn's message. Not what I'd imagined. He wanted me to teach the boy the proper way to hunt. Later on, I'd be a huntsman like Iolo. Breed a pack outcrossed with the finest hounds in Britain. Treat with dignity the passing of each fox.

The major's chair creaked noisily. 'Can't you answer, child? Are you deaf or what?'

My eyelids snapped apart. The major frowned, every bit as bleary as a drunken uncle. 'Are you deaf?' he asked again. He hadn't heard the pack. Like his tail male, he didn't have the gift.

Mam spoke inside my head. *For heaven's sake, act normal.*

'Sorry, Sir,' I said as the singing died away.

'Did you hear me, Jacqueline?'

'Yes. I think so, Sir.'

'I know you're tired,' he said in a kinder voice, 'but try and concentrate. We're depending on you, Jacqueline.'

'I'll do my best.' What else could I have said? I'd been blooded by the major.

He pointed at the door then swivelled to his journal. 'You're a little too old to be hunting in boy's clothes. I'll speak to Mrs Arbiter. Ratcatcher will do. She can put it on my Pownis's account.'

Chapter Twenty-One

ON Friday, as it thawed, we huddled in our classroom, trying to grip our pencils through our mitts. Outside, long icicles were dripping from the gutters, Sir slithered in the playground and hurt his gammy leg and we had to spend our dinner hour indoors. After school, I plodded down the street while rain like dirty pennies fell around my head. Tyres hissed behind me. A motor car shot past, indicator out. It swung left. The double gates stood open. As I reached the drive it was jouncing on the potholes that had deepened underneath the snow.

Tall in tweeds with baggy, knee-length trousers, his skinny legs encased in tartan socks, the major hovered by the open doors. A shiny black beetle, the motor car crouched on the gravel. Its door flopped back. A plump man wriggled out. The major cantered down the steps, throwing his tongue mid-air. 'Ballantyne! You've not changed a bit. You're welcome. Very welcome. I hope the roads were clear.'

Mr Ballantyne was staring at the house. It glared back at him through sullen, smeary windows.

'You've made good time. Is that your only suitcase?' The major's eager voice went wheeling round the dome. 'Leave it on the gravel. Mrs Arbiter will take it. It's cold now, don't you think, so come in and get warm.'

Collar up, peaked cap low, coat flapping round his knees, Mr Rumney slouched onto the carriage sweep. After peering through a nearby window, Mr Ballantyne stepped back to eye a hanging gutter. Mr Rumney climbed behind the wheel and the motor car choked into life and rolled across the grave. The visitor was staring at the dome.

'I know that one or two panes are missing,' the major said. Above his head, smoke drizzled from a chimney. While the visitor was prodding at a windowsill, the major shooed me off towards the kitchen.

Mrs Arbiter was pasting jam on a halved Victoria sponge. Not proper jam like you buy in jars but a lumpy, dark brown mess flecked with pale seeds.

'Where's Mam?' I asked.

'Gone to get some bottled plums. Run and tell her that I'm waiting.'

The bulb in the passage seemed dingier than ever, its light sucked into the cabbage-coloured paint. Back turned, Mam was kneeling in the storeroom. On the shelves beyond her, large shelled eggs hung trapped in jars of dirty water. Fingers spread above a bucket, she was staring at her knuckles, broken nails and damaged scarlet varnish.

I touched her collar. Eyes smudged with tears, she gasped and swivelled round.

'Mam! What's the matter?'

She hiccupped, blew her nose and gave a choky sob. Around her knees, plums lay in pools of goo. 'They give me all the dirty work,' she said, 'just because I'm prettier than them.'

'That's not fair. Can't you tell the major?'

'He knows – or thinks he does. He's part of it, you see. Oh, pet, it's things that happened a long, long time ago.' She trailed a cloth around the flagstones.

'Who's that man he's talking to?'

'Bunny Ballantyne-Brown. A stupid bloody name.'

'Is he some sort of doctor?'

Mam hurled a chunk of glass into a dustpan. I caught her Foxleigh smell of sweat and soda crystals. 'He's here because the major wants to sell the house.'

My heart filled with cold water. 'What about the hunt?'

'He won't sell that. Not him. He loves his bloody hounds.' A cut oozed on her thumb. I pulled hanky from my pocket.

'You want to stay here, don't you, Jackie, pet?' '

'I will if I can speak to Master Oliver.'

She watched me make a bandage from my hanky, then held out her thumb like a child. 'Be patient, pet. You'll get your chance. The major's on your side.'

Mam was right. I got my chance next morning. Polly knelt beside me in the drawing-room and pointed at a pile of empty Cornflakes boxes.

'Tear them into strips,' she said. 'Not like that. Much thinner. Now pile them on the grate.'

The visitor from yesterday scutted through the door. Bunny. A good nickname. He looked like Peter Rabbit in the book, with a paunch, short legs and a sticky-out behind. The major trailed behind him, still in his plus fours and gaudy tartan socks, blue wool with bright green diamonds joined by thin red lines.

'Ah! Polly,' said the major as if surprised to see her, 'any minute now we're going to tour the attics, and Master Oliver intends to come downstairs. Please go and check he's dressed and on his way.'

Polly slip-slopped to the door. The major glanced at me. My breath came in short bursts. He was giving me a chance. I tore a strip of cardboard and laid in the hearth.

'You train them young,' said Peter Rabbit with a wink.

The major didn't seem to get the joke. Peter Rabbit whisked a notebook from his pocket and trotted round the room on tiny paws. Trying to look busy, I tore more strips of cardboard while Peter stuck his finger through a moth hole in the curtain.

'Could be stitched,' the major said.

Peter Rabbit peered at a cabbage-shape of mould that sprawled beneath the nearest windowsill.

Polly slip-slopped back. 'He's going to the upper drawing-room.'

157

The major glanced at me again. Peter pattered off. The major left the room on creaking brogues.

'Thank gawd they've gone,' said Polly. 'Let's hope he hates it all.'

No need to hope. He didn't like the house and the mean old place disliked him back. Why else had rotten plaster dropped onto his bed? And why else had a chimney that had only just been swept puff a lump of soot into his slippers?

'Now while I clean that hearthrug,' Polly said, 'you can go and check the fire in the hall.'

I left the room before she changed her mind. Though smoke still draped itself around the mantelpiece, the logs beneath had stopped their dismal smoulder and were flaring up the chimney in the hall. Chrysanthemums, at breakfast-time still wearing tiny curls, were blooming on the chest beneath the bell pull. Made bolder by their spirit, I climbed the central stairs, not kicking off my shoes or even keeping to the side. Why bother when the major was going to sell the house?

Sir Walter's face looked pasty in the morning sun, as if he'd heard that change was on the way. But Ranksborough, for once, looked gaily optimistic by the golden buckle on his master's knee. His brow, I saw, was higher than Sir Walter's. His eyes, unlike his master's, were glowing and astute. I felt them on my back as I walked along the passage. I'd never get a better chance than this.

Near the upper drawing-room, I heard the major's bitch pack. Flirty little Ermine. Bumptious Quickly. Saucy Fable, proud of her good looks. Not thoughtful like Caradog or sagacious like Aneurin, but bred for centuries to please the Wetherals, read their slightest signals, understand their moods. And, what's more, they'd started making sense.

What if someone catches me? I asked them.

They spoke as one: *you're only doing what our Master told you.*

I looked along the passage. No sign of Mrs Arbiter. Outside the

158

upper drawing-room, I paused to catch my breath. Knock on bedroom doors, Mrs Arbiter had said, but never knock elsewhere. You'll never catch a gentleman doing owt he shouldn't.

All the same, barging in felt rude.

Master Oliver was reading in a wing chair by the fire, his feet propped on a stool and a rug across his knees. In a fortnight, he'd grown paler than skimmed milk and looked as if a puff of air might floor him. Feeling huge and clumsy, I faltered on the threshold. No wonder I'd been told to stay away.

Look casual, said Quickly, *when entering his habitat. Hands in trouser pockets, as if you're strolling past.* I bumped into a bucket placed to catch a drip, then clumped across the floor towards his chair. The corners of his mouth were flecked with white. I caught a whiff of sour, hungry breath.

Let him take his time, the bitches said. I grabbed the tongs and fiddled coal on to the fire.

'What's your book?' I asked as I replaced the tongs.

He gestured at a plate of biscuits on a nearby table. I took a plain digestive, not a chocolate. At last he pointed at the chair across the hearth.

'What's your book?' I asked again as I sat down.

He held it out to show a double spread of print and a tiny picture of a bird.

I shoved a bit of biscuit in my mouth. *Oh, Ermine, tell me things to ask about a goose.*

The fire smoked. Drips plopped in the bucket. 'That looks very interesting,' I said.

Forget the bird, said Ermine. *Just put him at his ease.*

'Last week the butcher's van got buried in a snow drift.'

He took so little notice I might have spoke in Welsh.

'And Threlkeld's ewes got trapped on Biddle Fell and Annie Threlkeld dug 'em out herself.'

You're boring him, said Ermine. *Look at him more closely.*

I saw his straggly hair, cracked lips and skinny neck. How on earth would I persuade him that it was good to hunt?

You must learn to spot the clues if you want to be a huntsman.

I looked again. His silk cravat exactly matched his primrose cashmere jumper and picked out a line of yellow in his pleated dogtooth trousers.

'Thing is,' I said, aware I'd used the major's pet expression.

Wary and sharp-faced, Oliver said nothing. Silence stretched between the splashes in the bucket. He'd get more leery if I shilly-shallied but if I went too fast he'd bolt or double back. 'Thing is, your father spoke to me,' I said.

Blue as Quink, a vein pulsed in his forehead.

'And I might be going hunting after all.'

He pecked the air and frowned. 'What's that got to do with me?'

'I want to be a credit to the Wetherals,' I said.

The corners of his mouth twitched slightly upwards. 'Not hard to do. You've seen my father's dreadful coat.'

He couldn't mean the magic jacket with its pale blue facings and little racing foxes on the buttons. *Stay upwind of him,* said Quickly in my ear.

'I know,' I said out loud. 'You're absolutely right.'

'And as for that old topper, so worn around the brim. Ma Arbiter has brushed it half to death.'

The cub had left his earth. 'I noticed that,' I said.

Although he'd closed his book, he kept his finger in its pages. 'But on the other hand, Jack was always smart.'

Let him take his time, the bitches said again.

'He always used to wear a canary-coloured vest, bespoke, of course, beneath his scarlet coat, cutaway, with double vent and tails with rounded corners.'

He paused as if to check I was impressed. I stayed upwind. 'That sounds very nice.'

'His boots were black, as you'd expect, with matching garter-straps. But you'll be wearing ratcatcher, I'm sure. All the same,' he eyed me up and down, 'you could look rather smart, even wearing tweed.'

I nodded as he reached out for a biscuit then stared at it as if he'd never eaten one before. Flames sputtered in the chimney. I shifted in my chair.

Talk to him, the bitches said. *He'll eat it soon enough.*

'That's what I'd like,' I said, 'but I don't know where to start.'

'You'll need to go to Pownis's.'

'Mrs Arbiter will take me.' Probably a lie. She'd barely spoke to me the last few days.

He took his finger from the book and snapped it shut. 'She mustn't choose your clothes. She'll only get them wrong.'

Agree with him, said Ermine.

'But so will I,' I said.

'Not in Pownis's. Mrs P. will sort you out.'

At a loss, I balked. *Keep after him,* said Fable. 'How can she when I don't know how to get there?'

His book dropped to his feet. 'Can't you catch the morning bus? Gosh! I didn't know that you were such a baby!'

Blood surged to my face. *Hold hard,* the bitches said. I sat in silence while he took a second biscuit. 'I need to go to Pownis's myself. I mean to buy a weskit with some money Maman sent me.'

A weskit? What was that? He finished his digestive. I eyed the plate that he'd forgot to offer. Never mind. The pack was on his heels.

'I could take you if you like and help you choose,' he said.

'Are you sure? Will you be strong enough?'

'Give me time. I'll do my best,' he said. 'I'm sick of Dr Madden and his mustard foot baths. And, besides, there'll be no peace upstairs now that Bunny fellow is poking round the place.'

'So when will we be going?'

'A bus leaves from the village every Saturday.' I fiddled with the scuttle while he scoffed another biscuit. 'Let's meet at ten o'clock on Friday week.'

Chapter Twenty-Two

I'D thought that time would drag but the week went by quite fast. Peter Rabbit poked his nose in every corner: kitchen, servants' hall, wash room, butler's pantry. One day, I even saw him in the stableyard.

'Pure Palladio,' he squeaked, paws clasped on his chest. 'Form and function match in ever brick! And that row of stalls! What a tea room it will make! Imagine all the home-made jams waltzing from the counter.'

At ten-to-ten next morning, I climbed the kitchen steps and hung around the corner of the house. A battered leather suitcase at her feet, Mrs Arbiter was waiting on the steps. An engine hiccuped: Peter's Rabbit's motor car. Mr Rumney parked it on the gravel.

'I hear you've got a date,' he said as he jumped out.

I turned away. MYOB. The double doors banged back. I jumped. A cheerful voice boomed out. Peter Rabbit bustled down the steps in gauntlets, flat tweed cap and overcoat. He nodded and said thanks to Mrs Arbiter who by now had stowed his suitcase in the boot. Earlier that morning he'd gave Mam half-a-crown.

'Thank you for coming to see us,' cried the major. 'We'll – agh - wait. We'll wait to hear from you.'

Peter Rabbit shook the major's claw then jammed his tubby body behind the steering-wheel. Mr Rumney shut the door and slouched away. The major raised his hand to the disappearing car, then, ignoring his bored foxhounds chanting in their kennels, set his face towards the Hall.

An east wind grazed my cheeks where Mam had scrubbed them. Her hairbrush had left scratches on my scalp. No sign of Master Oliver.

What if he'd forgotten? Or fallen ill again? Or didn't want to bother? The clock struck ten. The bus would leave at ten past. Wind rattled through the trees. Drizzle stained the gravel. Invisible and damp, I stood till five past ten.

The doors banged back again. 'Wake up! We're late,' called Master Oliver.

He must have been to the barber's. His face looked thin and young, with a short back and sides and a raw-looking cut on his neck. His overcoat seemed bulkier than ever, as if the boy inside had failed to grow into a man. It flapped around his calves as we hurried down the street. The women at the bus stop glared, a row of angry boilers: you have no right to walk with Master Oliver. A single decker bus churned through a puddle. He tutted at the splashes on his trousers. Its door whumphed back and brushed the steps with grubby ginger bristles. The women jiggled long string bags on board and smoothed their plastic rain hats into pleats. Oliver let me climb on first. I chose a seat at the back. The village rumbled past. A burnt-out plane. Puckered fields. Metal churns on platforms. A thrush sang on a fence post. Master Oliver took out a notebook. The fields turned to miles of scrubby grass. I squinted at a list of birds written in his elf-scrawl. We swooped downhill towards a regiment of chimneys marching on a stretch of wet slate roofs. The driver braked and slowed in a street of pebble-dash. The countryside had turned itself into a town.

First off the bus, Master Oliver crossed the road. *Let him lead you,* said the bitches. *You'll catch him soon enough.* He turned into a street of lit department stores and shoppers dragging toddlers by the reins. At last, he pushed through a revolving door. I met a blast of sickly-sweet warm air. He unwound his scarf. His head looked blue, like a sheep when clumsily shorn. We tracked past lipsticks in expensive-looking cases, pots of rouge and little jars of cream. How did ladies know which one to choose? He hovered by a stack of dainty boxes wrapped in pink and midnight blue with gold and silver ribbons.

'Can I help you?' asked a lady with pointy, blood-red nails.

He bared his wrist as if for her to slash it.

'What's she like?' the lady asked.

He stared back, eyebrows raised.

'I mean, what sort of perfume does she like?'

So he had a girlfriend: a pretty girl, I guessed, who flinched from dogs and mud. He said two words in what I thought was French. The lady chose a little crystal bottle.

'You don't mind?' she asked.

He let her spray his wrist. I smelt rose and tulips with an underlay of musk. Tom kittens in a bed of summer flowers. Beyond us, at the back, a lift was joggling downwards, a huge dumb waiter packed with tweedy shoppers. Oliver walked towards it, his wrist held to his nose. I caught a foreign word or two. Something to do with *Maman*.

We reached the second floor. He took my elbow as the gates clanked back on life-size dummies. He steered me through the hush of a huge, thick-carpeted room, past racks of tweed and mud-brown outdoor clothes.

A meringue-haired lady crossed the floor towards us.

'Ah, Mrs Prendergast.' He swept off his cap with a flourish.

'Master Oliver!' she replied, as posh as Lady Susan, though dressed, not in tweeds, but in a neat grey suit.

They talked about the weather and then he turned to me.

'This is Zhackleen,' he said. It made me feel grown-up. He told her that I needed riding clothes. Before I could dodge, she'd slid a tape measure round my waist. Wishing I'd had a bath the night before, I waited while she minced towards a rack of jodhpurs. Oliver followed, fussing about the size of the bags at the sides. She handed me three pairs to take to the changing-room.

'Come out here,' he called as I climbed into the first. He'd pulled up a chair just outside the curtain and sat, one ankle resting on his knee. I hovered beside him, glad the jodhpurs buttoned up the side. He twirled his hand like a motorist turning left.

I spun in a circle.

'The twill's too dark,' he said, his pernickety voice at odds with his kittenish, flowerbed smell. After I'd tried a second pair and then a third and fourth, he pointed at a row of hacking jackets. Mrs Prendergast chose a handsome, black and white check.

He pulled a face. 'We Wetherals can't abide a noisy tweed.'

We Wetherals! My face glowed in the glass.

'She doesn't want a dogstooth or a houndstooth, or anything lovat or brown.'

I nodded at Mrs Prendergast, pretending to agree.

He bounced towards the rack and riffled through the jackets. 'The tweed must be grey,' he said, 'to emphasize her eyes.'

'This one should fit her nicely,' Mrs Prendergast said.

I held out my arms for her to slide it on. Oliver shook his head. The lapels were far too wide. She found another. Its lapels were much too narrow. The third one would be perfect if it had a single vent and slanting pockets.

'And now she needs boots,' he said, satisfied at last. 'No, not black, thank you, Mrs Prendergast, and no, not a pair with elasticised sides.'

I wriggled my toes into leather as supple and soft as gloves. Oliver knelt to fasten the straps. Now I needed a crash cap: no, not brown or navy, thank you very much: Wetherals always wear black.

'And that should do for the moment,' he said when he'd added a buff-coloured *weskit,* a blue- and grey-striped tie and gold-coloured pin – plain, not fancy, thank you – and a pair of yellow string gloves. 'Would you please send our parcels to the tea room?'

Seeming to forget about a *weskit* for himself, he led me up two flights to a large, pink-painted room. A waitress led us through a maze of tables and sat us in a corner by a window. Oliver frowned at the chattering, middle-aged shoppers in their fox furs, soft felt hats and plastic overboots.

'In Derby,' he said, 'I go with my friend Felix to a place with proper booths and a machine that roasts the beans and grinds them while you watch.'

'Don't you miss Foxleigh?' I asked as the waitress brought our cakes: a chocolate éclair for me, a Madeira slice for Oliver, both of them chosen by him.

'Not since Maman's gone.'

I bit into my éclair. Oliver picked up a fork. Surely not for his cake? But yes. He carved a neat piece of Madeira, speared it with the prongs and popped it into his mouth.

'Besides,' he said, 'soon Father and I will be crammed like maids in the attic.'

I put down the éclair and licked my cream-splodged fingers. 'Your father and you? Why would you move up there?'

'Why do you think? The rest of the house will be open to the public.'

I stared at him, not understanding.

He laid down his fork. 'Have you not heard? Father is selling the house.'

'To Mr Ballantyne-Browne? I thought he didn't like it.'

Oliver's upper lip grew extra long and white. 'The best Palladian mansion north of Preston? What do you think? He grabbed it with both hands.'

'But why does he want to open it to the public?'

'Oh, Zhackie the Vackie, have you not heard of the National Trust? No? Well, never mind.' The waitress brought me a glass of Tizer with a straw, and a pot of tea for Master Oliver. He poured a cup and took a slice of lemon. 'The Wetheral family seat since 1792 and Father's getting rid of it to save his bloody hunt. Now my children will be homeless, and my children's children.'

My cake fork stopped mid-air. Which children did he mean? My fox had found a run I barely knew existed.

'But you'll have a flat,' I said, 'and one day you'll be Master.'

'I don't want to be Master. I'll sell the bloody pack.'

Oh, Accurate, oh, Quickly, tell me how to save you.

He refilled his tea pot from a silver jug. 'If I don't hunt, Father says I can't go back to Repton. He'll punish me by making me stay here.'

I sucked up my drink. 'When did he say that?'

'Just yesterday. He's found some namby-pamby tutor.'

Iolo used to tell me about a fox's brain: how it works just like our own but draws on different gifts. Oliver sipped his tea and talked about Latin, trig, Felix and his other friends in school. Not moving, barely breathing, I listened hard to what he said, stilling my thoughts, inhibiting my hound-smell.

'I could help,' I said when he'd finished. 'I could help you to like hunting. Then you could go back.'

Through tense grey eyes he peered into his cup as if he saw the fences in his future, bullfinches, raspers and five-barred gates with frosty downhill landings.

I shoved another piece of cake into my mouth. 'We could stick together and find the easy shortcuts and I'd never leave you on your own again.'

His fingered the barber's cut. 'It's fine for you,' he said. 'You don't know how it feels.'

'When you hunt, you learn about the fox.'

'I know about the fox. Just different things from you and Father.'

I stared at him, forgetting to chew. 'What sort of things?' I asked.

'A fox can catch a scent three feet beneath his paws. He can hear a ticking watch at sixty feet.'

At sixty feet? Did Iolo know? 'How did you find out?'

'By reading and observation,' he said in a grown-up voice. 'A fox will try to pounce in a north-easterly direction. He uses the earth's magnetic field to make a more accurate leap.'

Could Oliver be joking? I'd know if he met my eye. But, features huddled together, he stared down at his plate. The cake in my mouth turned to goo. Oh Orator, oh Spitfire.

'If you go hunting,' I pressed on, a hound in a thicket of brambles, 'you'll see different foxes and find more distant coverts.' Still wishing that he'd look at me, I plunged into the silence. 'And,' I said, 'you can find and unblock more earths.'

I caught his gaze at last. Wide eyes, fringed with thick lashes. 'I saw you from my window.'

He poured himself a second cup. 'And you never told.'

'No. Nor would I, ever.'

He punched my arm as if I was a boy. 'You can call me Ollie, like my friend in school.'

'And if we go hunting together, I'll help you unblock more earths. Every fox will have the chance of getting home.'

'And you'll never, ever tell my father?'

I crossed my fingers and waved them in front of his face. 'Honest Injun, Ollie.'

Back in the bus, he taught me four French words: *bon, merveilleux* and *absolument formidable*: all ways of saying good. Repeating them, I stared out at the scrawny sheep, their fleeces twitching in the fell-top wind. When Ollie was Master, he might let me be his huntsman, with the earths never blocked and the foxes never dug out. Each one we caught would be honoured at the moment of its passing. I could breed the pack I wanted, out-crossing with the Welsh, matching brains with beauty in the school of Gwyn ap Nudd.

Yet Ollie's face shut down as we reached the village. How to make him understand that it was *bon* to hunt, and even *merveilleux* and *absolument formidable*?

Gone to Ground

Chapter Twenty-Three

ON Sunday evening, Polly packed and washed her hair. Next morning, she sat in the kitchen, her suitcase at her side, a palomino mane around her shoulders. The major had found her a place in a home for unmarried mothers. In an hour and twenty minutes she'd be on the Kendal train.

'I know a lass who went there,' she said to Mrs Arbiter, who was stirring the major's kedgeree in a big, cast iron pan. 'They give you slop to eat, scrag end and mouldy cabbage, and you sleep in a room with twenty other girls and babies yowling their heads off all night long.'

A lump swam into my throat. In the beginning, she'd been kind, and saved me titbits from the major's dining-room. Then she'd tried to help me find things out – had trusted me to read his secret letters – to ask myself about my long white legs. But I'd told her to get out and saw her red face crumple. Now I'd never find out exactly what she knew.

The outside door crashed back. Her head jerked up.

'Don't worry,' said Mrs Arbiter. 'He's forty miles away. Driving the major to a horse fair in Carlisle.'

Boots clumped down the passage towards the servants' hall: some man had forgot his baccy or his snap tin. Polly bent to rub the veins twisting down her calves.

'So much the better. I'm over the blighter now. I only wish they'd let me keep the baby. Though it wouldn't have much of a start, poor little scrap.'

Mrs Arbiter tipped the kedgeree into a tureen and shoved past Mam to drop the frying-pan in the sink. Polly was leaving Mam to wash the breakfast things. Polly picked up her suitcase. The lid flopped back and a grubby white bra and a prayerbook spilled onto the floor. Why had she packed a prayer book when she couldn't read?

Mrs Arbiter shoved it back. 'You'll need some help with this.'

'I'll carry it,' said Mam. I knew she shouldn't have spoke. 'Jacqueline! It's time for school,' she said into the silence.

I left the room, the word goodbye jammed deep inside my throat.

I was skipping in the playground when Polly waddled past. I'd learnt to count in English. Arithmetic was easy. Brenda and the others could mostly understand me, and often let me skip with them in break. This time, the rope grew slack. Girls stopped to stare. One boy nudged another. Stiff-backed, her Sunday hat jammed on her head, Mrs Arbiter marched beside Polly, glaring through the railings and daring any one of us to shout or call out names. One hand supporting her bump, Polly kept her head down, the worn backs of her shoes slap-slap-slapping as she went.

Goodbye, *cariad,* I whispered. *Hwyl,* Polly *fach.*

A passage stretched ahead of me. Lights in tasselled shades beamed bright pools onto the carpet. On either side, stood chests bearing candlesticks, bowls of musty petals and old brown photographs.

The room on the left smelt of vinegar, mould and Mrs Bell's sweat. 'Watch your head,' she said, pointing at the ceiling. A ring of missing plaster showed a criss-cross of bare boards. Lumps of old plaster lay scattered onto the rug below. 'As for the bed,' she said, 'it'll give the man lumbago.'

'Who's it for?'

Her broad face settled in a look of disapproval, like a blighted turnip in a field. 'Who d'you think? A man from the National Trust. Probably worse than the first. Now shake the dust from them hangings.'

I jumped on the lumpy old mattress. Dust floated past my face from the cauli-shaped flowers that lolled across the curtains. As I shook them, moths flopped around my feet, waiting for me to stamp on them one by one. Smoke billowed out from the fire, just lit by Mrs Bell, who said there was a crow's nest in the chimney. We'd barely started the dusting when a motor car roared up the drive.

'Best go down and see who that is,' said Mrs Bell.

We arrived as the major was greeting a man on the step: Mr Fothergill, as thin as Peter Rabbit had been plump. The major showed him into the library, told Mrs Bell to bring tea, and left me to fetch the files and books crammed into the boot. Next day, Mr Fothergill stalked around the house. Maybe he hadn't slept well in his damp old bed or else his fire had smoked again, giving him a headache. This time, the major didn't trail behind him, just locked himself in his gunroom, wandered off to the kennels or paced along the terrace, up and down, up and down.

Later that week, Oliver's tutor arrived. I was the first to see him when he drifted past the playground, a small young man with hair in a centre parting and wire-rimmed specs on the end of his little snub nose. He carried his books himself up to the schoolroom, its row of desks all newly-shone and its blackboard newly-washed. Next morning, Mrs Bell took him his early tea. He was a pacifist, he told her, sitting up in bed, and an atheist-vegetarian who'd voted for Clem Attlee. He'd spend Christmas with his mother in Talkin Tarn.

Soon Ollie was spending his weekdays at his lessons. Meanwhile, in a notebook with squares meant for sums, Mr Fothergill listed the contents of every room, marking each item with different coloured stickers. Green: to be dry cleaned; red: to go for auction; pink: to be restored and yellow to be chopped for firewood. In the hall, he marked the chest and the grandfather clock with red and Lady Laetitia and Ranksborough with pink.

'When are they going to be sent away?' I asked one morning at breakfast.

Nobody answered. My ears buzzed. My scalp felt hot and tight. I stabbed a square of porridge with my knife. All right for Danny, Billy, Mr Hoad and the kennelmen. The major was keeping his hunters and the hunt. All right for Mr Rumney with his flat above the garage, for Mrs Bell with her cottage in the village, and for the hedgers and ditchers and the men who worked on the farm. And all right for Mrs Arbiter who, the major had told her, could live out her days at the Hall: all part of the deal he'd made with the National Trust.

'What about us?' I asked Mam when everyone else was talking. She shook her head and said she didn't know.

That night, when I was meant to be in bed, I remembered I'd left my shoebag in the tack room. As I passed beneath the arch into the stableyard, Mam was climbing the stairs to Mr Rumney's flat. I hovered in the shadows, saw the door swing back. Why was she there so late? She'd told me to ignore him but here she was, stepping into his room. The light went off. Keeping to the wall below the window, I slithered along to the tack room, grabbed my bag and slithered back again.

'Where have you been?' I asked when she came to bed.

'Nowhere. I've been sitting in the kitchen.'

'All on your own?'

'It's nice to get a bit of peace at times.'

'I wish Polly was here,' I said, half-afraid that Mam would hit me, 'and I wish that she'd got married to Mr Rumney.'

Mam sighed and sat on my bed. 'As you grow up, you learn that every story has two sides. Mr Rumney might be right and Polly might be lying.'

'Then whose baby is it?'

'How would I know?' Mam jumped to her feet. 'Maybe someone else's. Now for God's sake stop with all your stupid questions.'

On the last weekend before the Christmas holidays, the major, Ollie and Danny were standing outside a loosebox. The major and Ollie were dressed in their usual tweeds, and Danny in denim jeans tucked into his gumboots.

'Ah! Jacqueline!' said the major as I crossed the yard towards them. 'It's good that you've arrived. I want you to see what I - '

A volley of bangs from the loosebox drowned him in mid-flow.

He nodded at Danny to draw back the bolts. A gingery pony shot past him onto the cobbles. His mane was hogged. A carroty poll flared between his ears. He baulked. Flung up his head. Stared round the yard. Danny grabbed his reins and swung him round towards me.

'He's here on trial,' the major said. 'Let's put him through his paces.'

'What's his name?' I asked.

'Tallboy, I think,' said the major. 'Not that it matters much.'

Tallboy's blaze swerved sideways down his face. The eye in the blaze glared blue and the other shone dark brown.

'He's got a ewe neck,' said the major, 'and he's a bit corned up. But Danny's been up in the plate and didn't come unglued.'

I made myself look at the brown eye, not the blue. Danny laced his fingers and boosted me into the saddle. It felt slippery and small. Ollie dashed out of the tack room with a crash cap.

'Be careful, Zhack,' he whispered as I jammed it on. 'His owner can't hold him. That's why he's for sale. He bolted every time she took him hunting.'

A chance to prove myself! Tallboy pawed the ground.

'Remember he's only on trial,' said the major. 'If he's too much for you we can always send him back.'

No chance! I ran my hand along the rigid neck. The major told me to walk then trot round the edge of the field, giving me time to get used to Tallboy's strength, and his habit of stretching his neck whenever I tried to rein him in. Ollie stood beside the major, watching from the middle, a small, tense figure in his outsize coat.

'Give 'un a job in the mouth,' said Danny.

Tallboy jerked his head so high he banged me on the nose.

'Sit farther back,' called the major.

Annoyed with myself for needing to be told, I lifted my hand to my face. Blood splattered my new string gloves.

'Canter in a figure of eight,' called the major.

In the middle I tried to get Tallboy to change his leading leg. No luck. The second time I threw my weight and managed, a stride or two late. Danny heaved a red and white pole onto a pair of drums.

'Over you go,' called the major.

I stood in my stirrups, too startled to count the strides. Tallboy took off early. I went spinning over his ears. The ground blazed up and knocked the air from my chest.

'You'll need a bit of practice,' said the major. 'We don't want loose ponies careering around the hunt.'

Danny grabbed Tallboy and helped me back into the saddle.

'Are you okay?' called Ollie.

Before I had time to answer, Tallboy tore off again.

'Take the jump again,' the major called to me.

I grabbed the reins and this time counted the paces. One. Two. And a half. Up we soared. I lurched onto the pommel.

'Once more,' the major said, 'and this time grip with your knees.'

We cleared it with a foot to spare. I landed in the saddle.

'So what do you think?' The major turned to Danny.

'Well, he's a lepper, but I'd say the lass will get the riding of him.'

I glanced at the major. Did he agree? How long would the pony be staying?

'He's yours,' the major said. 'An early Christmas present. That is, if you want him.'

Want him! The field lit up. Already my heels hung down past Pixie's elbows. Tallboy looked 14.2 or more, would take any jump in his stride and, to judge from his spirited manner, would match the bigger horses. I slithered down from the saddle and kissed him on his blaze.

'He's a bit of a brute,' whispered Ollie, brushing the mud off my jodhpurs. 'Are you sure you'll be okay?' He licked his snow white hanky and wiped the blood off my nose. The day slowed. A crow flapped overhead, as sure as a questing hound, its steady wing beats steering it to the wood. I started to speak in a voice I hadn't expected. A voice that knew what to do and when to do it. A Wetheral voice that sounded like a ghost inside my mouth.

'Let's saddle Micah and try the ponies together.'

The major smiled and stroked his moustache with his claw. 'Danny will saddle him up, but don't take stupid risks. Tallboy's not even paid for yet.'

As soon as the major and Danny had left the paddock, we trotted our ponies side by side in a circle close to the fence.

'Relax,' I said to Ollie, 'and keep your heels down.' We trotted round again. Tallboy stopped lashing out. When we'd cantered peacefully round a few more times, I dismounted and laid two barrels on their sides.

'I don't want to jump,' quacked Ollie in a voice like Donald Duck's.

I slackened Micah's reins to let him graze, then lifted the pole and set it down again. 'See, it'll drop to the ground if one of us hits it.'

'So why did you fall off?'

I swatted a crust of blood from my lip and jumped back into the saddle. 'We'll start with the pole really low then raise it when you're ready, just an inch at a time.'

After another turn or two round the paddock, I steered Tallboy towards the jump, and beckoned to Ollie to follow. He wrapped both hands in Micah's mane, leant back as the pony took off, then landed in the saddle with a bump.

'Why not get rid of your whip?' I said, pulling up beside him. 'He only needs a nudge behind his girth.'

He gave me his new leather whip and we cantered up to the fence.

'One, two and a half,' I shouted from behind.

He grabbed Micah's mane, leant back and shut his eyes. I clapped as he landed with a slightly smaller thud.

'You cleared it really well and hardly jobbed his mouth. Let's stop for today and go for a ride.'

We clopped through the village, past lit-up trees in cottage windows, and the orange crepe paper streamers in my classroom, twisted by Miss and Sellotaped to the ceiling. For a week and a half we hoisted the pole one brick at a time. Soon Ollie saw that he'd been clinging on too hard. He learnt to bend forward as Micah launched himself, and stopped landing in the saddle with a thwack.

One mid-December morning, as we were training, a van stuttered up the drive. It halted outside the paddock with a burp. A man jumped out. Broad-shouldered, loose-limbed, dark curls, a baggy jacket.

'*Cariad,*' he said.

Iolo! I flung my arms around him, buried my face in his smell of damp wool and digestives. Before I knew it, I was speaking Welsh, the warm and friendly words rolling off my tongue, words from long ago, covered in hide and fur. '*Beth wyt ti'n wneud yn fan ma?*' I asked. What are you doing here?

'I've come for Llywelyn,' said Iolo. 'And for a chance to see you. My cousin was glad enough to be spared the trip.'

I heard a silvery yelp inside the van. 'Llywelyn is going already?'

'His job for the major is done.'

'You mean – '

'Three bitches in whelp, your huntsman says. And the pups will be woolly and white. He's the boyo who always stamp his get.'

The pack would swap their matching coats for Llywelyn's magical fox sense. Micah whinnied, reined in beside a jump.

'That's Oliver,' I said. 'I'm teaching him to hunt.'

'What are you saying?' asked Ollie, drawing near.

'We were speaking in Welsh,' I said, 'and this is Iolo who taught me to hunt. Why don't you show him how well you've learnt to jump?'

Ollie wheeled Micah round and pointed him at the pole. A schoolmaster of a pony, Mr Hoad had called him. 'One, two and a half,' I called. Iolo watched, intent.

'Aren't they doing well?' I said when they'd cleared the pole. 'Ollie was jumping with his stirrups crossed.'

Iolo's eyes stayed fixed on the boy and his pony.

180

'Your best jump ever,' I said as Ollie reined in beside us. Over the last ten days he'd lost his sissy, indoor look. His face was lean and bright as he ruffled his pony's mane. Iolo said nothing, just breathed in Micah's nostrils then ran his palm down his withers. Content, the pony dropped his head and snorted. Ignoring Ollie, Iolo crooned in Micah's ear in words that even I couldn't understand. Ollie waited politely, reins slack on the pony's neck.

'Let this go no further,' Iolo said to me in Welsh.

'You mean we should stop? But why?'

Dydi o ddim wedi cael y ddawn.' He hasn't got the gift. 'You must protect him, *cariad*. That's your job.'

'But you saw how well he jumped. And his father wants him to hunt.'

'The major will never change. But the boy should stay away.'

'He'll only go out the once.'

'The god has a vicious intent when an animal's wrongly killed.'

Leaving Ollie in the paddock, we walked towards the van. For the first time, Iolo had misunderstood. Ollie wanted to conquer his fear, not to kill a fox, and both of us wanted his father to see him do it. Iolo climbed into the driver's seat. No hug. Not even a word.

'Da boch,' I said uncertainly. Goodbye.

'O cariad,' was all he said. *'Da boch.'*

Llywelyn yelped. The hounds in the kennels yelped back. Which bitches had he chosen? Ermine? Fable? Quickly? I waved at the little grey van bucketing down the drive.

''What was he saying?' asked Ollie as he waited by the gate.

What was so special about the truth? 'He said that you looked great.'

'He seemed nice, and your Welsh is as good as my French. Can you teach me a few words?'

School broke up on the Friday before Christmas, which fell that year on a Thursday. Ollie's tutor had already left for his mother's in Talkin Tarn, so we could practise each day. On Christmas Eve, I

181

balanced the pole on the upright drums. Ollie's face turned sharp. Not giving him time to protest, I jumped back onto Tallboy. No need for the bitch pack to tell me that Ollie had come to the end of his pluck.

'Keep right behind Tallboy and me,' I called. 'Micah's not going to swerve.'

We thundered up to the fence. Though I gripped hard with my knees, Tallboy as usual jumped me half out of the saddle. On the other side, I wheeled him round and turned as Micah took the fence. Ollie leant forward, landed without a bump, cantered Micah round the field and reined him in at my side.

'You did that well,' I said, 'and Micah, too – so happy and relaxed. You'll easily manage to jump in and out of fields.'

'I'm not going hunting.' Ollie paused, as if inviting me to speak.

Now, said the bitch pack. Now's your chance, straight after his success. 'Oh, please,' I said. 'Just for the Boxing Day meet.'

His Adam's apple jerked. 'You know I don't want to.'

'We don't have to stay very long. And the major - your father - would love it, and so would Lady Susan.'

'I couldn't care less about them.'

'And I would love it, too.'

He drew a sharp breath. His eyes shone under the brim of his cap. Grey eyes, with thick black lashes. 'I'll do it for you and nobody else,' he said, 'just to let you see me mastering my fear.'

I felt a soft rush of air in my chest: for the first time, he'd told me he felt scared.

'But remember this.' He paused and raised a finger. 'I solemnly swear that after that meet I'll never hunt again.'

No one who'd hunted once could think of giving up. Hunting took you over. I knew it in my bones. Ollie would become a hunting Wetheral.

Chapter Twenty-Four

SMELLS of roasting goose larded the air. The windows dripped steam from the saucepans on the Aga. After I'd scrubbed the carrots and taties, I took up my post by the door bell. At a minute past one, Lady Susan stumped in holding a stack of parcels wrapped in snowman paper. She handed them to me and tussled with her headscarf. Craning my neck round the tottering pile of boxes, I watched her smoothe her big blonde buffalo horns.

'Now, tell me, Jacqueline,' she said, 'what did Santa bring?'

As if I was a child. I played along because I liked her. 'A pony,' I said as she slithered out of her fur. 'A beautiful pony called Tallboy who'll take any fence in his path.'

'Clever Santa.' She wore her emerald twinset and gathered tartan skirt, an outfit mocked by Mam because the colours clashed. 'We'll see Tallboy at the meet.'

'And Master Oliver, too.'

'The major will be pleased.' She peered at herself in her compact mirror. 'Now take those prezzies to the drawing-room, dear girl.'

The flaps of his jacket lifted to the blaze, the major stood bent, as if waiting to be caned. When he saw me hovering in the doorway, he nodded at a spindly tree in the window. I dumped the presents on the floor among a sprawl of parcels, some wrapped in shiny paper, others with big silk bows. Firelight danced in the decanters on the sideboard: three different kinds of sherry for the ladies and, for the gentlemen, two bottles of London gin.

Colonel Tunnicliffe trudged up the steps, a nondescript elderly man without his topper and scarlet coat. A band of guests filled my arms with furs, Gannex macs and Barbours. Ollie stuck his head out of the drawing-room. Bursts of laughter floated through the air behind him. I caught a whiff of pine and the zesty smell of gin. Glasses clinked. Someone struck a match.

'Let me take those coats,' he said. 'It's as boring as hell in there.'

He grabbed the macs and darted ahead to the cloakroom: the Ollie who'd learnt to jump, friendly and energetic. He even seemed to have grown an inch or two. 'Pooh!' he said. 'Don't these Barbours pong!'

'I don't mind. Most of them smell of dog.'

'I wish I could go below stairs. You'll have much more fun.'

Somebody called from the hall. 'Oliver? Where are you?'

'You won't forget tonight?' he said as he dashed away.

When everyone had arrived, I ran down the household passage. Opened the kitchen door. Hit a greasy wall of steam. Ollie wouldn't have liked it as much as he thought. Mrs Bell basted the goose on top of the Aga. Mrs Arbiter slid a salmon onto a plate. Mam was rinsing a colander of sprouts.

Mrs Bell looked up from the oven with a cross red face. 'Where have you been, Jacqueline?' she said. 'Get yourself over here and cut them lemons into quarters. No. Not like that.'

Time raced by in clouds of shouts and steam, people ringing down for fires to be stoked, scuttles filled and drinks to be refreshed. Drinks upstairs, they meant. Here in the kitchen, nobody even snatched a cup of tea, just paused to mop a sweaty brow or blow a dripping nose. At three, Mrs Arbiter changed her apron, settled her hat and left to serve the dinner. Laden trays creaked up the shaft. Dishes rattled down, piled with scraps of salmon skin and half-eaten bread rolls. Mrs Bell set the Christmas pudding on the tray beside a miniature bottle of brandy and a box of Swan Vestas. My stomach griped. I snatched a leftover roll.

'Get on with that washing-up,' said Mrs Bell.

I set the roll aside and filled the sink.

When the Wedgwood was stowed in its cupboard, it was time to fetch the coats. Weak-kneed, I watched the motor cars chug slowly down the drive, as if they, like their drivers, were full of Christmas pud. By five o'clock the guests had gone, apart from Lady Susan. The hunt staff trooped in with Danny. They hadn't had much of a Christmas. No money for a goose, or even to heat their kitchens. Too tired to go the servants' hall, we slumped round the kitchen table, apart from Mam who was wiping the counter tops. We hooked scraps of goose from the carcase and munched cold sausages and stuffing.

Mr Hoad burped and shoved back his empty plate. 'Come on, all of you,' he said. 'We'll natter in The Arms.'

'I won't be ganning,' said Danny. 'I've not got any lolly.'

'Me neither,' said Billy. 'I'm broke.'

'You can get your drinks on tick,' said Mr Hoad.

'That landlord says me tick is running out.'

Mr Hoad tilted his chair and pointed at the ceiling. 'So what did that dobby upstairs give his pals?'

'Sherry Fino in the drawing-room and a Dry Madeira with their soup.' Mrs Arbiter ticked off the drinks on her fingers. 'Then for the goose he said to fetch up the '33.'

'Thirty-three bloody bottles?'

'That's the year of the major's special claret, only twelve bottles left, laid down before the war.'

'By God he's doing hisself proud - especially when you bear in mind we've none of us been paid or even given a bloomin' Christmas box.'

I kept my eyes on a sausage I'd half-eaten: yesterday the major had given Mam two pounds.

'Me da wants a taste of the major's sup,' said Danny.

'Not a chance,' said Mrs Arbiter.

Mr Hoad jerked. His chair legs banged the floor. 'Why not, when his nibs drinks whatever takes his fancy?'

'Some of them bottles are priceless. Mr Arbiter told me so.'

'Maybe, but the major's clogging it over us and Mr Arbiter – God rest his soul – would have been quick to say so.'

For once, Mrs Arbiter seemed at a loss. 'I don't know, Bob. I just don't know.'

'It's what he'd do hisself, Bet, if he'd survived, that is, and you don't even have to gan to the cellar yourself. I'll bring up a couple of bottles and his nibs won't know the difference.'

Mrs Arbiter pressed her knuckles on the table and heaved herself to her feet. Everyone watched her cross to the mantelpiece and grope for the key in the innards of the clock.

'I don't think you should give him that,' said Mam as she turned from the sink.

'And what's that to you, *Mrs* Elton?' asked Mrs Arbiter.

Mam blinked and straightened her spine. 'The major's wife has left him and his eldest son has died and he's doing his best to make a family Christmas.'

'You shut your trap,' said Mr Hoad, 'and don't tell tales upstairs. If the major gets to hear we'll know damn well who blabbed.'

Mam turned back to the sink as he left the room. The cellar door squeaked. Footsteps thumped below. Mrs Bell set out seven glasses. One for me. Would Mam snatch it away, like when a customer bought me a drink at The Fleet? Mr Hoad came back with an armful of cobwebby bottles, dumped them on the table and dug an opener into a cork. I waited for Mam to tell him not to thump the handle. But no. Back turned to the room, she cleaned the draining-boards. Mr Hoad clamped the bottle between his knees. His forehead bulged. Bits of cork tumbled to the floor.

Danny squinted at the label. 'It's twice as old as me.'

'Then we're doin' the family a favour,' said Mr Hoad, slopping wine into the glasses.

A dog fox barked, a hoarse, challenging note.

'There's Charlie,' said Danny, pinching my arm, 'daring us to chase 'un.'

'Why do you call him Charlie?'

'If he overhears us when he's lurking by a window he won't rightly know it's him we're out to catch.'

I gave a wine-flavoured burp. No fox would be deceived. I tilted my head like Danny and dribbled wine into my mouth, not really liking its sour Ribena taste.

Mrs Arbiter pulled a card from its envelope. I glimpsed an ox and an ass behind a manger. 'Polly's had a baby girl,' she said.

Somebody else who'd never know her dad.

'What's she called?' asked Danny.

The skin beneath Mrs Arbiter's eyes turned soft and bruised. 'Maeve. A pretty name. And Polly's got a good job at the army base.'

'If it wasn't for them 'osses,' said Danny, 'I'd be headed there meself.'

Everyone talked about the jobs they'd have if they weren't stuck at the Hall, except for Mam who'd vanished and Mrs Arbiter who stared into her wine. Above her head, salmon moulds were skidding across the wall, three, four then five with bulging eyes and copper scales. Billy reached to put his glass on the dresser. It crashed on the tiles. Mrs Arbiter wiped her face with a towel. The fish on the wall sparkled and wove downstream.

'You've drunk too much,' said Danny to me. 'Now get yourself to bed or you won't be fit to hunt tomorrow morning.'

I tottered out of the kitchen and up the stairs to the hall. The pendulum clacked wheezily to and fro. Smells of coffee and cigars hovered round the library door. Behind it, Lady Susan whinnied. The major fluted like a questing hound. Muffled in coat, cap and scarf, Ollie sat in a chair beside the empty hearth.

'I've told them I've got a sick headache,' he said with his downturned grin. 'Now they're scared I won't turn up tomorrow.'

We ran down the path to the stables then paused beneath the arch. No lights shone out of Mr Rumney's flat.

'Gone to The Arms with your mother,' said Ollie. 'I saw them scuttle off.'

He fumbled for the light switch in the garage. On a shelf above a dusty manger, a bicycle lamp sat among tins of old keys, rusty cans of oil and unravelling balls of twine. I grabbed the lamp and a box of matches. Ollie seized the biggest jack from a row hung in order of size on the opposite wall.

We ran down the drive. On our right, the cottages, curtains drawn. On our left, the entrance to a lane. I struck a match and lit the Naphtha lamp. Its bright white beam waltzed us through a maze of narrow paths. The covert was easy to find: past a derelict farm and rusting jeep, then up a steep rise to a stand of trees dark against the sky. A briar-free track led to a hole tucked in a tangle of oak roots, with a scatter of quills and whitened bones outside.

Mr Rumney had done a good job, blocking the earth with a wooden square stapled with sturdy mesh. Ollie dropped to his knees and prised it away with the jack. I stuck my face in the hole: not musty, as I'd expected, but gusty and fresh with the tang of soil and leaves.

'Pass me the light,' said Ollie, springing to his feet. He placed it in the centre of the clearing, swung the jack high above his head and brought it down on the frame.

'You could have just left it,' I said.

He swung the jack again, bashing the frame into kindling held together by wire. 'If I'd left it,' he panted, giving the frame another whack, 'Father might think a badger had done it, and then he'd start culling them.' He hurled the frame high above his head. It clattered through some branches then thumped down out of sight. 'Besides, I want him to know that somebody hates his hunt.'

My head spun. I sucked in more air from the earth. Ollie lay flat on his back a yard or so away. I inched along the ground until I lay beside him, then locked my hands and cushioned the back of my head. In the sky on my left I saw a smear of light: Gwyn ap Nudd, the hunter god, rising sideways through the branches. The base of my spine jerked. I was sprouting a tail. Ollie pulled out his notebook and started to write by the light of the lamp he'd placed by his knees.

A nightbird whirred and fluttered.

'What was that?' I asked.

He didn't seem to hear me, just sat, head bent, writing or sucking his pencil. Spreading my hands, I sank into the roots that held the tree, no matter how big the wind that troubled its crown. When my eyes opened again Gwyn was shining through its branches, his belt a spangle of stars and Dormach, his faithful hound, crouched at his feet.

Ollie shut his notebook and reached to take my hand. 'We will be all right, won't we, Zhackleen?'

Wind in the branches rocked the god into a dazzle. 'Of course we will,' I said. 'Micah will see you through and Tallboy and I will be staying right beside you.'

His fingers gripped mine, bony and thin through his gloves. 'D'you think I'll manage the fences?'

For a second, he looked like the boy he used to be.

'You have to believe that you will. Just throw your heart over the jump. And if it looks too high we'll go the long way round.'

Chapter Twenty-Five

OLLIE and I reined in on the edge of Rosely village green. We'd ridden here from Foxleigh, following the major, the hunt staff and the pack. Mr Hoad and Danny both seemed out of sorts. Earlier that morning, passing through the kitchen, I'd counted twelve dusty bottles on the draining-board. The end of the major's precious '33.

Ollie hadn't spoken on the ride. Just tired, I told myself. We'd both been late to bed. Though I hadn't reached my room till one o'clock, luckily Mam wasn't back from wherever she'd gone with Mr Rumney. But I knew that he'd promised to drive her to the meet.

The grass was damp not wet. The air on my cheeks felt neither frosty nor muggy. The weather-vane on the smithy pointed south: good signs for the day ahead. Across the green, a horsebox stopped behind a row of trailers. Its ramp crashed to the ground. A boy untied Colonel Tunniciffe's strawberry roan. Head up, ears tense, it looked down its roman nose at nearby grooms whisking rugs off glossy hunters or unravelling the bandages protecting bony legs.

Men holding tankards bundled out of the pub at the head of the green. I scanned the crowd. No Mam. Three farmers jingled up the road, their boots jammed deep in their stirrups, ignoring the children chattering on their ponies. On lively, powerful Tallboy and wearing proper clothes, I felt as smart as anyone of them. The Pony Club mothers stood in their tarpaulin macs, well away from the village women in hats and winter coats. A figure wavered between the groups in a headscarf and bulky tweeds.

'Mam!' I shouted. 'Mam!'

She steered a circle round the horses and riders, flinching as Tallboy tossed his carroty mane.

'He's not going to hurt you,' I called. 'It's just that he wants to get going.'

She pointed at the splashes on her stockings. 'The Wolseley's brakes have gone,' she said, halting five yards away.

The landlady crossed the pavement bearing a tray of whiskies. Mam grabbed one as she passed. 'What a lot of dogs,' she said, glancing at the pack. 'You'd wonder how the major manages to control them.'

'Sometimes he doesn't,' said Ollie. 'Sometimes they riot and snaffle a villager's tabby.'

The first joke I'd heard him make: well, not so much a joke, more a way of teasing Mam. She frowned and drained her glass. The reins thrummed in my hands. Two army men on skewbalds talked about eight-mile points. The major slid his horn from between his jacket buttons. Ollie peered out then ducked back in again. From on top of their matching greys, Mr Hoad and Billy rounded up the pack.

'Be careful, won't you, Jackie, pet,' said Mam. 'That animal of yours has a horrible look in his eye.'

'Don't worry. We'll be fine.'

The hunt moved off the grass, followed by Colonel Tunnicliffe and Ella, his eldest daughter, the Reverend Beale, Lady Susan and a Pony Club instructor. I steered Tallboy alongside Micah as we jostled down the lane. Now that we'd got going, Ollie was riding well: heels down, back straight, elbows in and hands light on the reins. Seeming to sense his rider's new-found confidence, Micah was trotting calmly on the bit, neck arched, ears lightly pricked, a gentleman of a pony.

We passed the derelict farm and rusting jeep we'd seen last night. Was the dog fox crouching deep inside his earth, slowing his breathing, inhibiting his scent? Or had he already heard the hounds and run? We cantered over a field towards the stand of trees.

'Leu in, Spitfire, leu in Churchill, eleu in, Matilda.'

Soon the hounds were crashing noisily through the brushwood.

The major dismounted and vaulted the fence, followed by Lady Susan, leaving Billy and Mr Hoad to patrol the covertside. Deep inside the wood, a robin gave its alarm call. Had the major reached the earth? I pictured the look on Lady Susan's face. Why would anyone hate the major and his hunt?

Gaze fixed on Ollie, the Reverend Beale reined in his knock-kneed cob. I opened a packet of chocolates that looked like rabbit droppings and, holding out the box, moved to block the Reverend's view.

'Not yet,' said Ollie. 'But thanks.'

The sun sailed out of a cloud. Hounds yelped inside the covert. Miss Tunnicliffe lifted the veil of her topper and jiggled a cigarette out of a turquoise packet. A lady astride a thoroughbred brandished a lighter. Smoke curled in the sun. The yelps in the spinney grew scattered and subdued as if the fox had melted into the earth.

'Let's hope we draw a blank,' said Ollie. 'I rather like hanging around in the sun.'

'Huic halloah, huic halloah,' shouted the major beyond the wood.

So the fox had decided to run. Ollie frowned and pecked the air. 'He should have stayed put, with no Rumney to dig him out.'

The hunt staff cantered away, leading Fives or Better and Lucy Glitters. The rest of us listened as the pack began to bell, the confident note of hounds on a breast-high scent. After five minutes or so, Colonel Tunnicliffe let us move off, a band of horses and riders jostling past the wood. Ollie and Micah flowed smoothly, pony and boy as one, but Tallboy was jerking my arms and fighting for his head.

'Slacken your reins, Zhackie,' said Ollie with a wink.

The major was trusting the pack to drive through a flock of sheep. We crowded through the derelict farmyard towards another field.

'Jolly poor sport for the Boxing Day meet,' said one of the Army men.

The riders kept to the edge of a field of curly leaves. The pack hopped, ears flapping, over the crop. Micah's head drew level with my knee as Ollie stared across the blue-green rows.

'What is it?' I asked.

'Keep your voice down, Zhack.'

Ears bobbed up. Vanished. Bobbed again on top of a broad brown head. Ollie put his finger to his lips.

'View halloah!' I cried before I could stop myself. I snatched off my cap and waved it after the fox. 'View halloah.'

'I wish you hadn't done that, Zhack,' said Ollie.

The major pulled up on a patch of grass in the corner, stood in his stirrups and stared. 'You were seeing things, child,' he said to me. 'Hounds never find in kale.'

The head bobbed again. 'View halloah,' shouted the major. Hounds dashed through a gate and cast on the edge of a pasture. The major spurred Fives or Better along the headland. Neck and neck with an Army man, Lady Susan followed.

'Let's stick together,' I said to Ollie. He didn't meet my eye. The pack began to bell. I struggled to rein in Tallboy but his neck had turned to iron. After a ten-minute run hounds checked beside a sheepfold. Tallboy was blowing hard and even the hunt's twin greys were dark with sweat. Micah galloped up with Ollie firm in the saddle. Micah whickered but Ollie's face stayed closed. I lost and fought for my stirrups as Tallboy started to gallop, overtaking a farmer on a pounding dapple grey. The going turned soft as we cantered downhill to a five-barred gate. Billy stooped from his saddle to unhook the latch.

'Dammit!' he said. It was bound to the post with wire. The major drove Fives or Better at the gate, followed by Mr Hoad, the colonel and Miss Tunnicliffe, all on horses two hands higher than Tallboy. His neck still hard as iron, he crowded so close behind them that I had to duck the divots flung up by their hooves. Ollie at least would be safe, I thought, gathering my reins. Micah would never take a jump he wasn't asked to.

Tallboy leapt high but clipped the top and landed steeply.

'Ware road,' the major cried ahead.

Hounds milled round a ribbon of tarmac fifty yards away. Clever

Charlie. His scent had been smothered by tyres and petrol fumes. Turning, I saw a band of riders hurtling down to the gate.

'Hounds have checked,' cried Mr Hoad. The breeze snatched at his words.

A farmer pelted side by side with the Reverend Beale, followed by Lady Susan on Lucy Glitters and Ollie in the rear, leaning forward like I'd told him. The gate was higher than anything he'd tackled in the paddock.

'Don't jump! No need! Hounds have checked!' I yelled.

Whether or not he'd heard me, the farmer wheeled away. I prayed that Ollie would follow, but he raced after Lady Susan. They drove at the gate with Lucy Glitters a head or two in the lead. The mare caught her hoof on the bar and slewed in front of Micah who launched himself at an angle as Ollie clung to his mane. The mare slithered over and fell on her knees with her rider still in the saddle. Micah tumbled after them, flung Oliver onto the grass, then spun and rolled on his back.

'Somebody help him,' I screamed.

Ollie lay in a heap while Micah flailed beside him. The major jumped down from his horse. 'Fetch Dr Madden,' he shouted, 'and somebody with a van.'

A farmer spurred his cob across the field to Rosely. The major knelt by Ollie and pulled off one of his gloves. Though his hand fell white and limp, the major took his pulse. Micah's legs thrashed then flopped to one side like sticks. I jumped down from Tallboy and hooked my arm through his reins. An army man appeared and knelt beside the major.

'Let's make the boy a bit more comfortable,' he said.

They eased Ollie onto his back. The major took off his jacket and folded it into a pillow. Lady Susan left Miss Tunnicliffe holding Lucy Glitters, fetched Ollie's cap from the grass and laid it beside his head. Other riders dismounted and stood a few yards away.

'Get back! Get back!' Colonel Tunnicliffe called.

Mr Hoad blew the horn for home. The mournful, drawn-out

notes echoed round our heads. Hounds were clustering round his horse's hocks, ears back, sterns carried low. The riders climbed onto their horses and moved towards the road, with Billy Boustead leading Fives or Better. Ignoring them, I looked at the still, pale face.

Colonel Tunnicliffe touched the major's shoulder. 'Have some of this,' he said, holding out a flask.

The major shook his head, unbuttoned Ollie's jacket and put his ear to his chest. 'His heartbeat's growing faint.'

'Where's the bloody van?' asked Colonel Tunnicliffe.

A farmer cut the wire on the gate and jiggled it off its hinges. The few remaining horses flung up their heads. A Land Rover was rumbling along the road towards us. The colonel flagged it down. A startled face appeared at the driver's window. No, he hadn't got any message. He'd come from counting his sheep. And yes of course he'd take the lad to the doctor's.

The driver jumped down and opened the jeep's rear door.

'Don't lie him on the gate,' said the colonel to the farmers, 'just lift him straight into the back.'

The major climbed in with Ollie and shut the door. Micah raised his head and whickered to Tallboy – a throaty sound as if he lay underwater. Tallboy whickered back. Micah's neck flopped in the mud. He lay at my feet, neck outstretched, his legs in a tangle, his saddle slipped and broken. He gave another chesty whicker. I dropped to my knees. He blinked and rolled his eyes.

'Micah!' I said to him. 'Micah!'

Reins slack on the grass, not straying or even grazing, Tallboy whinnied to Micah from deep inside his chest. Though his soft brown eye still fixed itself on mine, Micah didn't even twitch his ears. A scream burst out of my mouth, and then another, not giving me time to breathe. Lady Susan knelt beside me and laid her arm on my shoulder. I shook it off. 'Leave me alone. He's in pain.'

'I promise you he isn't.'

I jumped to my feet. 'I'm going to get the vet.'

'No point, Jacqueline.'

'He's alive,' I yelled. 'He is! I saw him blink.'

'I swear to you he didn't feel a thing.'

Sobs jerked out of my mouth and dribbled down my chin. Lady Susan picked up Ollie's hat. We stood together, Micah at our feet, and watched the Land Rover jolting down the road.

'I'm staying here,' I said. 'I don't want to leave him alone.'

Lady Susan dabbed her eyes with her crunched-up glove. 'You'll have to, dear. Tallboy needs you now.' She handed me the pony's reins. 'See, he's feeling chilled.'

We climbed into our saddles and trekked across the field.

'The major knows a famous surgeon,' Lady Susan said, 'and hospitals these days are very good.'

Now and again I turned to look at Micah, alone in the field, stretched out as if asleep, with Ollie's saddle sandwich box flung open at his side. My eyes blurred. Rain stung my cheeks. It hardened into hail that had whitened all the gardens by the time we reached the village.

Lady Susan turned her mare for Kellaway. 'I'll telephone you later to check that you're okay.'

Tallboy whinnied as we reached our drive, as if he hoped that Micah would answer from the stables, then wound his way, head low, among the potholes.

Chapter Twenty-Six

DANNY sheered off to the tack room as we reached the stableyard. I glimpsed his fat red face as he shut the door behind him. He'd been crying, too. Don't look at Micah's loosebox. Turn away from Micah's loosebox. I hauled off Tallboy's muddy tack and groomed him, made a hot bran mash and filled his water bucket.

Mam was waiting in the kitchen. I told you so, she'd say. I told you he was scared, and you didn't even bother to protect him. But no. She sat in silence at the table, staring at a half-drunk cup of tea. Not daring to ask for news, I fiddled with the buckles of my mud-caked boots: we Wetherals wear brown, not black, thank you, Mrs Prendergast.

Mam raised her eyes to mine. 'They've taken him to the R.V.I.'

'The Arvie Eye? What's that?'

'The Royal Victoria Infirmary in Newcastle. He's going to need a major operation.'

My heart felt too small to beat. But at least he was alive. Up in my room, I pulled off my jacket - grey, not lovat or brown - hung it in the wardrobe and found my oldest clothes. I would have liked a bath but couldn't face the freezing room. Every muscle ached as I wandered past Ollie's nursery and into a passage we'd searched while he lay in the icehouse. The keys had been removed from all the doors but one. I turned it, crossed bare boards into another room, and then a third and fourth, all silent and dark, with drawn blinds. I felt buried alive. If only I hadn't persuaded Ollie to hunt. If only I hadn't shouted the Huic Halloah. And if only, if only, I hadn't taught him to jump.

Ahead of me reared a pair of mahogany doors. What if Ollie

197

lay beyond them, muddy and neglected? I'm starving, he'd croak as I poked my head inside.

I pushed the doors apart. The room had been emptied apart from cardboard boxes stacked high against the right-hand wall. I pulled one down and raised its lid. Two blank eyes stared out. I put my chin in the gas mask like we'd been taught at school. The dusty room wobbled beyond the eyepiece. The gong rang below, muffled by three ceilings. I packed the mask back in its box and carried it down to my bedroom.

At supper, all the men talked about Oliver: what a wonderful boy he was, how sensitive and brave, and what a sense of humour. And they all said how sorry they felt for the major.

Mrs Arbiter spoke from her seat to the right of her husband's chair. 'Why should we feel sorry?' Her voice sounded breathy and hoarse. Two rows of heads flung up like startled cattle. She lifted off her hat and set it by her plate. 'Why should we feel sorry when he brought it on himself?' Light gleamed on the sweat now beading her round, white scalp. 'He took one son to war and made the other hunt. He's punished for his foolishness, say I.'

Men finished their suppers in silence and left in twos and threes. Mam cleared the dishes. Hat still at her side, Mrs Arbiter sat staring at the empty table top. When the clump of clogs had faded, I wandered down the passage.

A man stepped out of the shadows by the boot room. 'Your mam is going to spend the night with me,' said Mr Rumney. 'Come over to the flat and have a nice hot bath, and then a cup of Horlicks by the fire.'

I shook my head. Mr Rumney blocked my path. 'She's already made your bed up.'

In a room that overlooked an empty loosebox?

'Your place is there with us, you know,' he called as I walked on.

A light shone through a crack in the butler's pantry door. I passed it without pausing - no ghost could hurt me now – and climbed up to the empty corridor. The pack was baying as I got undressed, great gouts of sound that tracked across the field. Dogs or bitches? I had no idea. Half-hoping Mam would bring a pitcher of hot water, I climbed between cold sheets. Pain throbbed through my scalp, as if a smith had knocked in nails. I chafed my hands. Hail rattled at the windows. The telephone shrilled through two levels of bare boards.

I dreamt I had four limbs and tramping hooves and fetlocks. Next morning, I woke with my body a mass of animal wounds and my mind ablaze with painful animal deaths. I had to wait till breakfast for the news: soon Ollie would undergo a six-hour operation.

I shoved my porridge bowl aside.

'Come to church with us,' said Mrs Bell, 'and you can pray to the Lord that the op will be successful.'

No point in praying to the god of Mr Beale. I climbed back to my room, put on the mask and stared into the mirror. My eyes stared back, dark and terrified. My nostrils flared in panic as if I was a ghost horse. Church bells chimed. I sat on Mam's bed and breathed the stale air. In. Out. In. Out. Was Ollie breathing, too? Was he breathing through a mask? Did the effort seem as pointless as it seemed to me?

An hour passed. Voices chattered on the drive: people back from church. As if he guessed I didn't want to see the empty loosebox, Danny had told me that he'd care for Tallboy. Dishes clattered in the kitchen. I caught a whiff of roasting pork. My stomach clenched. How could people eat? A motor car was braking underneath the window. I lifted off the mask and ran down to the hall. Still in his hunting pink, his face soft and damp, the major leant against the chest by the bell. Mrs Arbiter puffed in and slammed the double doors. The crash bounced off the marble. Tears dripped down the major's cheeks.

'To your room, please, Jacqueline,' Mrs Arbiter said.

'Leave her be.' The major put his arm around me. The musk smells of his coat were overlaid by petrol fumes. He gripped my hand and led me to the gunroom. The pike had vanished from the wall, the rifles from their rack, the Barbours from their hooks and the gumboots from their place beneath the window.

'Here. Sit down,' the major said and pointed at his chair.

He was going to tell me that Oliver had died. I sat and watched him lean against the gun rack.

'Poor boy. Poor boy. They've done their best,' he said, 'but his spine is broken, and he's still concussed. No one knows if he'll come round or not.'

Noise poured out of my throat, high like a run-over cat. When the *wah-wah-wah-wah* had stopped the major gave me a hanky. 'I should have waited for an ambulance,' he said. 'If he hadn't had that jolting in the jeep, my poor boy's spine would not have been so damaged.'

I blew my nose into the linen's starchy hardness. On the ghost square where the desert photograph had hung, somebody had daubed four different shades of pink.

'His mother is on her way, escorted by her brother.'

'Are they staying here?'

'No. She doesn't want to. She blames me for what happened. She's right, of course. Can't say she didn't warn me. They've booked into a Newcastle hotel.'

Not knowing what do with the snotty handkerchief, I folded it in four and laid it on the desk.

'My son is brave like you and Jack,' the major said, 'You've seen him try to prove that for yourself. And now that he's laid low he'll be as brave again. I'm sure of that. You'll see. All the Wetherals are fighters.'

'If he does come round,' I asked, a wobble in my voice, 'will he walk again?'

'If he does, it won't be for a while.' The major grabbed a journal and flung it at the door. It landed on the flagstones with a crack. 'No more hunting for the season.' He hurled another journal. 'No more hunting ever, as far as I'm concerned.'

'What about the hounds?'

'Tunnicliffe is going to take them over. He's promised me that Hoad will keep his job, and so will Billy Boustead and all the kennelmen.'

Colonel Tunnicliffe who couldn't hunt a thimble.

Instead of mucking out or hanging round the kennels, I spent the day sitting in the gas mask, head down, eyes shut, just hoping time would pass.

'You're taking things too hard,' Mam said to me at supper. Mam, who'd never said I told you so.

'I wish I'd died instead of Micah.'

'That's because you're not yourself,' said Mam.

Myself? How could ever I be myself? With no Ollie and no Micah, I had no self to be.

Mam popped an extra slice of bacon on my plate. 'Here. You missed your dinner. You must keep up your strength.'

I stared at streaks of flesh in shiny, oozing fat.

Next morning, after choking down my breakfast, I dragged on my outdoor clothes and set off down the drive. Frustrated by a lack of exercise, hounds were baying loudly in their kennels, dogs and bitches, all mixed-up, an ugly, jangling sound. Mrs Bell stood in her garden, throwing cabbage stalks to her hens.

'Any news?' she called. I tried to speak but couldn't. 'I was saying to my Gilbert, he was really really brave.' She threw another stalk. 'And Major Wetheral. First Master Jack, now this – and no French wife to help him see it through.'

My face bunged-up from trying not to cry, I bit my cheeks and walked towards the playground. Everyone stared as if Oliver hovered beside me. In class, head down, I blundered to my desk. Chalk marks smudged and vanished off the board. Miss's small pink mouth shut and opened. If by chance I caught a word it drowned itself at once in the pointless, pent-up babble of the hounds.

Chapter Twenty-Seven

I NEVER tried to find the empty rooms again, but the ones downstairs grew cold and hollow-sounding. Each day that week, a removal van drew up on the gravel. Watched by Mr Fothergill, clipboard in his hand, a team of men loaded the furniture and carpets. And still we had no proper news of Ollie. He'd had an operation. He wasn't coming round. No one seemed to know exactly what would happen next.

On Saturday, a gale punched the windows. A relief. Its roaring drowned the clamour of the pack. I crossed the hall. Ranksborough had vanished. Gone for cleaning, Mr Fothergill had said, but I felt as if he'd left us for a better pack. Caught in the wind from the chimney, ash drifted round the grate, and a draught sliced down the gunroom passage. Mam had said that I was wanted by the major. Three words in curly writing sprawled across the gunroom door: Ladies' Powder Room. I hovered in the doorway, newly painted pink. Odd and out of place against a pattern of gold roses, the major sat in his ancient swivel chair, groping through a desk drawer with his lobster claw.

'Come in, come in,' he said. 'We're going to visit Oliver.'

'Is he getting better?' I blurted out.

The major hooked a stick of sealing wax tangled up with string, crumpled bills and oily rags. 'Not quite yet, but I know he'll want to see you. Now that Jack has gone you're all he's got.'

All? When he has two parents?

The major cleared his throat. 'There's something else you need to know. Fives or Better's off to Kelso at the weekend. He's only six years old and needs to work.'

'Can't he stay? Yarico will miss him.'

202

The major turned his head towards the window. 'Poor Yarico. He knew that Jack had died. Went off his feed before we'd even got the telegram.'

First the bullet in the brain, then the knacker's yard. The major kept on staring at the windswept drive. 'Pixie can be sold to someone local. She'll make a decent pony for a nervous child. And Tallboy can stay here, for when you want to hunt.'

'I won't ever want to hunt.'

'Whyever not? You've done nothing wrong. Not at all. You did as you were asked.'

No point in trying to explain about Iolo's warning. I left the major staring through the window. His pack began to clamour as I climbed the servants' stairs. Saying what? They felt confused? That they'd been cut adrift? Ollie's bed was stripped and the photograph had vanished, but his battered teddy-bear was lying on the chest. Even though I guessed he wouldn't want it, I picked it up and took it to my room. The wind whipped my face as I struggled to the sweetshop and bought him an Aero he wouldn't be able to eat.

At ten o'clock I climbed into the Wolseley. The major crashed the gears. We ground down the village street. An early morning snowfall had whitened the road on the fell, and hungry-looking rooks flocked black against the woods. The major said he'd have to take it slowly but that we'd be in Newcastle by lunchtime. He judged it right. Soon after twelve we crawled through narrow streets with soot-black buildings high on either side. The R.V.I. looked a bit like Foxleigh with steps up to the entrance and rows of gloomy windows, but built of brick, not stone. We squeaked down polished lino through air that ponged of Dettol till at last we stopped outside a door.

'They've shaved his head,' the major whispered as he turned the handle, 'but don't worry, Jacqueline. His hair will grow again.'

I followed him to a bed with blankets raised in a tunnel. An Oliver-mask lay on a pillow at the top and a hand on the blankets looked waxy and white as a dummy's. Ollie's face? Ollie's hand? I couldn't feel quite sure.

I sat the bear on the locker beside the pillow and propped the chocolate bar between its legs. The major pulled up two chairs, one on each side of the bed.

Belted into a starched blue uniform, a red-faced nurse swished into the room. 'I'm Nurse Brunty, Mr Wetheral. Why not hold his hand?'

The major knelt and touched the waxy-looking fingers.

Nurse Brunty's little eyes shone at the dials on a machine beside the bed. 'Say something to him, Mr Wetheral.'

The major whispered to the side of Ollie's head.

'Louder,' said Nurse Brunty, 'then he might be able to hear you.'

The major gulped, looked at the nurse and then looked back at Ollie. 'I'm sorry, son,' he said. 'Really, really sorry.'

Ollie breathed deep inside his earth.

'Come on,' the major murmured. 'I'm here and so is Jacqueline.'

I took Ollie's other hand.

'Is he coming round?' asked the major.

'Not quite yet,' said the nurse.

As we drove us back across the dusky fells, lights from distant farms winked up and down the valleys. We passed a cattle wagon on a bend. Our headlights caught pink nostrils gleaming at the slats.

'This damn government, you know. They've taxed us to extinction. 'Well, no need for you to bother with such things. I hear your mother's gone to live with Alan Rumney so for the moment you can stay with them.'

'Thank you, Sir,' I said. Did he know what he was asking? For me to live above an almost empty yard? I'd rather sleep in my old attic room, alone on the top floor of the creaking, sighing house.

That evening, Mr Rumney took Mam for a drink. She deserved a break, he'd said at supper. When they'd gone, I visited the stables. Danny had worked hard: the cobblestones were spotless, the windows clean, the midden nicely squared. Out in the fields, a vixen called, a single wailing cry. She moved closer and called again, her cry flung up to the clouds then drifting downwards. Oliver's vixen. Had she sensed his absence? Like Yarico had sensed the death of Master Jack? I stepped inside his loosebox. He lowered his head for me to rub his poll, as if he knew that evening was his last. I didn't dare get close to Five or Better. Danny claimed he dumped him whenever he tried to ride him. He'd probably lash out at me from lack of exercise. Steering clear of Micah's empty box, I gave an apple core to Tallboy and stroked his sprouting flaxen mane. Tomorrow night, he'd be the only pony in the yard. Last of all, I said goodbye to Pixie, stroked her mushroom-coloured muzzle and said I'd see her soon. A local man had bought her for his son who'd lost his nerve out hunting on a fiery pony.

Next morning, Mr Rumney said he'd drive me to see Ollie.

'Is the major coming?'

'No. He's hanging round the Hall.'

I settled myself in the front seat of the car. As usual, when out of uniform, Mr Rumney wore the major's cast-offs. Although they never seemed to fit the major, on Mr Rumney they looked tailor-made. And he drove the Wolseley better, too, without a single jolt or grating gear.

As we climbed beyond the village, thoughts raced around my brain. I guessed the reason why we'd left so early: the major didn't want me to hear the vet arrive, or the shot and frightened whinnies from the other horses, or to see the body on the knacker's cart. But the knowledge weighed me down as we crossed the fells and dipped again to wind through blackened streets.

'Here at bloody last,' said Mr Rumney in the car park. He rummaged on the dashboard for a pack of cigarettes. 'You know your mam and I are going to marry?'

She hadn't told me, but I didn't feel surprised.

'When will you do it?'

'Not quite yet. It wouldn't be respectful.' He lit his cigarette and blew a smoke ring at the windscreen. 'But I want the three of us together. Always have.'

'Always?' I echoed before I could check myself.

'Always, Jacqueline.' He paused and caught my eye. 'I wish you'd call me dad. And even more I wish I'd got to know you sooner.' He blew another smoke ring. My eyes began to itch. 'There's certain things your mother hasn't told you.'

'I think I'd best be going.' I opened the car door.

'As you wish,' he said. 'You know the way?'

I nodded. He opened his *Express*.

I'd lied. I had to stop and ask. Turned right. Turned left and left again. Passed a porter with a trolley, a row of closed doors, three buckets and a mop. Where was I? No idea. No windows. No daylight. Just strip lights overhead. A girl without a pack has only half a brain.

As I neared a corner, I heard the clack of heels. Walking on, I caught a whiff of roses, musk and tulips. *Tom kittens in a bed of summer flowers.* A woman appeared in a navy skirt and jacket, its waist nipped-in, the skirt just skimming her knees. She walked on the arm of a man with a trim moustache and a camel overcoat hanging from his shoulders. *Maman!* She looked older than the woman in the photo.

'You're Zhackleen,' she said. A statement, not a question.

'Yes,' I croaked, not knowing what to call her.

'*Petite idiote,*' she said, and clacked away, her arm still tucked inside the gentleman's.

Sifting the air, I followed her scent round the corner, down another passage then left into another. It stopped at Ollie's room. Not a nurse in sight. I sat beside his pillow, where I caught another whiff. 'It's me. Zhackie the Vackie,' I whispered in his ear.

His eyelids flickered but stayed shut.

'I brought your teddy bear,' I said. 'And a bar of Aero.'

Both had disappeared. His eyes jerked open like a doll's. Too scared to call the nurse in case he sank back to his earth, I stayed beside the bed and said the first thing I could think of. 'Your father sends his love. He's been here every day.'

Ollie's eyes steadied and focused on the ceiling. Did he know his mother had been here? He mumbled a word I didn't understand, then two more with a long gap in between. After five minutes he fell asleep again.

Mr Rumney sat in the car, eating fish and chips. 'Did you see Her Ladyship?' he asked. The inside of the Wolseley stank of greasy cod.

'Yes. I met her in the corridor.'

He tossed a balled-up paper through the open window. 'No wonder his nibs stayed away. Not that I blame him, of course. Typical Frog. She don't half have a temper. And as for that Philippe Granel, the one who worked for Veeshy – '

'Who's he?' I asked. The car choked into life.

'Do they teach you nothing at that school? V-I-C-H-Y. The Frogs who gave in to the Nazis. No wonder them and the major don't see eye to eye.'

On the way home, I thought about Ollie's *maman*. Lady Susan had said her portrait flattered her. She was wrong. *Maman's* hair looked glossy and well-cut, and she wore a figure-hugging suit. Her shapely legs in see-through nylons ended in small feet, neatly shod, in shoes with pointy toes. Whereas Lady Susan looked bulky, blonde and square, with straight, stout legs encased in lisle stockings. Mam detested Lazy Susan, as she called her, though now she dressed like her and not Félice.

Next Saturday, and each weekend throughout the early spring, the major drove me to the hospital himself. One day in March, he went to look for the consultant and I arrived alone at Ollie's room.

Though flat, he was staring at the door. 'Zhack,' he breathed, so faint I hardly heard.

I gabbled about the weather and what I was doing at school: anything to block the question I was dreading.

In May, I was made to move into the flat, not by Mam and Mr Rumney but by Mr Fothergill. The attics were about to be repainted. I packed Iolo's letters and my lucky badger's claw, then wandered with my suitcase through the other attic rooms. Though their yellows and pale greens should have made them fresh and airy, they seemed to trap the heat beneath the eaves, and the stink of melting tar from what was once the carriage sweep.

Ollie stayed till midsummer on the surgical ward, and had three more operations, one on his legs and two on his spine. Then they moved him to a nursing home in Gosforth, a turreted brick house beside a noisy road.

During a hot July when school had ended, the major drove me to see him nearly every day. 'He'll need you more than ever,' he said. 'Poor boy. He's so cut off from everything he knows.'

Lady Susan had invited me to Kellaway, where I could hack round the lanes with her and Lucy Glitters. She'd said a distraction would be good for Tallboy who stood, head low, in his paddock, listlessly flicking his tail at clouds of flies.

I said no to Lady Susan. My first debt was to Ollie.

At first, he lay on a high, hard bed with machinery underneath. Later, each afternoon, they strapped him into a wheelchair, first for half an hour, then for two or three. One muggy day we sat beside an open window that overlooked the lawn between us and the road.

Stiff inside his neck brace, Ollie clucked. He was staring straight ahead at the dried out, thirsty grass. 'You never mention him,' he said.

The major had told me to lie – say that Micah been sold – gone to a riding school somewhere near Carlisle.

'Don't look so worried. I've already guessed,' said Ollie.

I gathered my wits and managed a single lie. 'He died straightaway. He didn't suffer much.'

Ollie sat in silence, still staring at the lawn. After a while, he swivelled his chair towards me. 'Poor staunch, courageous Micah. I should have known better,' he said.

'Better than what? It wasn't your fault he fell.'

'Oh yes it was. I was trying to prove I was brave. And now he's gone.' Oliver's voice broke. 'He only jumped because I asked him to. Left to himself, he'd have baulked. I'll never forgive myself. Never.'

I said nothing. What was there to say? We both knew how I'd egged Ollie on to jump – me, who'd ignored Iolo and tried to please the major. And I'd never warned Ollie what the god could do.

Chapter Twenty-Eight

NEXT morning, Mam perched on a chair in the tiny sitting-room. Eyes tight shut, she clutched a list and muttered. 'John Varley, 1778 to 1842. Edward, no, Paul Sandby, 1731 to 1809. Thomas Girtin, 1775 to 1835. No, not 35, 39 … or should that be…?'

I set a cup of tea on the table at her elbow.

Her eyes snapped open. 'Oh, Jackie, pet, I wish I had your brains. I'm trying to learn the names of all these artists.' She handed me the list. 'Will you test me?'

I recognised an artist's name: the one who'd painted Ranksborough. 'What year was Sandby born?'

'1778? No! 1732?'

I shook my head.

'You're looking peaky, pet. You need a bit more sunshine. You can't spend all your summer in a nursing-home.' She sipped her tea, paused and fiddled with the spoon. 'Me and Alan want to send you back to Wales.'

'What? For good?'

'Don't be daft. For a holiday. You can stay with that Iolo feller.'

'I thought you didn't trust him.'

'I may have been too hasty. I know you better now. And Uncle Bernard wasn't really helping.'

I thought about Caradog and my cosy kennel bed. 'I can't go back. Ollie needs me here.'

Mam shook her head. 'He needs a proper nurse.'

How to tell her what I'd promised: to visit Ollie every day, not to leave him, ever and then, when he was better, to live with him at Foxleigh.

That summer, the major often left Ollie and me together, no longer seeming afraid that we would grow too close. At the start of September, two physiotherapists levered him from his chair. He stood for only a moment, too busy keeping upright to joke or even talk. Next day, he managed a minute, hands clamped on the physios' arms. Next week, when I arrived on a rainy Autumn day, he sat alone in his chair.

'Will you help me, Zhack?' he asked, and pointed at a metal frame waiting in the corner. 'I've got to build the muscles in my arms.'

I walked it to his wheelchair like a spindly metal colt. 'Do the physiotherapists know what we'll be doing?'

'The physios don't matter.'

He took a deep breath. I levered him to his feet, the boy who I'd once called a scaredy cat. He stood and gripped the bar. Breathed in. Breathed out again. His legs slumped at the knees. He clenched the frame so tight his knuckles shone, eight tiny skulls beneath his pale skin.

'I told you he'd be brave,' the major said as we drove home. 'When he comes back to the Hall he'll need a special room. The library will open onto our private garden so tourists can't stand gaping through the windows.'

'That's nice,' I said.

'Nice? I had no choice. What must be must be. It's not what he expected. Nor I, cooped up like a maid in my attic flat. But Mrs Arbiter will still be housekeeper, you know, and have her same old rooms close to the kitchen. As for you, we'll need you in the Hall.'

'Mr Rumney says I've got to live with him and Mam.'

The major puffed air into his scrawny moustache. 'You'd better have a word with her,' he said.

She was drying her new Pyrex dishes in the kitchen of what still felt to me like Mr Rumney's flat. No scrubbed pine. No copper pans or salmon moulds. No airing rack above a cranky Aga. Just a Baby Belling and pink Formica tops.

'There's things I'd like to know,' I said. The blood thumped in my ears.

She sat beside me at the little table. 'You're right,' she said. 'It's time. High time you knew the truth. That is, as much as anybody knows.'

I gulped. It seemed impossible to say. 'I think that Polly thought I was the major's daughter.'

Mam's finger traced a pattern in the Formica. 'I believe you are and so does he. You have a look of him at times. Not him now, of course, but as he used to be.'

'You mean when he came to that pub?'

'Aha! So you remember.' She lit a Kensitas. 'Yes, that was it – well before the war. He looked so handsome in his uniform. He never was an uncle. I did it all for love. And then, when you were born, he loved you, too – came to see you each time he got leave.'

The stupid doll. The big black motor car. Mam swung off her feet as he grabbed her in his arms.

'Why does Mr Rumney say that he's my dad?'

'He wants it to be true. An outside chance, I'd say. You'll understand things better when you're older. Times were hard in Bootle during the Depression and Alan was a sergeant, out for a good time. If you want food on the table you do what you have to do.'

My cheeks felt hot. Why? I didn't feel quite sure.

'I brought you here as soon as I could,' she said. 'And then, when we arrived – well, I got a shock. I knew Alan had become the major's batman – after poor old Arbiter had died - but I'd no idea he'd come to Foxleigh, and even less that Polly had got pregnant.'

As if she'd done it by herself, I thought. 'Do you have to marry Mr Rumney?'

She glanced around as if to check the flat was empty. 'Oh, pet! Why can't you understand?' She rubbed the lines on her forehead.

'Like I said, I've never had much choice. You're lucky. You can decide who you want to be your dad.'

Foxleigh Hall had changed. It had lost its chilly meanness. The mould had vanished from the dark old rooms, brightened now by bulbs in all the sockets, pastel paint and velvet drapes at every window. In mid-September, when it opened to the public, it basked in autumn sunlight like a pampered cat, bland and neutered, pleased to be admired. At two o'clock, the first small group assembled. Three farmers' wives, Brenda Watson's dad, Dr Madden's nurse and two cousins of Constable Coulthard leading Borzois. Mr Fothergill waited on the steps. Sideways on, flicking back his hair, he pointed out the beauties of the Palladian façade: its symmetry, Doric pillars, capitals and portico.

I followed the group up the steps into the hall. Mam, in twinset and tweeds, stood beside the gong. Voice shaking a little, she talked about the marble, quarried in Italy, loaded onto ships then carried by mule from Dover. Sir Walter had built his mansion on the site of a Tudor farm. Her notes no longer shaking in her hand, she led the group up the stunning double staircase – nobody told to take off their shoes - and pointed out the portraits on each side. The visitors stared at Félice and Lady Lætitia and clucked at the fate of brave young Master Jack.

They reached the end of the tour in the household passage. Spotlights had replaced the dingy bulbs, and pale buffs and greys blotted out the cabbage green. In the laundry, an actress in a mob cap mimed shovelling slack on the fire that heated the coppers. Her little white hands danced sopping, imaginary linen through the mangles. She finished at last. The visitors' faces relaxed. They chatted among themselves or rummaged in their handbags. You could tell they were longing to take the weight off their feet. Mam led them to the tea room in the stableyard to scoff the village women's cakes or buy their jams with gingham caps or dusters made from feathers dropped by local hens.

That same week, I began at Appleby Grammar. They left me even more alone than in the village school, as if everyone knew my part in Ollie's catastrophe. When fields and trees had turned to the colour of foxes, Colonel Tunnicliffe held the opening meet. That day, and on every hunting day that followed, the major sat indoors with all the windows closed. As for me, I barely heard the hunt and what I heard I didn't understand. I'd become a girl and not a hound.

In mid-November, Ollie came home to Foxleigh. On weekend and holiday afternoons, I'd read to him in his room. Then, when the last of the coaches had rumbled out of the car park, I'd take his arm and steer him to his zimmer, promising him that soon he'd walk unaided. We wandered slowly down the passage and crossed the empty hall with its bulletin board and table stacked with brochures. Every day we walked a little further, touring rooms now open to the public. Locked away in cabinets we'd never seen before, Waterford crystal and show-off silver lined the walls round Turkey carpets and damask-covered chairs roped off to stop them being sat on.

We didn't step outdoors till school broke up for Christmas. In the last of the daylight, we crossed the frosty gravel. Under his thick tweed coat Ollie wore the clothes Mrs Prendergast had helped me choose: a shirt of palest primrose silk, a sweater as soft as a rabbit and a paisley cravat in colours that glowed like jewels. A long, sad winding note echoed round the park: Billy Boustead blowing the Going Home. Ollie's arm tightened on my hand, clamping it against the ribs beneath his coat and sweater. He'd been unconscious when it sounded on that day. Had its mournful echo lodged inside his brain? Without a word we plodded through the car park and underneath the arch towards the tea room.

'God love you both, the pair of you,' cried Mrs Bell behind the counter. 'Now, let me bring you some cakes and a pot of tea.'

'Earl Grey for me,' said Oliver, 'and a Tizer for Jacqueline, if you will, and two substantial slices of your nice Victoria sponge.'

For all his white, exhausted face he sounded every bit as bossy as in Pownis's. Mrs Bell didn't seem to mind, just bustled off to boil a kettle. I steadied the zimmer. He slumped onto a chair. As we waited for our tea, the hunt clopped through the village.

'I've been thinking,' I said, 'that Major Tunnicliffe's old and Mr Hoad has said he'll soon retire. In a few years' time, you must take control of the hunt.'

Ollie sat up straight. 'What do you mean, control?'

'You can be Master – non-riding, if you like - and I will be your whip. The hunt depends on Wetheral money, after all.' I ticked off the points on my fingers. 'First, no digging out. No terriers. No Mr Rumney. Secondly, the earths will not be blocked. Third, we'll ban barbed wire throughout our country. Fourthly, every field will have a working gate so no one will need to jump who doesn't want to, and each farmer must ensure that his gates are in good order. Fifthly, if a fox is killed, the pack is not allowed to tear its body. The animal's remains will be treated with respect.'

Mrs Bell brought a jammy Victoria sponge. I would have liked a slice of chocolate cake. Ollie stared across the empty tables. 'Your ideas are good,' he said, 'but not quite good enough.'

I clanked down my spoon. 'They're the things Iolo always did.'

'Maybe. And they will do for now. Together we'll patrol the fields and coverts.'

I tried not to look at his wasted legs stretched beneath the table. Two useless sticks. It might be months – years – before he'd walk unaided.

He caught my glance. 'I know,' he said. 'I know just what you're thinking. That's because you're a Wetheral, you see.'

Startled, I flushed. How much had he heard about Mam?

'Did Polly never blab to you?' he asked.

Them long white legs of yours. You should be asking questions. 'She tried,' I said. 'I didn't want to listen.'

He gave a hoot of laughter. 'I don't blame you, Zhack. Who'd want to be descended from this accursed line?' He brushed my knuckles with his fingertips. 'Our father is rolling in dosh now he's sold the house. I need him to buy me an old, reliable pony. Although I can barely walk, I'll soon be able to ride.'

Ollie no longer sounded bossy. Just grown up, and brave enough to climb into the saddle with less than half the strength he had before. Taking up the reins. The words rang through my brain. Somebody needed to, what with the major spending most of his time at Kellaway: courting Lady Susan, Mrs Arbiter had said. I reached across the table and thumped Ollie on the arm.

He picked up his cake and frowned. Jam leaked on his fingers. No cake forks here, just teaspoons and paper serviettes. He cleared his throat. I listened, ignoring the ache in my chest. I already knew what he was going to say.

'The hunt must be run down.' He took a dainty bite.

'You're right.' Micah dead. The major gone away. And Danny soon following Polly to the army base. Worse, all three of the bitch pack had miscarried. Llywelyn's pups refused to live away from Wales.

'We'll wind it down together,' Ollie said. 'It should only take a year or two.'

'*C'est absolument merveilleux,*' I croaked.

One breezy day that spring the major called me to the stables. 'Meet Rory O'Mor,' he said. A shapely head was hanging over the half-door of what had once been Fives or Better's box. Inside, I saw a solid Irish cob with dappled coat and lightly feathered heels.

'He's bomb-proof,' said the major as he led me to the tack room. He'd had a special saddle made for Ollie, extra-broad, with roomy rubber stirrups, a solid cantle and two handles on the pommel for Ollie to grab if he felt insecure.

Not that he ever did. Rory understood his duty. Tallboy liked him, too. Soon Ollie and I were roaming the Saturday country, checking the gates and coppicing, and chatting as we rode.

Though Ollie grew stronger every day, I still felt scared at times.

I knew I'd spend the rest of my life at Foxleigh and never forget the terrible thing I'd done. Though we never mentioned Micah, I sometimes dreamt of him, looking up from the mud and trusting me to make him well again. And sometimes I thought that Tallboy remembered him, too, when he went off his feed for no reason or jibbed at a fence that once we'd jumped with Ollie.